The Man at the Caffè Farnese

BY JANET S. SIMCIC

The characters and evens portrayed in this book are fictitious. Any similarity to real persons, living or dead is coincidental and not intended by the author. The Caffe' Farnese and other historical places mentioned in the book are real.

Caffe' is the Italian word for coffee. Café's are a place to drink coffee. The small coffee bars use the two words interchangeably.

ISBN-10: 0983592101
EAN-13: 9780983592105

Dedication

This book is dedicated to my sister survivors of breast cancer. May we all remember we are still women…even with body parts missing, estrogen deprivation, temporary baldness… Know who you are. I'm confident we are the bravest of women.

To my dear husband, who stuck by me and still loves me for myself. Thank you for your support.

And to the one person who has run the Race for the Cure in my name, Barbara Whipple, THANK YOU.

And my wonderful oncologist, Dr. Tariq Mahmood

Chapter One

Spending the month of September in Italy had been my idea. I would have come alone if I'd had to, but I'd worn Liz down, urging her to run away with me. And now, here we were, along with Liz's friend, Mary, jet-lagged and jammed into a car with too much luggage, hurtling toward central Rome.

From the moment my feet touched the ground at Leonardo da Vinci Airport, I felt at home. The language, the gesturing, the scent of coffee, even the dreaded customs lines fascinated me. I was in love with everything Italian.

We made our way through the double doors past the customs inspectors and were greeted by unsmiling armed soldiers. I searched the myriad of drivers, looking for the sign with my name.

"There it is," said Liz. "The tall good looking guy over there." She pointed, waving her arms.

"I see it." In large block letters, the sign read, 'JULIE WALDEN'.

The gentleman smiled and walked quickly to assist with our bags. He shook his head at the number of suitcases.

"Scusami," he said. He lifted three of the smaller bags and placed them in the back seat where Mary and Liz would sit.

We piled into the black Mercedes while our driver hefted over-sized suitcases into the trunk.

"Buon giorno. My name is Marco. Are you comfortable?"

Answering for everyone, I said, *"Si."*

I pulled out my compact and made an attempt to freshen my makeup. Unsmiling gray eyes stared back at me. *So this is what fifty looks like.* I was appalled that my neck was ringed like a pheasant and relieved no one could see the rest of my body. I snapped the compact shut and stared at the passing scenery of rustic farmhouses centered against an olive green horizon. My thoughts drifted to my husband, Ted...missing him. The feelings of distance and disconnection between us this past year had stressed me out. I was relieved to be free from the emotional tensions that seemed to hover over our marriage like a dark cloud. Yet I felt great concern about his tiredness of late. His response over my worry was always the same.

"I'm eighteen years older than you are, sweetheart. What do you expect?"

Not much you can add to that. Still...

The landscape changed from airport hotels and open fields to ruins contrasting with new stores. We dodged in and out of traffic on the busy *autostrada*. There were four clearly marked lanes; yet the drivers seemed to hover on the lines, creating five lanes as they vied for space and speed. My heart raced at the excitement of our September escape allowing me to ignore the anxiety in the pit of my stomach.

Reaching into my leather tote bag, I pulled out the folder containing my correspondence with Gabriella Windsor. We'd exchanged many friendly e-mails after I signed the rental agreement for her penthouse in Rome. I couldn't wait to meet her, and I was curious about the "lover" she'd mentioned in her last e- mail.

The driver jerked the car to avoid a motorcycle, pinning me against the front passenger door. I glanced at Mary and Liz huddled in the back seat, their eyes wide with fear at the chaotic driving. We were an unlikely trio, having met two years earlier in Italian class at a local junior college in Costa Mesa, California.

"Hey, Julie." Mary furrowed her brow. "Tell this guy to stop driving like a maniac."

Mary Scarpaci, unpredictable and hard to read, was the wild card in the trio. I'd met her through Liz and liked her. Liz had assured me this tiny but feisty woman would be fun on the trip. Her petite face, framed with chestnut cropped curls, enhanced her soft coffee-and-cream colored eyes. She had a tendency to be negative about life. Not to mention a tad bossy. I hoped she'd loosen up on this trip.

"It's okay, girls. Relax," I said, grateful they couldn't see how terrifying the ride was from the front seat!

"Oh, my goodness!" Liz pressed her nose to the window. "Look at that billboard for the Prada shop."

Liz MacArthur had divorced her husband three years ago, and her determination to remain mute on the details, combined with her sad expression whenever the subject came up, told me there was much to learn about her. I was sure she'd open up when the time was right.

Tall, about my height, five-feet-nine, Liz had riotous red hair and arresting green eyes that turned many a man's head. Liz was fun-loving and easy to be with, but her obsession with shopping, combined with the inability to make decisions, could be annoying.

I smiled, thinking about the two women sharing my get-away vacation. Our Italian heritage and our love of the language were our only bonds.

"Hey!" Mary tapped my shoulder. "Where are you? Hello?"

"Sorry. I was just thinking about how we met."

Liz unglued her nose from the car window. "Who knew that taking Italian would change our lives?" Liz sighed. "At least we learned enough Italian to give directions to a driver."

"Aren't you excited? Look at this," I said. I waved my hand at the ancient aqueduct we'd passed. "We did it. We're here. Take in the ruins, smell the rosemary, look at the tiny speeding cars."

"I can't take it all in," said Mary, pulling on her hair. "Remember, this trip might cost me my marriage."

The driver jammed on the brakes and threw Mary and Liz forward.

"What the heck!" Liz jumped.

The driver shouted at the helmeted young man on a Vespa. I understood his crude hand motions, followed by a loud, "*Imbecile!*"

Liz and Mary looked pale. "It's okay," I said. "He knows what he's doing." I smiled at him.

He grinned back at me with eyes as brown-black as espresso. He gave me a Roman shrug which in Italian meant, "Oh, well."

I pointed to the rosary beads and a large cross hanging from the dash of the car. "Hey, he's covered. It's obvious all the saints and angels in heaven have protected this car for a long time."

"Yeah, sure," said Mary. "Did ya happen to notice the dents on the side of this black beauty? And they're all on the passenger side in back...WHERE I'M SITTING."

I rolled my eyes and ignored her.

Marco turned off the main highway onto a road that led to the center of Rome, driving along claustrophobic streets. Soon, we were navigating alleys where no car could possibly fit, yet did. We marveled at the pedestrians narrowly avoiding death from cars and *motorinis.*

"Look at how these women dress," Liz whined. "I didn't bring the right clothes."

"Forget the clothes," Mary said, pushing aside a piece of luggage that had slid off the pile beside her in the back seat. "How the heck are we fitting this car down this so-called street?"

The driver screeched into an ancient alley barely wide enough to allow the doors to open. A shoe store stood on the left side and a pizzeria with two small outside tables blocked my side of the car.

"*Arriviamo,*" said the driver, his toothy smile revealing several gold crowns. Inching the Mercedes forward, he stopped in front of a fountain.

"*Numero quattro cento tre,*" he said, pointing to a faded red door with small brass numbers—403.

We unwound our cramped bodies and stepped out onto time-worn cobblestones to survey our surroundings. Mary harrumphed. Not a good sign.

"What's wrong?" I asked.

"*Graffiti.* Look at the *graffiti.*" She put her hands on her hips. "It's all over the building near our door." She scowled. "What on earth did you get us into?"

"Relax," I said, fishing in my purse for the wad of euros to pay the driver after he unloaded our bags. "Where's Liz?"

"Drooling at shoes," Mary answered.

I turned to see Liz gazing into the window of the shoe store, completely unaware she'd left her luggage sitting on the piazza. I rang the doorbell of 403. Glancing up, I saw a woman waving from a window on the top floor.

"I'll be right down," she shouted to us.

Surrounded by enough suitcases to outfit an Italian Countess, we waited for our hostess. The door swung open, revealing a tiny blond woman, hair softly framing a face that held large amber eyes. She wore snug, peg-leg jeans and a pink-tailored shirt that strained at the bust line.

"You must be Julie," she said in a clipped British accent. She greeted me with the two-cheeked Italian kiss. "And Mary and Liz? My name is Gabriella. Just call me Gabby." Mary blinked like an owl and Liz said, "Hello, Gabby."

A young man, wearing only string-tied lounging pants and no shirt, slipped his arms around her and drew her against him. "This is Antonio, my lover." She turned and stroked his shadowed jaw. My knees went weak. *Her lover! How bold.* His sculpted body, dark curly hair, black eyes, and sensual lips left us speechless. I sighed, remembering the sparks that used to fly between Ted and me. A shiver went through me as I shoved the image aside.

"Antonio will deliver the luggage to your rooms," she said, scooting out of his arms and motioning us inside.

"Wait a minute. What's that doing here?" asked Mary, pointing to the *graffiti* beside the red door.

Gabby laughed, deep and throaty. "Don't be concerned. *Graffiti* is political here. She waved her hands to the foyer, marble floors, and elegant framed mirrors on the walls. "As you can see, it's lovely inside."

Stepping in, Mary asked with suspicion, "Where's the elevator?"

"There is, uh, no lift." Gabby glanced my way and realized I'd kept that little detail a secret.

Mary and Liz stared at me.

"Aren't we on the top floor, Jules?" Mary asked, squinting her eyes.

"Yup. The top floor. We have our own Italian stair master." We followed Gabby up the marble steps.

Antonio passed us twice with luggage, not breaking a sweat. Gabby talked non-stop, never winded while the three of us paused at each landing, gasping for air.

Mary glared at me. "I've counted sixty-eight stairs so far, Jules." She bent over, took a deep breath, and wheezed, "And I'm not happy about it."

"You'll get used to the stairs," Gabby said. She held out her arm to signal our arrival at the penthouse. "We're here."

Once we entered the apartment, the climb was forgotten. If the living room was any indication of the rest of the penthouse, we were in paradise. Yellow-hued walls trimmed with white molding, sofas of gold and yellow tapestry, antique sideboards, and an elegant Venetian glass chandelier took our breath away.

"I forgive you for failing to mention there was no lift," said Mary.

"Oh, by the way, Julie," said Gabby, "your husband called."

I gazed at her, startled.

"Something about test results. He said to call."

A chill floated over my skin as I felt under my arm for the newly-found lump. The constant swelling of the lymph nodes from the lymphodema was driving me crazy. Always scaring me, imagining the cancer was back. I pushed harder against the lump.

Dear God! Not again. I just got my hair back.

I talked myself down from the panic. This was my time and Rome was my city. Nothing was going to come between us.

Okay, Jules. The doctor gave you a clean bill of health along with his blessing to make the trip. Stop worrying.

I smiled at Gabby.

"Thanks. I'll call him after I get settled."

Chapter Two

Rome beckoned. But jet lag had exhausted us.

"Antonio made a snack for you." Gabby motioned for us to follow her.

We walked into a bright, spacious kitchen filled with hand-painted Italian pottery of bright yellows and blues. Antonio, still shirtless and delicious looking, sat perched on a stool in front of the espresso machine. He grinned lazily. "Ready for coffee?" His accent was thick, his voice low.

Gabby pointed to a round table covered with a bright yellow cloth. A bouquet of flowers stood in the center along with bowls filled with fresh fruit and a tray of crackers.

Gabby handed me a folder. "Here's a list of restaurants, tourist attractions, maps, and, in case of an emergency, my cell phone number. Antonio and I are at your disposal while you're here."

"Thanks, Gabby." I swept my hand to include the others and said, "We all appreciate this." I thumbed through the information-packed folder.

"Please, enjoy your food," said Gabby. "We'll leave you alone for now." She stood and walked to the door. "Remember, we're just one floor down if you need us. Now unpack, explore the penthouse, and be sure to take a nap." She glanced at me. "Will you need a wakeup call?"

"Absolutely." I winked at her. "Call us an hour before you want us to be ready." I could feel my energy waning.

"Dinner will be at eight. I'll ring you at seven. *Ciao*." She and Antonio left, arms encircling one another.

I yawned, stood up, thanked her and turned to my new roommates. "I'm going to take a nap. Right now." I wandered down the long narrow hall searching for the blue and white bedroom Gabby had assigned me.

The image of my office flashed through my mind when I entered the tranquil room. I'd left my blue office haven at my home in disarray cluttered with papers, discarded magazines, and scattered files. Editing notes and Masters Theses were piled high under glass paperweights. The usually beautiful home office with its lovely artwork and calm-hued walls was in shambles, just like my life. I stared out the window. Something niggled in the back of my mind. Ted. I'd been avoiding calling my husband.

I yearned to get under the covers and sleep. Instead, I walked to the ornate sideboard in the corner of my room and with a trembling hand, dialed home. Ted picked up on the third ring. I took a deep breath.

"*Ciao*, it's me."

"Hi, honey. Good to hear your voice."

"Wanted to let you know I got here safe."

"Well, I figured you were still alive. I hadn't heard about any plane crashes." He laughed. It sounded forced.

"We had a great flight." I paused, uncomfortable. "You'd love it here."

"Hope you enjoy yourself." An awkward chuckle, tight and controlled. I knew he resented my trip to Rome.

"So, is everything okay, hon?"

"You've only been gone a day. Nothing's changed, Jules. Relax. Enjoy Rome. Take time to laugh. Find the old Pennsylvania girl I fell in love with and bring her home to me."

"I'm not looking for myself. I'm right here. As for change"—my voice rose—

"I'm not going to change for anyone. I just want to feel whole again."

Silence.

"Ted?"

"I miss the other Julie." His tone softened.

"I miss her, too, Teddy. Don't you get it? No one can go through what I've been through and not change." I paused. "Is this a good time to call you?"

"Good as any. What time is it there?"

"I haven't changed my watch yet. Four or five in the afternoon."

"Rats. There goes my cell phone. Sorry, Jules. I really need to take this call."

"Wait. What about the test results."

"Oh. Sorry. The doctor called and said they'd been delayed, and he'd have them in a couple of days."

"I hate waiting on blood tests."

Silence followed by a sigh that sounded irritated. "Julie, this is routine. Your cancer markers came in before you left. This test is just a check on your sugar levels. They were normal a month ago, they'll be normal now.

"Okay. I miss you, Ted. A lot."

"I miss you too, Jules. More than you know."

I heard him take a deep breath.

"It's hard on me, too, Jules. What you've been through."

"I know that, Teddy. I love you. And I'll call soon."

"Love you, too, Babe." A dial tone.

I re-cradled the phone and shook off a wave of emptiness. I flung back the blue duvet, slid onto the bed and fell asleep.

❦

The dull, flat droning of the phone jarred me awake. It was an odd sound, different from the high ring in America. I grabbed the phone, and it bobbled in my hand.

Gabby's cheerful voice brought a smile to my face. "Time to get ready for dinner, Julie."

My head felt stuffed with cotton. I mumbled sleepily. "Where?"

"Just be downstairs and outside the front door at eight o'clock."

"How should we dress?" I asked, leaning on one elbow.

"A skirt, slacks, whatever you like. The restaurant is a three-minute walk." Gabby laughed. "The people-watching will amaze you. *Ciao, bella.*"

My stomach felt queasy. Then it hit me. Sadness! Despite the tepid relationship with Ted, I missed him and felt lost and lonely without him. A sob caught in my throat.

"Good grief, Jules," I mumbled to the empty room. "Deal with it. That's why you're in Italy."

Willing myself to move, I strolled to Liz's room and knocked. "Liz? Are you awake?"

No answer.

I knocked louder. "Liz, wake up."

"I'm awake," said Mary, opening her door. She walked across the hall, hair askew, and rapped on Liz's door. "Liz. I'm coming in."

"Be gentle, Mary," I said.

"Gentle? You weren't sitting with her on the plane, Miss Upgrade. Liz goes into a coma when she sleeps. Gentle doesn't do it." She turned the handle, opened the door, and marched on tiny bare feet to Liz's bedside. I followed her.

Liz was buried under the sheets and duvet, her form barely visible in the darkened room.

"Liz." I nudged what might be a leg.

Mary fumbled with the shutter and swung it open, revealing the buttercup walls of the room. She marched to Liz's bed and yelled, "Wake up!"

Liz moved, slowly at first. "Where am I?" She squinted into the light of the window. Her long graceful body uncurled, and she stretched.

"It's seven, Liz." I touched her arm. "You have one hour to pull yourself together, Red. Come on."

She swung her feet to the floor in one elegant movement. "I'm up." Without another word, she padded into her bathroom.

"See ya," I said to Mary, turning to my room.

An hour later, we met in the living room, all of us dressed in black slacks and tops.

"I'm not changing," Mary said, voice firm.

I chuckled at our black outfits, walked to my room and yelled, "I'll add some color." I quickly switched my sleeveless top for my favorite aqua blouse and returned to the living room. "*Andiamo.*"

We clicked and clacked down the many marble stairs, trying not to twist our ankles on the indentations evolved from years of use. We opened the door and stepped onto the cobblestones of the Piazza Farnese and into our first night in Rome.

"This is stunning," Liz said. Her eyes darted in every direction.

Several *carabiniere* guarded the doors to the brightly lit French Embassy across the piazza on our left. The opened windows on the second story revealed wall and ceiling murals by Michelangelo. The white marble of the building sparkled in the spotlight and Italian chatter surrounded us. What teased my senses the most, though, were the pungent aromas of sauces and Italian spices that filtered from every corner.

"I feel like new Rome has disappeared and ancient Rome is illuminated. Wow!" I exclaimed. The Romans had bathed each antiquity in spotlights, the fountains, embassy and church blotting out any hint of new construction.

Gabby and Antonio sat sipping an espresso at the Farnese Caffe', on the corner of the piazza, directly across from our front door. They waved when they spotted us.

"He has a shirt on," Liz whispered, clearly disappointed.

Gabby wore jeans, turned up to the knee, her top a deep crimson, setting off her blonde hair. She looked like a runway model. I knew from her emails she had to be at least forty. She looked half her age.

She stood up to greet each of us with the two-cheek kiss while I wondered how on earth she walked on cobblestones in spike heels. "Ladies, it's the custom in Italy to walk about before dinner, stop for a drink, talk, then eat. I hope this is okay."

"Non c'e problema, Gabby," I said.

Antonio rose. He left the most incredible cologne scent of citrus trailing after him as he kissed each of us. He wore casual black slacks and a long-sleeved black shirt open down to the third button. It was oh-so-hard not to stare at him.

Gabby signaled the waiter and ordered in rapid fire Italian. She glanced at us. "I just ordered still water and cappuccinos. Hopefully, you'll become true Italians and graduate to sparkling water and espressos at night time."

"Don't worry, Gabby," I said. "My goal is to become Italian, espresso and sparkling water included." I knew it was un-Italian to drink a cappuccino after twelve noon.

Antonio smiled at me, his dark eyes twinkling.

I glanced at my watch.

Gabby reached over and touched the time piece. "No. Time is a foreign concept in Rome. Enjoy," she said, waving her hand about. "In fact, don't wear a watch while you're here. Italians are never on time anyway. . .especially Romans.

Gabby pointed to a nearby restaurant, explaining that Julius Caesar had been murdered on that very site. She told the story of the fountains in the center of the piazza, the bathtubs of the evil emperor, Caligula, and how both had been found perfectly preserved and moved to this piazza a hundred years ago. We listened, watching people stroll by: impeccably dressed couples, children, all out for their evening *passegiata*, laughing, cell phones attached to ears, hands gesturing with vigor.

I felt an unexplainable happiness sweep over me.

"Come," said Antonio, tossing some bills onto the table. He took Gabby's hand to pull her up. "We go to my shop, and then eat."

We followed. Sounds ricocheted from building to building, cobblestone and back, like a movie set. We turned down another alley, plastering our bodies against the stone walls to avoid speeding *motorinis*.

We stopped at a tiny shop tucked back on a narrow lane, with doors under an ancient arch, windows filled with pencil sketches of Roman buildings and Roman faces.

A round, dark-haired woman yelled, "Antonio!" She rolled toward him—a ball of energy. She grabbed his face and pinched his cheek. "*Mio figlio.*" More kisses.

Gabby watched with amusement. "This is Antonio's mother, *Signora* Colleto. Antonio is famous for his pencil and charcoal sketches of everything Roman."

Gabby chattered rapidly in Italian, introducing each of us to the rambunctious little mom. She two-cheek kissed us, and we grinned. I loved the Italian's easy affection.

Mary and Liz held back, but I tried my basic Italian.

"*Piacere*," I said. "A pleasure to meet you."

"*Anche lei*," she responded.

"*Mama, per favore. Inglese.*" He explained our Italian was minimal and she must try to speak a little English.

"Okay." She beamed. "Come, I show you my son's work."

The space was impossibly small, but every nook held artwork framed and displayed against plush black fabrics, spotlights beaming on each Roman antiquity. Standing next to a large display in the corner stood a man in the shadows, his striking profile exposing a straight nose, square jaw and thick curly hair. He turned, stopped, and held my eyes with his. Every nerve in my body stood at attention. I glanced away to catch my breath. When I looked up, he'd vanished. I scanned the area and caught a glimpse of him outside the door. My visceral reaction to him frightened me.

Chapter Three

The sun brushed my face through the crisp white organza curtains as they moved tenderly in the morning breeze. The writing desk gave me a perfect view of the Piazza Farnese. The splashing of the fountains comforted me. The French Embassy glistened in the first blush of the morning sun.

Two nuns walked across the piazza holding tight to their rosaries, heads down.

A leggy blonde strode across the stones, a *motorini* helmet under one arm. It was eight a.m. and, with each minute, The Caffe Farnese came more alive. The scent of fresh coffee and *cornetti* floated through the open window.

I ripped a blank page from my journal and wrote a hurried note to Liz and Mary telling them I could be found at the Café having coffee. I threw on my black capris and a soft pink blouse, left the note for the girls and five minutes later found myself seated in the warm sun on the café's patio. I ordered my first *cappuccino* and *cornetto* in faltering Italian.

"*Scusami, Signora.*" The male voice was so resonant it vibrated my bones.

I turned to my left and saw a pair of incredible eyes the color of the Mediterranean Sea peering at me over the headlines of *La Stampa*. I sucked in a breath. *The man from Antonio's shop.*

Lowering the paper, the owner of those eyes smiled, showing even white teeth, dimples beside his full lips and a glorious head of thick dark brown hair, woven with silver strands. My heart thundered. His hair caressed his neck, brushing the collar of his shirt several shades bluer than his eyes. The stubble on his face gave him a sexy sinister look. I wondered how his face would feel against my skin. "Stop it," I told myself.

"*VORRAEEE.*" He repeated my order, R's rolling.

"Oh, *si, vorrei.*" I would like...

"You said, *VORRIIIE.*" He purred. And winked.

Great job, Julie. You're impressing the heck out of these Italians.

"*Grazie, signore,*" I managed.

"*Prego, signora.*" The newspaper once again covered his face.

My breakfast arrived. Taking my time, sipping, savoring the cream-filled pastry, I felt the presence of Mr. Blue Eyes. *Should I turn around? Ah, push the chair back and pretend you're fetching your purse. Get a grip, girl. You're too old for these games. This is embarrassing.*

With as much grace as I could muster, I slid the chair back and to the left, reached for my purse, pulled out a pen and small notebook, and positioned myself for unobtrusive observing of this breathtaking man.

I studied my blank note page, as if inspired, and started to write thoughts. From the corner of my eye, I noticed a movement of the newspaper being folded. I took a sip of coffee and glanced toward Mr. Gorgeous. He looked straight at me.

I smiled.

He smiled.

A blush started in my neck and flushed upward, traveling to my hair line.

He adjusted his shirt collar with well-manicured hands, placed some euro under his cup, gathered his paper and briefcase and walked away.

Drat.

Then he turned, and my heart dipped over a cliff. Slowly, he pulled his Armani sunglasses down onto his nose. "*Buon giorno, bella signora.*"

I nodded.

I watched him walk until he turned the corner and disappeared.

Okay. So I'm an unhappy woman of fifty and he intrigues me. Who is he? *He was a conservative Italian, reading La Stampa; about my age. He carried a briefcase...maybe a businessman. His tailored suit fit his slim frame well. And he'd noticed me.* I tapped the pen against the notebook.

Was I so needy that this small gesture made me feel like a woman again? But then, he couldn't see ALL of me.

"Wipe that dreamy look off your face!" Mary ordered

"What?" I'd never noticed their arrival.

"We've been watching you." She looked at Liz, who shrugged.

"The coffee is fabulous." I motioned them to sit.

"Do they have tea?" Liz pulled her chair back and in a single fluid motion sat down. She lowered her face to the side and flipped her hair, managing in those few seconds to transform into a model.

"How do you do that?" Mary stared at her. "And it's really rude to shake your hair around food."

"*Signore?*" The waiter interrupted to take their order.

Mary pointed to my breakfast. "*Lo stesso, per favore.*" The same please.

"*Ha te caldo?*" Liz asked. Do you have hot tea?

"*Certo.*" He smiled. "*Americane?*" He nodded toward me, asking me if my friends were also American.

"*Si.*" I smiled and ordered another cappuccino.

The waiter left, shrugging his shoulders. I had a feeling we'd see a lot of that since we'd never quite conform to the Roman ways. As he walked away, I thought I heard him mumble "Crazy Americans." He was, however, smiling. I think he liked us..

"So, back to your flirting." Mary's brows arched. "You have a nice husband."

"Yes, I do. He's a great guy." I raised my brows right back at her. "And I wasn't flirting. Can we not talk about home right now? What happens in Italy stays in Italy."

"We'll see about that," snapped Mary.

I sipped my water and faced Liz.

"So, Red, what are your plans for today?"

"I'm going to the *Via Condotti* to shop."

"What a surprise." Mary rolled her eyes. "I'm going straight for the culture, St. Peter's. And I'm walking there."

"Mary, for goodness sake," I said. "Take the bus or a taxi. You'll wear yourself out your first day."

"Don't want to waste money on transportation. And I need the exercise."

A shadow of something crossed her face. Fear? Not exactly. Vulnerability. That was it.

"Something wrong, Mary?"

"No."

"It was the look on your face."

"I'm fine." Mary smoothed her cropped hair behind her ears.

The waiter arrived with drinks and food, and the conversation changed.

"So, are we still agreeing we're doing our own thing?" Liz curled the string around her teabag and pressed it into the spoon. Her bronze jersey top blended into her hair. "I don't like to be alone much."

Liz lived a comfortable lifestyle as a divorced woman. Between the first year of Italian and the second year, the change had been dramatic. Although she didn't talk about it, she must have been the victor at the end, because she bought a new car and a new house. Her wardrobe consisted of elegant name-brand clothing. And each week, the class would wait with anticipation to see her latest outfit.

"We'll all meet back at the apartment about four for a nap. Or whatever you want," I said.

"Well," said Mary, "I'm sticking to my original plan." She took a bite of her roll, the cream filling oozing onto her fingers. She wiped off the cream, touched the arm of the chair and sighed. Holding her purse with her clean hand, she maneuvered inside the purse and retrieved a tiny bottle of gel hand cleaner.

Liz and I watched the familiar routine. We'd observed it many times in Italian class.

"Mary, you're such a clean freak." I laughed.

Mary didn't laugh back. "Do you realize how many germs are on all public surfaces?" She frowned. "I can't help it. My perfectionism comes from…" She waved her hand. " Never mind."

"Just tell me one thing." I took a sip of coffee. "Do you microwave your kitchen sponges?"

"As a matter of fact, I do," she snapped. "Have you ever seen the movie, Sleeping With the Enemy? Well that's my life. See you this afternoon."

ꟹ

I watched her walk away, head held high as she blended into the crowd. She looked Italian.

Liz leaned forward. "Is that the movie about the psycho neat freak?"

"Yup. Come on, Liz." I pushed back from the table. "Let's go together."

She looked grateful. "Thanks. Just take me to some shops."

"If you dawdle too long, I may have to leave you, *capisci?*"

She nodded.

I noticed her intense gazing at a shoe store on the corner. "Later for the shoes, Red. Come on."

"Do you remember the location of Antonio's store?" she asked. Her tone had forced casualness.

"You want to find the man across from his store, don't you?"

"He was handsome."

"I agree. But look around." I waved my hand toward the men clustered on the piazza, dressed with Italian flair. Hair in place, sexy sunglasses perched on their Roman noses; they were obviously comfortable in their skin.

"Do you think…what was his name again…was flirting with me?"

"His name is Matteo and I don't know. What happened to you in the divorce, Liz? You've done a one-eighty in what you want in a man."

"I just don't trust white-collar men, and I don't feel like talking about it." She swung her hair and put on her sunglasses. The flip caught the eye of several men standing nearby. It was no wonder. Her flaming hair and long legs provided an intriguing contrast to dark-haired Rome.

"Please, could I just look for a minute. I'll be quick."

"Fine. I'll wait here." I leaned against the window while she fished through the shoes and thought of last night when we'd left Antonio's shop.

We'd met a stunning older man, with a mop of white curly hair and bronzed face belying his age. Antonio had introduced him as Matteo.

During the introduction, there was a flurry of cheek kisses leaving me wondering how Italians stayed healthy.

Matteo spoke broken English. Still in his work clothes of stained white coveralls and sandals, he wiped his hands on a cloth and shook our hand. The whiff of varnish and wood wafted from the shop door.

"Matteo refurbishes furniture. An artist in his own right. Look." Antonio pointed to a table and chairs of rich mahogany, gleaming through the illuminated window. "*Domani,* Matteo," said Antonio.

Liz couldn't take her eyes off him. And from Matteo's wide smile, the attraction was mutual.

"Hey, Jules...just a couple more minutes, promise." Liz popped back into the store.

I thought about dinner last night at the *da Giovanni Trattoria.* It had been mouth-watering. Despite Mary's grumbling at the late hour for dinner...we'd sat down at nine-thirty...it was a delicious experience.

"This is a famous *Trattoria,*" said Antonio.

We'd sat at a table facing the French Embassy.

The table linens were blue on blue. White linen napkins were folded into flower shapes and peeked out from the sparkling crystal water and wine glasses. Candles twinkled in the faceted glass hurricanes and fresh flowers sat to the right of each table setting. And for one moment, I wished Ted were there.

Liz tapped me on the shoulder interrupted my memory of the night before.

"She's holding a pair of shoes for me," said Liz.

I smiled. "Okay, let's walk. You can window shop and I'll just follow."

As Liz and I strolled in silence, I thought more about last night. The air had held a humid balminess, and the aromas of cheese and garlic filled the night. The view through the open windows of the French Embassy stunned the senses. Chandeliers sparkled highlighting the frescoes of Michelangelo. Large cabinets of dark carved wood peeked through the windows. Fountains splashed quietly, interrupted only by chatter, laughter and an occasional buzzing *Vespa.* I felt an anger build inside me. It was ugly. I needed to find out why.

"Hey, Jules? I asked you a question."

"Oh, Sorry, Liz. What?"

"Do you mind if I just go through this jewelry shop? Please."

"Sure. I'll wait for you right there." I motioned to the tiny café on the corner. "I'll order a drink. Take your time."

I sat down and a waiter took my order.

"Vorrei un espresso, per favore."

He smiled and went inside to make my coffee. And I continued to ruminate about our first night in Rome. Not only had the surroundings been overwhelming, but the conversation tiring after such a long flight. I tried to remember the conversation.

Liz had bubbled with excitement at the beauty of the piazza at night.

"I don't know where to look." Liz turned her head with dizzying speed.

"Forget looking," said Mary. "Something smells good, it's past my bedtime, and I'm starved." She grabbed the menu. After a cursory glance, she turned to me. "What the heck does this say?"

"Mary. Good grief." I picked up my menu and translated. "We've covered the food over and over again in class. *Vitello* is veal; *pesce* is fish, *vedure* are vegetables." I looked at Gabby. "Do you have recommendations?"

"*Si. Con permesso*, I will order for all of us."

"Call me a strange Italian, Gabby, but I don't care for fish or seafood," I said.

"But I do," said Liz, still glancing at Mary.

"Me, too," said Mary. "I'll try anything." Her lips were pursed when she looked at me.

Mary was beginning to get on my nerves. What was going on with her? Probably just me. She seemed kind of snarky.

Antonio summoned our waiter. After much shrugging, gesturing, and high-speed Italian, the waiter walked away, shaking his head.

"Antonio, what's wrong?" I asked.

"Nothing." He smiled.

"No, really, Antonio. I want to know."

Gabby touched my shoulder. "Because this place is family owned, usually the menu is limited. The waiter had specials featuring shrimp and various fish in many of the pasta dishes." She patted me. "It's okay. He's making one dish without seafood and one with seafood."

"Well, Princess Upgrade." Mary's said. "What about your lecture on 'When in Rome, do as the Romans do?'"

"So I don't like fish. Deal with it, Mare." The waiter arrived with our water and wine. Mary's clipped tone was getting on my nerves.

Gabby and Antonio raised their glasses; we followed their lead.

"Welcome to Rome. *Buon appetito!*" The clinks echoed in the piazza.

We saw the door to our building from the restaurant. I kept thinking how good my bed was going to feel. Stifling a yawn, I turned to Gabby. "Is that a garden at the top of your building?"

"Yes, and that's where we're going after dinner."

The waiter arrived with two steaming plates of pasta. The first plates held clams smothered in a rich white sauce. The second platter was laden with bow-tie pasta and a red marinara sauce.

The meal was a blur. Red wine and pasta quieted our stomachs.

"This food is fabulous." Liz yawned and stretched. "But I'll enjoy it more tomorrow. Right now, I'm exhausted." She stifled another yawn.

"It's okay," said Gabby. "We know jet lag all too well."

Antonio paid the bill, and we walked to our door.

Seeing the stairs, we'd groaned, and trudged upward. Gabby led, agile as a panther, Antonio followed. I paused at every tenth step. Exercise had not been a priority during the chaos of the last three years. My usually slim figure had bloomed in new places. Carrying an extra twenty pounds was like hefting a twenty pound infant. I just didn't understand why most chemo patients lose weight while chemo for breast cancer...it tends to pack on a few pounds. Maybe it messed up the hormones. When I stopped to catch my breath, Mary and Liz joined me.

Liz pulled both hands through her hair, sighed, and vowed, "I'll be running up these steps by the end of the first week."

"Whatever," said Mary, giving us the 'look'.

"Hey," I said with an evil smile. "We all need to lose a few pounds. Think of these stairs as aerobic exercise."

"Easy for you and Liz with your long legs," Mary retorted. "At my height, this is more like mountain climbing."

I took a sip of the espresso and smiled, thinking about all of us entering the penthouse. We'd gazed with longing toward the hall that housed our bedrooms.

But Gabby rallied us with a, "One more flight to the rooftop. We have a surprise for you." I'd suppressed a groan.

The wooden staircase at the end of the kitchen was narrow and circular, not for the faint of heart. Tired to the bone, we climbed and went through the door to the rooftop. One glance at the view and our fatigue floated away.

From the rooftop, we could see ancient Rome, the Coliseum, the Forum, St. Peter's dome. The white marble wedding cake, the Roman nickname for the Monument to Vittorio Emmanuele II with Italy's Tomb of the Unknown Soldier, glimmered.

In the corner sat a small table and chairs enclosed on three sides by a wooden arbor entwined with vines and blooming purple flowers. An ice bucket held a frozen bottle of *limoncello.* Wrought iron candle holders round and tall, were scattered between clay pots that cradled of blue, yellow and red flowers. The citronella candles glowed, guarantying no mosquitoes, leaving wispy trails of smoke that disappeared into the night sky. I felt like I'd traveled through time. Rome. Italy. The Eternal City wrapped me in its arms. I was home. I could feel the rhythm of the city.

Gabby and Antonio held out the chairs for us, and poured the lemony *digestivo.*

"To Roma," I said. The strong cold taste of lemon slid down my throat. I sipped it slowly.

"This is your secret place," said Gabby, "where you can rest before retiring, or feel the sunshine during the day. *Buono notte.*"

"*Grazie*, Antonio and Gabriella."

Gabby turned and reminded us, "Don't forget to write in your journal. Days blend into each other and can confuse the memories."

"Rest tomorrow," said Antonio. "You have many days and Rome must be experienced slowly."

Antonio slid his arm around Gabby's shoulders, leaned in to kiss her neck, and they disappeared, leaving us to gaze in wonder across Rome's rooftops.

"This is beautiful," I said. "I hope I can settle down and sleep." I sipped more *limoncello*, savoring its coolness and warmth.

"If you think I'm writing in a dang journal tonight..." Mary's voice trailed off.

"I wonder," said Liz, "if their friend Matteo has been up here." A dreamy smile graced her face.

"As lovely as this is," I said, "I have to sleep. See you in the morning."

Chapter Four

I felt a hand on my shoulder.

"Earth to Julie." Liz hit my arm, breaking my train of thought. "Where are you?"

"Still thinking about last night in Rome, the dinner, the view," I said.

"Yeah," said Liz. "It was fab. Now let's find some more shops."

I laughed and swallowed the last drop of espresso. "I'm ready."

We turned in the direction of the Spanish Steps. What should have been a twenty-minute walk took an hour. After asking half a dozen fully armed *carabiniere* for directions, dodging Vespas, and gawking at sculptures and fountains and very un-Orange County buildings, we arrived at the Steps. The antiquities connected me to history. And every corner held something ancient that captured my eyes. It sure beat looking at row after row of tan or peach-colored tract homes.

Liz gasped when she saw the steps. The Spanish Steps, the great stairway leading up to the heights of *Trinita' dei Monti* with its French church and small obelisk, takes your breath away.

"I'll race you to the top, Liz."

"No way. We'll walk. I don't want to sweat. Look at the people. I wonder how many steps."

"I know. I looked it up. There are one hundred and thirty seven in all. What a view." I tapped Liz's shoulder to draw her eyes back to the Steps and away from the Gucci store on the Via Condotti. "Can you imagine the beauty at Easter when the steps are filled with flowers?"

We made the climb to the top, sidestepping fingers of tourists now sitting on almost every step, stopping often before reaching the top.

At the summit, I felt excited, almost like I was already part of this city.

"Let's sit for awhile, Liz." We meandered between hands and feet. Locating a space about half-way down, we sat and threw ourselves into serious people watching.

"What a feast for the senses," I said, almost tasting the gelato being licked by a young Italian boy sitting next to me.

The visitors to Rome wore casual clothes. Young lovers caressed each other, workers gestured with phones connected to their ears. Others sat and relaxed. Lunchtime scents of pasta sauces permeated the air. And conversations in foreign tongues added an exotic flavor.

"It's better than a movie," said Liz.

But she threw long wistful looks toward the Via Condotti, a narrow street that began at the bottom of the Steps, and was known as the wealthiest shopping district in Rome.

Her restlessness was palpable. I yearned to just sit and watch people. She was determined to shop. I heaved a sigh and gave in reluctantly.

"Red, if you're not going to relax and enjoy the moment, it won't be enjoyable for me. Let's go." I offered my hand to help her up.

Fifteen minutes later, after Liz had fingered and lifted every silk scarf in the store, I began to wring my hands together out of sheer boredom.

I pulled a scarf from her hand. "I'm sorry, Liz. I'm out of here." I gave her my 'I'm sorry' look. She barely glanced my way, asking to see a bright red scarf in the furthest corner of the display.

"See ya later." She spoke to the scarf as though I weren't there.

With Liz safe in shopping heaven, I slipped out of the store and onto the narrow, noisy Via Condotti. Tucked away somewhere on this street was the famous Greco Bar. My eyes glanced up searching for the famous landmark. I ran my fingers through my hair in a gesture of frustration. I needed some time alone. My stomach had tightened and I felt my shoulders slump with sadness. It seemed like my life was a rollercoaster...exciting and thrilling going up, followed by a huge drop into a pit. At the end of the ride, all I had left was a lack of emotional happiness.

Thinking was best done while sipping coffee. And I'd walked off the nourishment of the morning roll on the way to the Steps. My stomach growled. I looked at my watch. One-thirty. Where had the day gone?

I spotted the sign barely visible between the elegance of Gucci and Bulgari. *Antico il Caffe' Greco*, coffee house to the rich and famous. Established in 1760, the café had hosted Dickens, Lord Byron, and Keats. Thanks to my diligent research, I, Julie Walden, would join them today.

The servers wore black suits and white gloves. A distinguished host, with graying hair and steady brown eyes led me beyond the ornate wooden bar in the front through a series of salons, finally seating me at an elegant marble table beneath an ornate antique mirror. The seats were red velvet, the walls a rich gold.

Instead of great writers and philosophers of old, the café was filled with tourists, Italian businessmen and women and Japanese ladies laden with Gucci and Armani bags. And me.

I ran my hands over the cool marble surface of the table and picked up the burgundy menu, fiddling with the gold tassel. I held back a quiet gasp when I looked at the prices. Ten euros for a macchiato...espresso with cream served in a doll's teacup, three times the size of a thimble. Water an astounding fourteen euro (although the bottles were deep blue and quite lovely) and a pastry of any kind averaged twelve euros. Including tip and taxes, a treat at the famous coffee shop cost more than dinner for four. Some would say it was a ridiculous waste of money. But not me. Time was valued here. The coffee shop's motto was 'A place to sit and wait for the end.' The end of what, I wasn't sure. But I intended to linger.

A white glove touched the corner of the table. I ordered a salad and espresso. I handed him my menu, acting as though I always spent this much money for a place to sit and wait for the end.

In my salon, the tables were full of English-speaking tourists. It disappointed me. I yearned to be surrounded by Italians, wanting to breathe in the language. The white tennies and black stretch travel pants with twenty 'hidden' pockets were a dead giveaway that they were true tourists. The bulging belly bags around their waists brought a smile to my face.

My diminutive drink, salad and water arrived. The cup sat on an elaborate plate with gold scrolling. Three tiny bowls were filled with chocolate shavings, sugar, and thick rich cream. A sterling silver fork and demitasse spoon nestled among a display of yellow flowers. The waiter poured my water into a clear crystal goblet, bowed and walked away.

I'd been occupied with my coffee, glanced up, and noticed the Americans were gone, replaced by a flock of handsome men. Well, a couple of them weren't so handsome. But they were intriguing.

Taking a sip of my *macchiato*, I noticed an older man watching me. The direct eye contact of Italian men took some getting used to. But I liked it. Bravely, I held his gaze while I placed my cup on its elegant saucer. He spoke to his companions. One man looked familiar. But I could only see the back of his head, his long dark hair curling into his...oh. I dropped my gaze. But not quick enough.

The man from the Caffé Farnese that morning, with eyes the color of the sea, turned and raked a hand through his thick hair. I held my breath.

Great, Jules. He probably thinks you're stalking him. And there goes my thinking time.

Feeling awkward, not knowing where to look, I said a silent thank you when the waiter brought my bill.

Fishing in my purse for my favorite plastic card, I handed it to the waiter and stared at the table, waiting for him to return. I tried to ignore the blue-eyed man as I scribbled my signature on the card receipt. I got up from the table, and started to walk.

The man said, "*Ciao. Domani*? Tomorrow? Caffé Farnese? *Nove*?"

I managed to choke out a "*si*, nine" and continued toward the exit, my heart pounding.

Thirty minutes later, getting lost only once, I arrived at door number 403, my Roman penthouse, and climbed the many marble stairs. I plopped into the first chair I found.

A blinking red light caught my eye. I struggled off the chair, walked to the phone, and hit the message button.

"Just wanted you to know your blood work came in all complete and normal just like I said. Stop worrying. With the best oncologist in Southern California giving you permission to go to Italy…I think you should feel pretty good about everything right now."

A pause, followed by a cough. "I love you. Good blood tests for you are good news for me. Pretty soon everything will be back to normal." Then a click.

Relief. Then my stomach knotted. "You're such a jerk," I yelled at the phone. I hammered the erase button, wanting to cry. But I was too angry.

After the first rush of relief at the good news, my emotions plummeted to the ground, leaving me feeling frightened and vulnerable at the desperate lack of closeness we once had. His demeanor when I asked to take this trip was one of sheer relief, almost as though he felt a weight had been lifted from his shoulder that he wouldn't have to deal with "us."

An older friend had told me, not too long ago, that marriage is made up of seasons. This season felt like a cold barren February where even a blast from a well-run furnace couldn't keep me warm.

Mary found me crumpled in the chair, face tear-streaked.

"What happened?" she asked.

"Nothing. It was just Ted's phone message." I rubbed my eyes with my knuckles, spreading the black streaks.

"You look ghoulish. What's the problem, raccoon eyes?"

Mary pulled the ottoman next to me. She sat there, staring.

"Ted called."

"And..." She shrugged, waiting for the dramatic moment.

"He told me my blood work came in fully normal, cancer markers were in the normal range." I hugged myself tightly to hold back more tears.

"That's great. Really. Aren't you relieved?" Her tone of voice was as stern as her jutting chin as she faced the window.

"Yeah." I avoided looking at her.

"So stop crying. It'll get you nowhere."

"I never realized you were so mean, Mary. You remind me of Ted. No sympathy, no—-oh crud—-I don't know. And I'm well aware I'm overreacting."

"So we're having a pity party? Buck up, baby. You're not the only woman in the world who's had breast cancer."

I choked back a sob.

"Look." Mary's tone softened. "I'm not the warmest person in the world." She took my hand. "But you have to understand; I see your world and envy you, breast cancer and all."

I stared at her.

Lady, you're nuts.

"It's just that Ted didn't sound relieved or anything," I muttered.

"So help me out here. Explain." She pulled my face toward her.

"He said nothing about being happy for me or that he was relieved. Nothing. And that's what I've been getting from him—nothing." My voice caught in another sob. "He's been working so many hours, meeting with clients, playing round after round of golf…almost avoiding me." I looked at Mary and heaved a sigh. "We used to shared such passion."

"Jules, for goodness sake. He's watched you go through seven surgeries in one year, lose body parts, suffer through chemo, lose your hair. He stuck with you. He supported you, even though he must be scared to death." She paused.

"Then you go into a funk and run away to Rome to find the meaning of life in a luxury penthouse? And you want sympathy? He's a man. He doesn't have a clue. I don't think a man can understand how much this affects a woman."

Nausea twisted my stomach. "You're not seeing my side, Mary. I've done everything to make myself attractive and exciting to him. Even though my body has changed, my feelings haven't. He's shut me out of his life emotionally."

Placing my hands over my stomach, I mumbled, "Of course it's been my emotional withdrawal, too, I guess."

Hands on hips, Mary said, "Duh! Besides, when you've lived my life, there's no other side. It's just a big piece of misery."

"Wait just a minute." My jaw was so tight, I thought it'd snap. "We're not comparing lives here. I hurt for my own reasons. You hurt for yours. Don't compare. I'm so ticked at you right now, Mary. If things are so bad, why are you staying with George? I love Teddy. "

"Just before I came here, my husband threatened to wipe out my bank account and leave me if I went through with this little adventure."

"I feel bad for you, Mary." My voice rose in anger. "But you haven't been threatened with cancer."

"Oh get over it." Mary stood up, her tiny frame looming over me. "You have a nice husband, money, great kids. Stop whining."

"Stop comparing your life with mine. You made your own bad choices. I didn't choose cancer."

"And I did?"

"What do you mean?" I asked.

"I lost my second child to cancer when he was four, as if it's anything to you. Leukemia. Who chooses tragedy? We all suffer, Jules. Deal with it."

My jaw dropped. I stammered. "I'm sorry...please forgive me."

I looked at Mary in a new way. What was his name?"

"James." She folded her hands and studied them. "I don't want to talk about it."

"Whoa. We're having an argument about whose life is better, who's suffering the most, you share a terrible tragedy with me and now you won't tell me about it?"

Mary looked at me, eyes brimming. "I SAID, I will not talk about it."

Liz' entrance interrupted us.

She dropped her packages on the floor. "What the heck are you two fighting about? I heard you in the stairwell."

"Nothing," I said. "Looks like Rome made some money on you today."

The room filled with thick tension.

Wanting to ignore it, Liz gathered her bags and carried them to the dining room table. The packages shimmered against the table's deep mahogany.

Liz looked at me as if waiting for permission to share her joy.

"Mary and I were having a minor disagreement. We'll talk it out later, won't we Mary?" I glared at her.

She glared back.

I directed my full attention to Liz.

"Show us your stuff, bag lady," I said.

"Wash your face first, Jules," Mary said.

She scampered to the kitchen sink, dabbed a paper towel with water, returned to me, and reached up to gently wipe away the black around my eyes.

"There. That's better." Mary stood back to examine my face. "And here's a tissue." A half smile emerged through her pursed lips.

"Thanks, Mary." I exhaled, not realizing I'd been holding my breath during the argument.

Liz took long strides to the gold sofa, sank into it and gathered her purchases around her as though they were delicate ornaments and she, the Christmas tree.

One by one, she pulled the items from their lush bags.

"Fendi purse, silk scarves, Prada shoes, dress, trousers, Bulgari bracelet..." She tossed each treasure aside and folded the bags with care. "Souvenirs," she said, patting the pile of empty designer bags.

"Model them," said Mary.

"Yeah. Go for it," I nodded toward the pile of clothes.

Liz had chosen a theme of deep brown, orange, and yellow. Her green eyes sparkled as she preened and plucked the clothing together, mixing and matching, and wheeling around, displaying perfectly coordinated outfits. She rattled on and on about shoes she wanted to find that would set off every piece of her new wardrobe. I had to admit, the clothes were stunning.

But could she afford it? Didn't think she made that much money working part time as a travel consultant.

"So," she cooed, "what are the plans for tonight and will we be anywhere near Antonio's store?"

"Don't you mean Matteo's shop?" queried Mary.

"Gabby says Rome is best seen by strolling," I said. "Let's walk around and eat at one of the restaurants on the Piazza Navona tonight."

"Sounds good to me," said Mary. "It's close by and great for people-watching." She glanced my way. "Tell Liz the good news?"

"What? You saw that dreamy man again?"

"No, Liz. Ted called and said my cancer markers have remained within the normal range, all the blood tests perfect."

"So the mascara mask was from tears of happiness?"

"Yup. We should be ready to leave about seven-thirty, right?"

"Whatever." Mary squinted at me.

I sauntered down the hall to my peaceful bedroom and plopped in a heap on the soft blue duvet covering my bed. The piazza below was filled with the sounds of workers coming home, clipping over cobblestone, with scents of early simmering sauces wafting through my window.

I closed my eyes, took several deep cleansing breaths, and thought about the good news/disappointing news scenario. I touched my hair, playing with the soft dark curls, thankful for each strand. I touched my breasts, grateful for the miracle of plastic surgery. My fingers brushed against my eyelashes, each one a treasure.

So, why was I so miserable?

Tears slipped down my cheeks.

Nurturing. I need nurturing. I missed my parents and their unconditional love. Two years later and I still couldn't bear that they were gone.

I sat up, scooted back against the cool square linen-covered European pillows, closed my eyes and tried to picture my folks.

And Ted. *Is he afraid, too? Is that the problem? Does he not want to deal with it? Am I different to him?*

"Probably," I said aloud.

Cancer is an isolating disease. I remembered finding half of my hair on the shower floor, clumps on my pillow, sitting in a chair in the middle of the night and pulling out large quantities, and crying from fear and nausea and pain and loss. Alone.

Facing my mortality.

I thought of all the friends who'd sat by my side, held my hands during treatment. It'd been an overwhelming comfort. But in the end, I was alone with the disease.

I should be thankful I made it through the first year, this year, to hit that two-year mark. But turning fifty, feeling undesirable, less of a woman. There has to be more for me. I wanted to call Ted, but I feared he'd just say something that would leave me emptier, lonelier. Tomorrow. I'll wait until tomorrow.

I rolled off the bed and padded toward the shower. I removed my clothing and stood naked before the mirror. I looked like a woman. I was still Julie and looked pretty good.

I scuttled into the shower and let the hot water pour over me, hoping to wash away my fear. I scoured my skin, shampooed and conditioned my hair, and let the soft water of Rome rinse away my sadness.

Afterward, I wrapped myself in a thick terry cloth robe.

Tonight, Jules, you're going to be a Roman woman. Comfortable in your skin. I tapped the side of my forehead with my fingers. "It's all up here, babe," I reminded myself.

An hour later, scanning my reflection in the glass, I strolled into the living room, calling to Liz and Mary.

"Come on," I said. "Let's eat."

Liz and Mary's heels clicked down the hall. Both of them stopped, jaws dropping as they looked at me.

"Wow, Jules. You look stunning," said Liz.

"A knock-out," Mary said.

Fingering the red and black silk scarf draped around my shoulders, Liz said, "Red is your color." She pulled at the short sleeves of the silky texture of my sweater. "Look at the cut? It outlines your shape. And with cleavage!"

Liz walked behind me, admiring my outfit from every angle.

"Lose the earrings," said Mary.

"Why?"

"They're too long."

"No, they're not," said Liz, touching the filigreed gold drops hanging from my ears. "They're elegant, and elongate her neck."

Liz was a flame of fire with her new orange top. Mary wore her usual black.

"We're a good looking threesome," I said. "Look out, *Roma.*"

Liz led the way. And we knew where she'd take us. We meandered through the *Campo di Fiori,* now crowded with people. Young Italians clumped together, talking, laughing, cell phones nestled against their ears. Every restaurant patio was set for dining under the stars, the piazza brimming with tourists, eating and drinking. The scent of oregano and simmering garlic permeated the air. The Romans were dressed in the latest fashions. Their chatter and happiness beat against my skin like butterfly wings.

"Ah. There's that Roman rhythm again. Do you hear it? Can you feel it?" I squared my shoulders, confidence draping me with gossamer strands.

"It's so noisy here," said Liz. "Let's take the alleys to the Navona."

"What a surprise," intoned Mary, raising her eyebrows.

Sure enough, Liz led us straight to the Via Cancelleria and entered Antonio's shop.

"*Ciao,*" said Antonio, waving us into his store. The wall behind him displayed his dramatic sketches of Rome. Gabby stood next to him, leaning against a black marble counter, her arm linked in his.

Would Ted and I ever connect again.

Squaring my shoulders, I walked to them. "*Ciao.*" Kisses followed.

"Ciao, mi'amici". Gabby and Antonio spoke in unison. *"Ciao, Matteo."*

Liz froze.

We turned. Matteo stood there, almost unrecognizable. Work clothes gone, body clothed in fitted jeans, topped by a soft beige short-sleeved shirt. His tousled white hair, bronzed skin and wide brown eyes were enhanced by the smile lighting his classic Italian features. The only trace of the artist could be seen under one thumb nail...a trace of brown paint.

Liz stood in place, mute.

"*Ciao*, Matteo," I said and leaned toward him for a kiss. I recognized the scent of his cologne. Dolce e Gabanna. I loved it, had purchased it for Ted, who'd never used it. He usually slapped on some aftershave, screaming each time because it burned his face. I'd given up in my attempts to push him out of his comfort zone. Being eighteen years older hadn't mattered when we were young. Now, the age difference was telling, me fifty, Ted almost seventy.

Matteo reached down to Mary. "*Ciao.*" Then he turned to Liz. He walked over to her, held her shoulders and lingered longer than necessary as he kissed her, Italian style, on both cheeks.

"Hi." She lowered her eyes as though shyness had overcome her.

"*Ciao*, Liz." Mary looked at her and crossed her eyes. "We're in Italy. Say *ciao.*" Mary's tone was playful.

"Nice to see those brown eyes smile, Mare." I winked at her.

"Julie, Mary," said Gabby. "Would you mind if we borrowed Liz for the evening?"

"Take her," said Mary, elbowing me to emphasize I'd better not disagree.

"We close store in thirty minutes." Antonio gave Liz his lazy smile. "Then we go to dinner."

Liz nodded and smiled, a blush rising to her cheeks.

"Liz, we'll see you later, okay?" I waited.

Finally, a soft "okay" drifted from her. She flashed a dazzling smile and ran her fingers through her hair. I envied Liz and her natural grace.

I grabbed Mary's arm. "Come on." We scurried out the door.

I looked back at the foursome, catching Gabby's gaze. She waved and made the 'okay' sign with her thumb and forefinger. She'd planned well. I was beginning to wonder if Gabby was secretly crafting all our moves.

Chapter Five

Mary and I meandered down the alley that flowed into the Piazza Navona, our sandals clicking on the thick stones. We stood, inhaling the night-time aura of Rome. The Navona was an oval shape and presented an unusual ambience. Restaurants echoed with the low humming sound of satisfied diners. A church face was spotlighted and soft lighting accented the walls of the apartments, glowing dimly in the bronze and gold shadows. Even though filled with people, the piazza made me feel as though I stood in a lovely, cozy room in someone's home.

Bernini's Four Rivers sculpture and fountain dominated everything, its center a Roman Obelisk topped by the Papal Dove. One of the statues, a muscular man representing the Plate River, seemed to have an arm raised in protest toward the Church of Sant' Agnese. When standing near the fountain, the surrounding churches, palaces, and beautiful old rust-colored buildings shown in a surreal beauty. The lights hovered on terraces awash in flowers.

Alive and warm, I knew I belonged here. The afternoon spat between me and Mary appeared to have been tucked away--a distant memory as we breathed in the sights and sounds of this perfect oval art piece.

"Mary, look at this."

"I know. Just like the guidebook said. It's God's waiting room'." Her tone soft, Mary appeared relaxed.

We looked about, each lost in thought.

"Mary?"

"Yes?"

"Can we just pick a place to sit and sip?"

"Works for me," she said.

"I want to find the perfect spot," I said, scanning each restaurant patio for a front row seat.

"*Scusa, Signore.* I have place for you." An older man with thick silver hair and wire-rimmed glasses perched on his long nose bowed as he spoke. "Good to watch people."

"*Grazie*," I murmured.

"This is it," I said to Mary.

The waiter pulled chairs around the small round table, and we settled in front row, center stage.

"Mare, I need to throw myself at the Italian language. We have to use what skills we have and try."

"Okay," she said, rubbing the back of her neck.

No one was in a hurry. It seemed to be a sitting room for the locals.

I studied the menu. What grabbed my attention was the Tartufo. Dessert. It was hard to concentrate with hordes of visitors strolling around the center, as well as local Romans out for their pre-dinner walk.

The waiter returned, took our order, and chuckled at our attempt to speak Italian.

"*Parla Italiano molto bene.*" He held my eyes for a moment. Then, he swept his arm toward the piazza. "*Bellissima, si?*"

"*Si,*" I sighed. "*Molto bella.*" It was too lovely to be real.

"What's the name of this restaurant?" asked Mary.

I picked up the wine list and read "*Tre Scalini*" on the front. "I guess we're at *Tre Scalini.*"

I couldn't stop gazing at the cafés, restaurants, wine bars and small shops. The fountains next to the center were centuries old. Filling the center part of the oval were painters, mimes, and singers.

Since the piazza was closed to traffic, the absence of pesky scooters enabled us to hear every whisper.

"Jules," Mary said, reverent in tone, "I feel like I'm in a painting."

"Same here," I answered in a whisper. "I could stay for hours."

Our waiter brought water, wine, and *bruschetta.* We wanted to save room for the sweet treat.

"Here's to Rome, and..." Mary paused, "positive changes."

"To friends, to relationships, to healing," I said, clinking my glass against hers. I wondered, though, what she was thinking when she made the comment about change. Seemed odd.

"So Mare, my friend, what were you talking about when you said George was taking all your money and leaving you?"

She tightened her grip on the wine glass. "Let's not ruin the evening."

"No. It won't ruin the evening." I leaned forward. "We're pretty much stuck with each other. So lay it on me."

Her brows furrowed. "Well, okay." Mare took a deep breath. "Where to begin?"

At that moment a little man dressed in black, wearing a plaid fedora, strolled to our table and squeezed his accordion. *"O Sole Mio."* His eyes twinkled as he sang. Tourists from everywhere knew this Italian classic. Mary and I knew the Italian words and sang with him. His voice, rich and deep, moved me. My eyes felt moist. We were in Rome, enjoying its music. California and my sadness seemed to float into a puffy cloud, drifting high above the buildings of the piazza. I tried to envision my husband's smile. But all I could see was the intimate drama of life in front of me.

I sat with my chin on my hand, gazing into the chestnut-dark eyes of the street performer while he sang, lost in the moment.

When he finished, the patrons on the patio burst into applause shouting, "*Bravo, bravissimo*!" Many tossed coins into his accordion case, including Mary who added a generous five euros.

"What you lika me sing?" The musician seemed to ask just us.

"Back to Sorrento," I said.

A crowd gathered behind him for this song. His voice haunted. I noticed the worn material on his shirt and jacket. His tie was old and stained, but he took pride in his work. I thought of my grandpa and pictured him in his kitchen, singing old folk songs of Italy.

"*Scusa*?" A rich male voice, behind my right shoulder.

I knew it was him. The man from the Caffé Farnese. His deep voice sent an unfamiliar feeling to my stomach.

I turned away from the singer and gazed into a pair of deep blue eyes.

He took my hand. "I am called Dante. What are you called?" Never had a man looked me with such intensity. Once again, I fantasized about the feel of his face against mine. *Dante. The man had a name. I rolled the name over in my mind, loving the sound of it.*

"Her name is Julie," said Mary, hitting my arm.

I couldn't move, almost feeling like a fragile butterfly caught in a net.

She hit me again. "Are you mute?"

"*Si*, I'm Julie."

"*Ah, Giulia. Una bella nome.*"

My name had never sounded so lovely.

"*Permesso?*" He gestured for permission to sit and join us. His shirt, I noticed, matched his eyes.

"Of course. You speak English?"

"*S*i. I try." The smile began with a curve of his lips, long dimples exposed. It was electric.

"So, Dante," said Mary, glaring at me. "What brings you here tonight?"

"I live in the apartment over there, at the top, during the workweek." He pointed to a rooftop next to the Church of *Sant' Agnese.*

"Oh," said Mary.

"I see a garden from here," I managed to sputter.

"Yes, I have a rooftop garden."

Julie, for goodness sake, un-freeze. This conversation was sputtering from riveting and falling toward pathetic.

The waiter arrived with our *bruschetta.* He called Dante by name, and they spoke like old friends.

Breathe, Jules, breathe.

Mary hit my arm for the third time.

I turned to her and glared, mouthing, "Shut up." She returned the glare with pursed lips. Yes, the lips were back.

When the waiter left, Dante leaned close to me. In that moment, I knew how people fell into affairs. Given my mood and a couple of glasses of the house red wine...it was a very good thing Mary was with me.

"Jules?" Mary said.

Dante glanced at her, eyes twinkling, and then turned his attention to me. He leaned back in his chair, body open, and hands behind his head.

"Giulia, tell me why you're in Rome."

I drew my gaze away from him, hoping to settle down.

Another smack in the arm.

"Ouch," I yelled, annoyed.

"Trying to have a three way conversation here." Mary rolled her eyes.

"Well," she said, "we met in Italian class a couple of years ago and decided we needed to come to Italy and practice."

Oh, good, Mary. How lame was that?

"We came to Rome," I said, trying not to sound breathless, "to connect with our roots, our Italian heritage. All of us had grandparents that immigrated to the United States."

Dante listened intently, holding my already fragile heart with his eyes.

We chatted about ancestry and California, lots of small talk. I tried to eat. But my hand trembled whenever I picked up my fork. I'd noticed while in Italy, that wine was everywhere. It had never been my thing. I reached for my wine glass and took several gulps.

Dante laughed and touched my hand. The electrical jolt was almost more than I could bear.

"Don't drink the wine quickly, Giulia. Sip slowly, eat slowly, and walk slowly. Let the ways of Rome relax you."

"So," said Mary, leaning toward Dante. "Plans for tonight, have you already eaten with your family perhaps?" She inched into my space, trying to protect me from Dante. Yet he continued to surround me in the most pleasant of sensations. The wine melted me into a puddle.

"To answer you, Maria," said Dante, "I ate a very late lunch, no family, no plans." He motioned to the waiter for another carafe of the house wine.

The bells in the tower of the church chimed midnight. I had just spooned a mouthful of the amazing decadent bitter chocolate gelato into my mouth.

"Oh my goodness." I closed my eyes, savoring the taste.

The third carafe of wine had disappeared. I sat back against the chair, full, dizzy, and tranquil. The waiter arrived with our espresso.

Mary and Dante were talking like old schoolmates about Naples and the Amalfi Coast. The wine had not only relaxed her, but loosened her reserve. I watched as she exchanged words with this stranger named Dante. She'd revealed new sides of her complex self, humor, and a confidence I'd never noticed. Mary proved downright charming and fun.

She was so engaged with Dante, she failed to notice, as Dante leaned in to converse with her, he'd slid his hand onto mine under the table. My stomach was churning, but pleasantly. I couldn't DO this. I love my husband. But my hand didn't move.

"Hey, Dante. Don't people ever sleep here?" Mary waved her hand towards the piazza, and in doing so, tipped over her glass of wine.

Dante laughed. "I think we need to take a walk." He waved the waiters toward us. They chuckled as Dante placed some cash on the table and said, *"Buono notte, amici."*

Dante helped Mary first. I noticed how tiny she looked next to him. She wobbled.

"Good grief, Mary. You're a bit in the cups."

"Huh?" She started to giggle. Giggle!

"Mare, you okay?"

"I'm just fine." She stood still, grinned, pushing stray hairs from her face. "I think."

I stood and walked around to her, feeling a shade dizzy myself. Dante's arms held me steady. I leaned into him. Mary flanked him on the other side.

"Drunk in Rome," said Mary. "Great!"

"Don't worry," Dante said, gently. "We'll walk around the piazza and back to the Caffe' Farnese." He turned to me and brushed some stray strands of hair from my face. *"Bella,"* he said.

The three of us strolled around the center of the piazza, Mary and I in a dream-like state, Dante our escort. We passed through the *Campo di Fiori*, still crowded with people. There were lingering scents of marinara and espresso, and strains of Italian music. The stadium benches by the corner flower mart were jammed with young people calling out to their friends in the center. It seemed like they were watching a game at a soccer field, instead they were watching their friends eat, and talk, and drink. The Campo was filled with enough policemen to contain any possible eruptions of anger or pickpocket activity.

"Again, I ask," Mary said, standing on her tiptoes, flinging her arms wide. "Do people ever go to bed here?" Mary looked at Dante.

"Everyone's happy. They'll return home when it's time." He shrugged. "This is how it is."

We navigated the crowded alley connecting the two piazzas, watchful of wayward *motorinis.* The Farnese appeared empty. Dante led us to a table at the café, much to the dismay of the waiter who was in the process of stacking chairs and getting ready to close. Dante ordered a round of espresso. The dark flavor rolled on our tongues.

Mary yawned. "I can't keep my eyes open." She nudged me. "Let's go, Jules."

Dante touched Mary's arm. He leaned in to kiss her cheek. "Goodnight, Mary. Giulia will come in a moment."

"Whatever." Mary walked across the alley to the door, turned and waved.

"I hope for more time with you." Dante smiled, took my hand, rubbing his thumb across my arm.

"I'm very tired, Dante." Without Mary here, I felt vulnerable, tempted.

He leaned in to me and held my fingers to his lips.

I stood quickly, and he followed me to my door. Once inside, I sat on the first step.

Was my marriage so empty that a stranger could intrude so easily into my thoughts? Was it the wine? Or the fact I'd literally planned this trip to escape my reality?

I opened my purse and reached inside. The slim red wallet rested in my hand, burning my skin. I flipped it open to our family photo, taken three years ago. We looked so happy, so perfect. All of us dressed in Christmas red sweaters, faces widened with smiles. Sam, my blue-eyed boy, had his

JOURNAL - ROME

I'm supposed to be keeping a journal...working through the things in my life that are eating me alive. I need to find myself, the person I am right now. I need to focus less on myself and more on my husband. I'm feeling desperate, not in the sense of women who run away because they're feeling unfulfilled, but as one who is struggling to accept my circumstances.

My husband is unhappy, I am sad; our wonderful boys are unaware of our struggles. I'm feeling guilty and torn because of the relief of being miles away from my reality.

Ted and I have both changed. My biggest fear is that we can't be fixed.

Now, here I am in Rome, relief pouring over me like special cleansing oil, absent from the unease in our relationship.

Now this stranger enters...a man called Dante. I'm tempted. This feeling when I'm in his presence is frightening. But I am drawn to him as though hypnotized.

I need to understand myself so I can understand my husband, to avoid temptation, to see clearly, to not avoid my circumstances, but to embrace them.

I wonder if Ted is really okay. He's always been so strong. Yet, even before my cancer, he seemed tired, distracted.

Anyhow, I am glad I'm here in Rome with Mary and Liz. Funny how different people are when out of their familiar environment. It's going to be a great trip. I keep telling myself that over and over. And at the end, the three of us will really like each other or possibly not ever want to speak again.

One thing is obvious. We all have our dirty little secrets. Mary has a cruel husband and she lost a little boy. Liz acts like her divorce never happened which brings many questions to my mind. And I'm stuck in a "season" of marriage where the autumn chill starts to overshadow the warmth of summer. I'm not handling it well.

In a good marriage, the seasons flow quietly with periodic storms and rare bleak winters where sunshine never seems to light the day. And for me, during the year of my fiftieth birthday, my marriage is moving into a violent storm in the middle of a dark winter. I need to find my way through the storm and not around it.

I'll think about it tomorrow.

Tomorrow is another day.

Chapter Six

The next morning, or rather noon, I knew it would be too late to see Dante at the café. So with lingering regret, I ambled into the white kitchen. Here, Mary, hair tousled, was interrogating Liz, who looked inhumanly beautiful without makeup, hair awry, sexy green silk dressing gown draping her tall, slender body.

"Welcome to our first 'morning after' in Rome," Mary said, voice gravelly, speaking around the rim of her coffee mug. "I would have preferred some cappuccino from the café, but was too tired to get dressed." She hunched over the table, robe gaping open.

"Mary, cover up." I padded to the refrigerator to fix some fruit for breakfast, lunch, whatever. I gathered a knife and dishes, and started to peel a peach.

I paused and asked Liz, "Was your evening with Matteo wonderful?"

A soft smile. "Wonderful doesn't begin to describe it."

"We want to hear every detail. Now!" Mary propped her chin on her hands and raised her brows.

"In a few minutes," said Liz. "I need a shower first, and then we'll talk." She placed her cup back on the table, got up and left us sitting there.

Mary and I looked at each other and shrugged.

"Guess she's used to being independent." I said.

"Well it ticks me off. She's always walking away without a word. Kinda rude, don't you think?" Mary pursed her lips and threw up her hands. "Really, really ticks me off."

"She'll tell us when she's ready. Not to worry."

GABRIELLA

Chapter Seven

Gabriella prepared greens for a salad lunch. She loved working in the kitchen. The view faced directly into the windows of the French Embassy. The Piazza Farnese buzzed with activity. She felt the arms of her lover slide around her waist and jumped, startled.

"*Basta,* Antonio." She turned her head to look at him.

His deep-chocolate-brown eyes devoured her. He leaned toward her, kissed her on the eyes, brushed her body with his fingers.

"*Ti voglio, cara.*" He pulled the straps of the camisole off her shoulders, his fingers sliding down her arm.

Gabby dropped the dark salad greens, and turned to burrow her face into his muscular neck. "Stop, Antonio," she said. "Not now. I mean it."

He lifted her into his arms and carried her to the bedroom, saying nothing.

Afterward, their bodies still tangled, Gabby snuggled her face again into his neck. But her feelings had changed. An anger began to simmer inside her.

I'm no different than me mum. I hate this!

Gabby remembered the day her proper English mother told her she'd been the result of an affair with an Italian Count.

"The air, the food, the men," she used to say. "Italy is dangerous for a young woman."

She pictured her mum, blonde hair tugged back from her face, a tight bun at the nape of her neck. Her green eyes had filled with tears when she'd told Gabby her real father was dying. Gabby remembered the confusion. Her father had already died. What did she mean?

Gabby brooded about that betrayal by her mother...to her, her father, and this other man for whom her mother grieved. So much resentment and hate seemed to spring from that day.

She could still see her mother, trying to explain. "It wasn't just an affair. He'd consumed me. We loved each other with such passion and devotion."

Then she'd dropped the bomb.

"You inherited a goodly sum of money from your birth father. And he left you a building in Rome." Gabby thought her mother had gone daft.

Now, in the same building, she felt Antonio's hands stroking her. "*Ti amo, bella.*" The words blended in rhythm with his breathing.

"*Ti amo,* Antonio. God help me, I love you."

"Wish I had time to eat, Gabby." Antonio kissed her gently. "You have to work, and I have clients coming to the studio." He leaned over and nibbled her ear.

"My accountant is looking over the property management figures. So I have the day free." Gabby sighed, feeling restless.

"Then help your American tenants. They seem to be having fun, but they are all troubled," said Antonio.

"I know. You want me to help the American women find love," she said. "But Mary will be difficult."

"You'll find a way, my Gabriella." His fingers stroked her cheek. "You always do."

"Liz and Matteo...will it work?"

"Gabby, Matteo will never settle down. Why do you keep trying? He's not going to change." His fingers traced her cheeks. "Matteo will never marry again. Never."

Antonio dressed for his afternoon shop hours.

Gabby glanced at the photo on the bedroom wall. The father she'd never met gazed with love at her mum. "Well, Mother," Gabby said to the picture, "at least you knew real love. But you have royally screwed my perception of men."

She slipped on a soft shift and returned to the kitchen.

Antonio snuck up behind her, pressing his body against hers, holding her against the counter top. "*Ciao, bella.*" He kissed her neck and left.

Gabby stood at the counter, fixed her salad and sat alone at the table. She tried to eat, but her appetite for food had been replaced by an anxious feeling in her stomach.

Guilt. She felt pleasure, guilt, addiction, craving. Damn. Antonio was a good man. He loved her. And he was married.

Gabriella knew the women upstairs were awake. She'd heard the water from the shower filter through the pipes to her bathroom.

With Antonio back at work, Gabby could concentrate. She reached for her cell phone on the kitchen table and dialed.

"*Ciao.* This is Gabby."

"Hi, Gabby." Julie's voice sounded tired.

"I wanted to call and make sure everyone was rested and ready for another day."

"We're fine," said Julie. "Tired in a good way." She laughed. "But we can't keep this schedule every day we're in Italy. The late nights are exhausting."

"You'll get acclimated," said Gabby. "Italy is to be savored."

"Believe me, we are. I am...I mean, we are all savoring Italy."

"Listen, "said Gabby. "I've found a man whose family lives in Frosinone, the city by the little town where your grandfather lived. He's willing to take you there, talk with people in the town and look for your grandfather's records. Are you interested?"

"Absolutely," Julie said. "I'm excited to find family. Should be a flock of cousins there. Oh, can my friends come with me?"

"*Certo,*" said Gabby. It had been her plan all along. Gabby wanted them to discover their roots while in Italy. The search and finding her father's family had, well, almost healed her.

"In two days, this Friday, Roberto can take you, Julie. You must be ready very early to avoid the Rome traffic. His price is three hundred euro for the day, including breakfast and lunch. You buy him dinner."

"Perfect," said Julie.

Gabby could hear the excitement in her voice. "I'll firm up the arrangements and let you know tomorrow."

"*Va bene*, Gabby. Okay."

"By the way," said Gabby, "Dante was disappointed you did not come to the café for coffee this morning."

"Um, well, Dante is the reason I slept so long. He joined Mary and me for dinner last night, and we came home late."

"Ah, yes. He mentioned that." Gabby hesitated. "Julie, Dante is an important and powerful man. He's charming. He's quite taken by you."

Silence.

"Be careful, Julie, and wise. *Ciao*."

"*Ciao*, Gabby."

Gabriella sat for a moment, remembering the revealing emails from Julie...each one showing her depression, her battle with cancer, her feelings of emptiness, the growing fears of her relationship with her husband. Julie was vulnerable to someone like Dante. Gabby determined to speak with Julie alone.

She thought again about her father. Photographs were a poor substitute for a flesh and blood dad she'd never known.

"I will not let Julie make a mistake while under my roof." She pounded the table.

Gabby's eyes filled with tears at all her lost years without family; all her failed relationships with men. She blinked, stood, and walked to her bedroom determined to put her emotions aside. If she could, she would try to see that Julie didn't complicate her life. Had she, Gabby, ruined her own life?

"Back to work," she said to herself in the mirror. She pulled her fingers through her hair, applied blush and lipstick, and strolled to the door, looking more confident than she felt. She tried to push thoughts of Antonio away. "He's married, Gabby. Let him go."

She wondered if her mother had struggled with the same guilt. Gabby had never seen any evidence. She struggled between a feeling of empathy for her Mum and a disgust of being in the same situation.

Chapter Eight

After Gabby's phone call, I returned to the kitchen with a giant grin on my face.

"What are you so happy about?" Mary asked.

"That was our lovely landlady. She's arranged for me to go to Ripi on Friday."

"So what's Ripi?" Mary asked.

"Remember? It's my grandfather's town where he was raised. My, our, genealogy project…one of our reasons for coming to Italy. You're both coming with me, right?"

"Fantastic," said Liz, sipping her tea. She looked groggy and breathed deeply, inhaling the steam. She sat at the kitchen table, the sun pouring onto her hair, wet and fresh from a shower. She had wrapped a soft green terry robe around her body.

Mary tapped the table with her spoon. "Yeah, yeah, we'll go with you. Ripi. Hmmmm. That's right. I need to make arrangements to go to Naples for my family search." She quickly turned her attention to Liz. "Back to last night, Red. Details, please."

"Well, first of all, Matteo's very charming, although almost impossible to understand." Liz put her cup down. "When I spoke Italian, he smiled a lot. When I spoke English, he also smiled a lot. Goodness only knows what he thought I said. Thank goodness Gabby was there."

Liz mimicked Matteo's smile. "I think he has money. I also think Gabby has a thing for him."

"No way," I answered. "It was absolutely obvious last night that she and Antonio were trying to set you up."

"I concur." Mary splayed her hands on the table. "Continue."

"Well, we went to a tiny restaurant at the end of the alley from his furniture shop," said Liz, eyes wide. "The place looked like a movie set. The walls were done in a Venetian plaster, dark gold. Linens were gold brocade with little..."

"Those aren't the details we want, Liz." Mary tapped her fingers.

Liz ignored her. "The crystal glasses sparkled in the light of the chandeliers. It was small and held maybe thirty people."

"Get to the good stuff," said Mary.

Liz rolled her eyes. "Right. Well, the sexual tension between Antonio and Gabby was incredible. It was like..." Liz paused, as if trying to choose her words. "I've never seen a man devour a woman with a look. It took my breath away." She stared out the window, a dreamy expression on her face.

I don't think anyone has ever looked at me like that. Not even Teddy.

"Come on, Liz," said Mary.

"And Matteo." Liz's eyes brightened. "You know me and my attention to details. At first, I seemed to dwell on his job. I noticed a stain on his hand that he'd missed. Calluses. But by the end of the evening, I saw Matteo, a handsome and very sexy man."

"He's a furniture restorer, for goodness sake," said Mary. "Of course his hands are stained. Honestly."

"I know," said Liz, looking apologetic. "I like the strength of them. And his arms, the way his muscles stretched the fabric of his sleeves. Wow."

I laughed. "Liz, you need more than muscles and strong hands in a relationship."

"I know that." Liz fondled her tea cup, took a sip. "He's been married, has two grown children, and his father owns a place by the sea where he rides his horse."

"For someone who's never been interested in uneducated, always-covered-in-varnish, broken-accent-kind of guys," said Mary, "you seem quite taken by him. What gives?"

"I guess I've been a snob when it comes to men since my divorce. Only white collar, successful... But Matteo," she rolled her eyes heavenward and sighed, "he's delicious, intriguing...all in one nice package."

"Delicious is for food." I leaned my face on my hands. "The older I get, the more I feel like neither love, infatuation, or sexual attraction is enough."

"Well, aren't you the little ray of sunshine?" Mary turned away from me and leaned toward Liz. "What's he like as a person?"

"I don't know." Liz stretched languidly. "Love his accent. He kept touching me with Italian familiarity. He's gorgeous when he's dressed up. He looked into my eyes when he spoke, and I felt like a woman for the first time in years."

Sadly, I understood exactly what she meant!

Liz leaned forward, her expression intense. "And frankly, all those business-suit types at home are dull in comparison."

"Hey, Liz." Mary thumped the table with her spoon again. "You're in Italia. All the men ooooze charm. It's even affecting me." She pointed her spoon toward Liz. "And, we've observed your tendency to look for reasons to dump fairly nice guys."

Mary pushed her chair back and stood up to stretch. She walked to the refrigerator and pulled out a peach. Leaning against the counter, she took a bite. "I see you sabotaging every guy as soon as he gets close." She dabbed the peach juice on her chin with a towel.

"I agree." I leaned back in my chair. "Hey, Mare, throw me a peach, please?"

"Catch!" she said, tossing it toward the table.

"What happened with your marriage, Liz?" Mary pursed her lips and squinted.

I scowled at Mary. "Maybe she's not ready to tell us."

"No," said Liz. "It's okay. A few people know. But this info better stay here." Liz closed her eyes and took a deep breath. "I caught Brad in my bed with my best friend." Her face reddened; and the tone of her voice went harsh with anger and raw with hurt. "He was doing her in OUR bed. The look on his face when he saw me...I've never seen such total shock."

"I'm so sorry, Liz," I said. "I can't even imagine."

Mary didn't say anything for a minute. Then, "I'd have had to kill him."

Liz' voice became strident. "The idiot started to cry. He begged me to understand, that it had nothing to do with me."

"Nothing to do with you? *Bastardo!*" Mary sat down banging the table with her spoon.

"What happened next?" I asked, grabbing the spoon away from Mary.

"I immediately went into survival mode," Liz said. "I snatched my purse and laptop, walked out of what used to be my house, drove to my mom's. I spent most of the night on the computer going through our saved files, compiling a list of our financial records. Just like Santa, I made a list and checked it twice. In the morning, I called the best, meanest female divorce lawyer in Orange County." She clenched her fists. "I wanted a pit bull."

Her brilliant eyes grew stormy. "Twenty-five freakin' years together; twenty-four hours a day, working our business, feeling secure, knowing we were good together..." She twisted the ring on her finger. "Before the day was over, I'd wiped out our savings, checking and money market accounts." She smiled.

"He was so desperate to get me back, he didn't have a clue. Devious isn't usually my style." Her body stiffened. "He thought I was bluffing, that I would forgive him."

She pointed to each of us. "Advice? Your husband could do the same thing to you." Placing her hands behind her head, she said, "In fact, I believe most men rob their wives blind. Especially if a greedy mistress is involved. But then, I'm a tad bitter."

"And you got away with it, all of it?" I asked.

Mary and I were speechless. Mary stood and sat back down with a thump.

"Stop staring at me," said Liz. "What would you do?"

"I'm so sorry, Liz. I'm stunned." I reached over and stroked her arm. This wasn't the Liz I knew. She always appeared calm and dignified, glamorous, and beyond everything, totally in control.

"Oh that isn't the half of it." An evil grin enlivened her face. "I even cleaned out the safe. Forty thousand in cash."

Mary's mouth rounded in a silent "Oh."

Liz leaned back and laughed. "There's more."

She slapped a hand on the table. "There's a good reason why they say not to mess with redheads." She paused. "And I am, after all, a natural redhead."

"Uh huh. And?" I said, rolling my eyes.

"The next night I returned to the house and waited for him to come home, hoping he wouldn't be dragging 'the woman' in tow. I asked him to tell me details of his affair with Clare. They say what you don't know can't hurt you. But my hurt was so painful; my entire body was in pain.

When he finished talking, he cried again and begged me to forgive him. I remember smiling and casually handing my lawyer's card to him. The look of disbelief on his face gave me great satisfaction." Liz smiled. "God bless community property laws. Sometimes, the law works in a woman's favor." She inhaled the steam rising from her mug of tea. "The sweet smell of revenge."

"That doesn't sound right," said Mary. "My husband threatens me all the time! He says I'll be penniless if I leave him. I can't believe you got away with that?"

"I was quite generous with old Brad." She paused, baiting us. "I gave him our antique jewelry business with all of its headaches." She looked at me. "It's why I have an obsession with new stuff."

"Hmmmm," I had to point out a tiny flaw with Matteo. "You do realize that Matteo restores antique furniture."

"Yeah, I know," said Liz. "And don't think that didn't cross my mind last night while I salivated over his muscles and strong hands every time he moved."

"How long were you married to this creep?" Mary asked.

"I told you," Liz snapped. "Twenty-five years. Weren't you listening? And, the kicker is, Clare made sure I knew she wasn't the first affair. Talk about your best friend rubbing salt in the wound."

Mary looked at me, touched my shoulder, and said, "Think long and hard, Julie."

"I believe we're talking about Liz, Mary...not me." I pulled away.

"Liz, I'm curious. Is there a lot of money in antique jewelry?"

"Of course—if it's real....gold, rubies, emeralds, diamonds. Lots of money is involved when dealing with an estate sale of wealthy clients."

The phone rang.

I ran to the hall to answer it.

"Hey, Jules."

"Teddy! We were just talking about you." I smiled at the girls.

"So you havin' fun?"

"I am. Friday we're going to Ripi and hopefully find droves of cousins." I didn't have to force excitement. I <u>was</u> excited about our jaunt to my grandfather's town.

"What if they're weird?"

"Don't care. I love all this family tree stuff, Ted. Come on. Be happy for me."

"Uh-huh. I'm happy for you. Really. Look, I just wanted to let you know I'm probably going to fly to Indianapolis for a week to spend time with my brothers."

"Great."

A long pause. Chattering voices drifted up from the piazza below.

"You still there, Teddy? Hey, I'm here to see first-hand all the stuff I've checked on the internet. You know how many dead ends I've met looking for the Italian side of my family."

"Jeez, Julie, you don't have to defend yourself. Scour the nooks and crannies of Italy. I hope you find droves of relatives. Just don't invite them all to California at the same time." He chuckled. "You have fun. And at the end of the month, you come back to the only relative that counts. Me."

"That's sweet, hon. And thanks for the good news from the doctor."

"I figured it would ease your mind."

"Well, have a great trip. Say hi to your fam. I'll email you in a couple of days."

"Okay. Sure."

"Bye. And, Ted?"

"Yeah?"

"I love you."

"I know you do, Jules. Just...come back. Happy."

I placed the phone on the receiver. Teddy seemed a million miles away. I yearned for my normal feeling of contentment. Instead fear and uneasiness seemed to swirl around me like restless ghosts.

My legs felt leaden as I dragged myself back to the kitchen.

Liz sat quietly. The anger had disappeared from her face, but she seemed to be struggling to gain back her composure.

"I'm going to the American Express office to change some money," I said. "Care to join me?"

"I think I'll just hang out here, go to the rooftop and read my book," said Mary.

"I'm going to check out some of the shops near the Piazza Navona." Liz stood up, took her cup to the sink, rinsed it, and started for her room. "Dinner tonight?"

"Sounds good," I said with a cheeriness I didn't feel. A veil of depression slipped over me.

"I'm leaving now." I hurried back to my room to dress.

"What happened to us?" Ted's often asked question lingered in my mind.

I struggled to remember my life before everything changed. I caught my reflection in the mirror. I didn't see Julie. The Princess of Gloom stood in her place. Salty tears stung my eyes.

JOURNAL - ROME Entry:

Help. I'll have to destroy this journal. Don't want my sons reading this after I'm dead thinking I'm the woman in "The Bridges of Madison County." I need to understand why I feel so empty when I speak with my husband on the phone, to understand his pain and my own pain.

Liz's revelation tore me apart. Her husband was flawed...flawed in his character, his truthfulness, not to be trusted in any way. How do you survive that kind of betrayal? To see it in its raw form?

Yet she has made a new life for herself. I understand her more now. The way she seems to compartmentalize everything. Her total unawareness of her beauty.

Liz has made me realize I need to love my husband in spite of his flaws.

Tomorrow is a day I've yearned for, to learn about my grandfather, to see where he came from and why he came to America. My grandfather was everything to me growing up.

I'm thankful for the good news about my cancer...that it's in remission. Now I must concentrate on removing anxiety and dread from my mind.

Oh God, I feel so less of a woman. I struggle daily. I hate this feeling.

Chapter Nine

Friday morning. Early. I hadn't slept much in anticipation of this day. Mary was a morning person, but six-thirty posed a problem for Liz and me. Gabby had advised us to be ready for our driver early to maximize the day in Ripi.

I didn't know anyone in my grandfather's village, but I wanted to look my best in case I met a family member or two. I applied makeup and donned white linen capris and a simple red short-sleeved sweater. I walked to Mary's door.

"Mary," I yelled, knocking, "Time to get up."

"I'm up," she said, swinging the door open to reveal a perfectly clean room, bed made, and Mary herself dressed all in black.

"It's going to be a hot day," I said. "You might want to consider changing that top."

"It's sleeveless."

"But black draws heat."

"I guarantee you, Jules, that most of the older women in town will be wearing so much black you'll think the Pope has died. It's all my grandmother wore."

"Whatever." I strolled down the hall and knocked on Liz's door. "You awake?"

A muffled sound.

"Liz, seriously, get out of bed?"

Heels reverberated on the marble flooring. The door opened. Liz stood there, fully dressed in beige; slim gold chains hung from her neck. Chandelier earrings sparkled and framed her face.

"I can't believe it," I said. "You look fabulous. I mean you always look perfect, but I didn't expect you to be ready on time."

"Got a good night's sleep," she said. "I'm excited about today." She yawned widely and strolled past me to the kitchen.

I glanced into her room. It looked like a bomb had exploded. Bed covers were piled in a heap, clothes covered every surface of the furniture and floors. How could someone so put-together be so messy.

We met in the kitchen for a glass of orange juice.

The phone rang.

"*Pronto*," I answered. "*Si*, Roberto. We'll be right down." I motioned for them, and we gathered our purses and water bottles for the day.

The ungraceful clicking of our heels interrupted the quiet of the hallway as we approached the front door.

A slim man about my height stood outside, a cigarette burning in his hand, its smoke rising in wisps. He turned to us.

"*Ciao, sono* Roberto." He extended his hand to me.

"*Ciao*," I said offering my hand. "I'm Julie and this is Mary and Liz."

"I will not smoke in car," he said. "I know *American*i are strict about smoking." He flung his half-smoked thin cigarette down and carefully crushed it with his expensive-looking black leather shoes. "Come. We go to my car."

We followed him. I admired his flair with clothes. His slacks were neatly pressed, topped by a soft yellow shirt that accented his hair of the same color, and he'd hooked a black jacket over one shoulder.

"Glad we don't have to deal with his cigarettes," said Mary. She hurried to keep up with us.

We crossed the Piazza Farnese. Except for two embassy limos dropping dignitaries at the French Embassy and a few priests strolling toward the church, the piazza still slept in the warm morning sun.

We ducked into a small alley that led to the main road. We were pleased when Roberto approached a large, shiny black Mercedes Benz. Fiats were the norm in Italy. I'd worried about being squashed in a small car. I sighed with relief. "Ladies, please," he said, holding the doors for us.

I slid into a luxurious pewter leather seat.

"Why do you always get the front?" asked Mary, a hint of whine in her voice.

I didn't move an inch. "Remember our agreement? She who pays for the car, sits in front."

"Oh, yeah. Right," said Mary, nodding.

I swung my legs in.

"Ladies, please excuse." Roberto's tone was suddenly serious. "I not speak while in the city. I need to watch traffic. On *autostrada*, I talk." He turned to see if everyone understood. *"Capisce?"*

"Non c'e problema, Roberto." I waved toward the street. "We'll just enjoy the scenery."

"Roberto? *Scusa."* Liz spoke, eyes half-closed, voice sleepy. "Would it be possible to stop for breakfast on the *autostrada*?"

Mary interrupted. "Didn't he just ask us to not talk to him? Honestly."

Roberto ignored Mary's comments.

"Certo." He gave Liz an admiring glance. "Is okay with you if I make this day Italian style? We eat as Italy eats? *Va bene?"*

"*Si*, Roberto. It's okay."

"You'll see." He flashed a happy smile. "The Italian way will seduce you. Today is taste of small village, but a short stop first at *autostrada*."

He turned to me and shrugged. "It's different, the little town. All about family and enjoying life." He kissed his fingertips. With that, he leaned his head out the window, held out a hand, and glided onto the heavily trafficked Vittorio Emmanuele Corso.

Taking advantage of the silence in the car, I replayed my conversation with Ted. *Maybe he was right. Maybe this search would come to nothing. But I wanted to enjoy this adventure. I was so unprepared for life after fifty. Maybe that was the reason I needed to connect with my roots.*

Soon we were on the *autostrada* with Roberto pushing the Mercedes to the limit, zigzagging from lane to lane.

"*Servizio* ahead," said Roberto. "Breakfast?"

"*Si*! *Ho fame!"* I was definitely famished.

Roberto skillfully exited and pulled into a space near the front entrance of the service area. We piled out. Next to us was a bright yellow and black Smart Car.

"That's the cutest car I've ever seen." Liz ran her hand over the bumble-bee yellow hood. "Why don't we have these in the States?"

"It's half a car for goodness sake," said Mary.

"She's right, Signora. It's a half Mercedes. They are in America, I think." Roberto directed us to a glass door surrounded by steel. The building was practical in construction, simple lines, utility materials of concrete and tile.

Roberto explained the system of service, telling us to place our order with the cashier and take our receipt to the order counter. He slipped a cigarette between his lips, ready to light up. "I'll wait."

We entered the building, pushed through a turnstile, and were pleasantly greeted with heavenly aromas of coffee, simmering sauces, and cheese.

Within minutes, we had our cappuccino and roll and were lined up at the counter with businessmen and women on their way to work. We devoured the food and were back in the car, with me wondering...did I really just eat something? I concluded I'd rather sit and pay extra than stand and hurry. I'd just discovered the first thing in the Italian lifestyle I disliked. Standing, while drinking coffee. Although, I certainly appreciated the ceramic cup instead of the American Styrofoam.

Roberto drove the car back onto the main highway. The city disappeared and rolling hills took the place of multi-storied buildings. Ruins of farm houses and estates dotted the landscape. I noted a sign that said, "Frosinone."

Roberto turned to me. "You think you know Italy? You not know." He tapped his slender fingers on the dashboard. "I advise you watch at next exit. It's different world here."

The exit took us to a narrow winding road that by-passed the city of Frosinone, about thirty miles southeast of Rome. The hills, dotted with grazing sheep, rolled higher, greener. Stone houses were scattered here and there; laundry hung on lines in the sunlight.

"This is unreal," I turned to Mary. "The chaos of the city, and in thirty minutes, the serenity of the countryside."

Liz twisted the strands of her hair. "I love this. It's so tranquil. Suburbia in Orange County is full of traffic and noise...people rushing everywhere. I could get used to this."

Roberto pulled the car to the side of the road. "There. That's Ripi. He pointed to my grandfather's town, barely visible.

I opened the car door and stood in tall grass growing in clumps at the edge of the pavement. The small mountain rose like green velvet to a tower of stone buildings at its zenith.

I felt a tug of emotion. My grandfather had lived there. I had chills just thinking about it.

Mary's sneezing fit interrupted my reverie. She couldn't stop. She bent over, covering her nose and mouth, waving one hand wildly in apology.

"Olive trees." Roberto reached into the front seat and handed Mary some tissue. "*Allergia.* It's common." He pointed to a cluster of olive trees about fifty feet from the side of the road. He waved his hand toward the little town. "Ripi, this area, is a destination for Romans. They come here, relax, and escape city life. Many sheep." He turned to me, grinning. "I think your grandfather ate much *pecora.*"

"*Si,* Roberto." I smiled, remembering grandpa saying he never wanted to eat lamb again.

Roberto swept his hands toward the mountains. This region once Napoleon ruled." He shrugged. "Everyone rules at one time history. *Che sara', sara'.*" He inhaled deeply on the quickly lit cigarette, and after two more short hits, he crushed it with his shoe and hopped back into the car.

Liz gingerly pulled a few blades of grass from her sandals and eased into the back seat. Mary kept her nose covered with tissue. I slid into the car, barely able to contain my excitement, wondering if I'd meet family today.

Roberto shifted into race mode and the Mercedes glided around the dangerous s- curves. Now the towers took the form of century old buildings.

"How on earth did they manage to build so high?" asked Mary. "I mean, how'd they cart all the stuff up there to make the buildings and homes?"

"Modern doesn't mean better," said Roberto, holding a cigarette in his hand. "Everywhere are wonders that were built hundreds of years ago. They used the earth, rocks, mud. They found a way." He grinned, flashing his even white teeth. "Remember, Rome wasn't built in a day."

We groaned, laughing.

Soon, small signs appeared with arrows pointing to coffee bars, municipal offices, and the church. We drove into the town center. A statue of Vittorio Emmanuelle II, Italy's last king, stood proudly on a tall platform in a fenced area, the surrounding area covered with red geraniums. Roberto squeezed the car into a small open area next to a crumbling building and parked.

"Now, we walk." He glanced toward Mary. *"Permesso?"*

"Si, permesso."

He lit the cigarette.

"You know smoking is really bad for you, right?" Mary stood in place, shaking her head.

"*Si.* It's a bad habit. But one I enjoy. *Andiamo,*" he said, motioning us along.

It was like a movie set. We walked down a narrow alley on ancient cobblestones, stones that had been there for centuries, row houses huddled together, short doorways, large windows with shutters open. Women leaned on the windowsills, gossiping. No need for phones when an open window would do.

Mary hit my arm. "Told you," she said. "Black dresses."

Sure enough, most of the older women were covered in black down to their knuckles.

Aromas of garlic and onions wafted through the air reminding us it was lunch time. People eyed us with suspicion. We were strangers.

I took a chance and waved to a lady, dark hair drawn tightly into a bun, a stained apron covering a, yes, black dress.

"Buon giorno, Signora." I explained in Italian that my grandfather had grown up in this town.

"Ah!" Her arms opened and a smile lit her face. *"Paisana!"*

Roberto asked for directions to the records office. After much pointing and gesturing, Roberto said, *"Grazie, Signora."* She beamed.

"Signore," said Roberto. "Quickly. It's almost time for lunch and siesta. All will be closed for pasta and..." He winked at us.

After a few twists and turns, we found the street and the records office, a non-descript old building with *Ufficio di Municipale* printed in gold letters on an uneven though spotless window. Roberto led us through the door. It was like stepping back in time.

The office felt warm and closed in; musty scents of old pages hung in the air. An ornate but worn wooden countertop separated us from the office workers. Fans whirred, not cooling, but circulating the stale cigarette smoke and dust. One wall displayed floor-to-ceiling bookcases laden with old books, the binders written in script. I assumed they were hundreds of years of birth and death records. Four dark desks facing each other in twos were pushed together in the middle. Each one was occupied by a person...three men, their faces lined and bronzed, looking bored, and one woman, young and eager, with a ready smile. Papers were heaped in piles next to photos of family, an occasional statue of a favorite saint adding color to the dull desks.

"Buon giorno," said the bald man closest to us. His tone was curt as he glanced at his watch and then at Liz, who stood there, arms stretched, lifting her hair to cool her neck. The open boldness of Italian men continued to engage me. They stared but in a nice way.

Roberto commenced with the questioning. The woman, an attractive brunette with large brown eyes and flawless bronzed skin, listened intently.

"Scusa," said the older gentleman, his reading glasses perched precariously on his rather large nose. He touched his watch. *"Pranzo."* He ducked through a door near the records, hurrying home for lunch.

Lunch! He's thinking of lunch while I need information. I reminded myself that this is Italy, not the USofA, and tried to be patient.

"Vai, vai," said the woman, telling the men to go home. "I'm Laura," she said, motioning us to sit.

Roberto and Laura talked for quite a while, the three of us getting only bits and pieces of their conversation. But Roberto referred often to the three-by-five card I'd given him with the facts about my grandfather.

They walked to a small shelved area. Laura took an old book, covered in dust, and flipped it open. They talked quietly while she leafed through pages. At one point I noticed Roberto looking at me and shaking his head. His cell phone rang.

"Pronto.

"*Si.* Dinner. Eight thirty." He snapped the phone shut.

"What's happening?" asked Mary. "He looks puzzled."

"Don't know. But I'm not getting a warm, fuzzy feeling." Liz stood up and walked to the window.

"They're just looking up records," I said, my confidence draining away. "They'll find where my grandfather's family lives and we'll meet some of them. I've heard this explained to me so many times from friends who've come to Italy."

Roberto sighed and walked to my chair. He bent the card I'd given him and his face crinkled with puzzlement.

"Julie, your grandfather. Adopted?

"What?"

"Adopted. Did he talk about family?"

"All the time. But he never said anything about adoption."

In the back of my mind, however, I remembered seeing the ship's log at Ellis Island. And in the column of "Who did you leave?" were the words, "I left no one."

Chapter Ten

Sitting at the desk overlooking the Piazza Farnese, I seemed unable to overcome the gloom and shadows outside my window. Even the single ray of sunlight gleaming through parted clouds of silver didn't brighten my mood.

Yesterday's news about my grandfather had shocked me. I'd examined the documents given to me by the Officials in Ripi late into the night and compared them to the papers I'd brought with me. After hours of mapping out clues, I'd tumbled into bed still wondering...who was my grandfather? Why would he have kept such a secret from us? In reality, from my studies of the time period, it was probably shame. He felt shame about his origins, shame because he didn't want his family to know the sadness of his life in Italy. Or that he was discarded by his birth family.

I put away the journal, which had now turned into pages of petitions to God, put on a minimum of makeup, and crept out of the apartment. I crossed the alley to the small café, sat at my favorite table, and ordered a cappuccino.

"*Buon giorno.*"

His familiar low voice sent a chill through me. "*I didn't need this distraction.* I grabbed my sunglasses to cover my eyes. "*Buon giorno.*"

Dante's eyes studied me as though he could crawl into my head and read my innermost thoughts. He nodded.

I hesitated and asked, "Would you like to join me?"

"*Si.*" He sat down and dropped his newspaper on the table. Dressed in casual black slacks and a muscle-revealing black shirt, he resembled a panther, his every move sinewy and sensuous.

"Giulia?" He pulled his chair closer, his cologne nudging me with each move. "This is foolish. This pretending." Tucking a finger under my chin, he locked his gaze with mine. "You are sad, no? That I don't like. Tell me."

"I am sad, Dante." I looked away.

He touched the back of my hand. *"Dimmi*, Giulia."

I shared the disappointment about my grandfather.

"I really want to find his family, to solve the puzzle."

"Listen. I will help you. It's better if an Italian helps find the information. I know people." He leaned in and kissed my hand, holding it to his lips, his eyes never leaving mine. In the grayness of the cloudy morning, I ached. But Dante's kindness gave me hope. My heart, in that moment, flew to him like a humming bird, then left as quickly. My conscience tumbled off my shoulder. And one layer of the old Julie peeled away.

"Well, you look like heck this morning." Mary's voice cut the air like a chain saw. "Sunglasses don't hide anything, you know."

Dante stood, pulling out a chair for Mary. *"Ciao, bella."*

Liz followed, looking embarrassed at Mary's rudeness.

"Nice shirt, Dante." Mary chattered.

My hands tightened into fists.

Dante, tuned into my tenseness, distracted her.

"Mary," said Dante. "You look lovely. *Bellissima.*" He kissed her hand. "Your company the other night at dinner was delightful." He gazed into her eyes. She was unable to look away. "You have a wonderful sense of humor."

"Thanks," she said, pleased with the compliment.

"Any plans for today, Jules?" Mary waited for my answer, smiling pleasantly.

"Mare, I'm still digesting yesterday. I need a break."

Liz sat with elbows on the table, chin resting on her hands. "Matteo invited me to go for a drive with him." She blushed. I looked at her outfit. She sported a pair of jeans, a simple yellow t-shirt, and on her feet, a pair of ugly, sensible shoes. I was astonished. Her normal footwear was elegant. She noted my surprise.

"We're going on his motorcycle."

"Are you crazy?" Mary stared at Liz. "You are NOT riding with a stranger on a bike in Italy ALONE." Lips pursed, she thought for a moment. "Aha! You don't have a helmet."

"Matteo has one for me," Liz said quietly.

"He barely speaks English. And for that matter, your Italian isn't so hot. How will you communicate? What if he comes on to you, and he's your only ride back here? Huh? Then what will you do?" She poked Liz on the shoulder.

Mary reached inside her bag for a cell phone. In mother-hen mode, she punched in numbers. "I'm calling Gabby. Maybe she'll talk some sense into you." She looked at Liz. "It's ringing."

"Oh, hi, Gabby. This is Mary." She shook her head in disgust. "Liz is planning on traipsing around with Matteo on his motorcycle. Can you convince her it's dangerous?" She handed the cell to Liz.

Liz took the phone. "Uh huh." Long pause. "Hmmmm. Okay. I'll tell her." Liz handed the phone to Mary. "Antonio and Gabby are meeting us at Matteo's home near *Osteo Antica* by the sea. I'm going."

"But it's Saturday," said Mary. "Everything in Rome is closed by noon." She looked at me, waiting. "There's nothing to do but eat dinner. And dining alone is no fun."

"Giulia's going to be with me this afternoon and for dinner." Dante said.

"Really," said Mary. "Well, since I'm alone, I guess I'll go back to the Vatican."

"Why the Vatican?" I asked. "You've been there at least four times since we've been here."

"Confession is good for the soul," said Mary. She gave me a knowing look that said I had no business being alone with Dante. She pulled one lower lid down, the Italian gesture for, "Be on guard."

Dante laughed.

"Well, you go confess your little heart out, Mare. I'm going to send off some emails." I turned to Dante. "What time?"

"I have some business to attend to. I come for you at four? *Va bene?*"

"Four, it is. What should I wear?"

"Dress for dinner, Giulia." He held my hand as he leaned in, kissed my cheeks Italian style, and walked away.

"Dang, you're in trouble, Jules." Mary glared at me. "Going to write an email to hubby?"

"Yes, I am. Want to come with me?"

"I'd rather go to church. Maybe you should wait until after dinner to write to your husband, if you know what I mean."

"Thanks for the advice, Mary."

"I'll see you all later," said Liz, her face filled with anticipation.

I watched her cross the piazza unaware that every man turned to look at her red hair, a contrast to the gloomy day. I wanted her to enjoy her time with Matteo.

"You watch yourself tonight, Jules," said Mary.

"Yes, mother."

"Jules. You're playing with fire." She leaned in closer. "I'll be there at dinner with you. Remember that," she said, pointing her finger and shaking it in front of my nose. "And don't you forget it."

"I'm off to my room." I waved. "After emailing, I'll be spending the afternoon on the rooftop reading if you want to join me."

I began composing in my head. What was I going to say? *Dearest Teddy, Yesterday made me sad. It was such a disappointment to discover my grandfather was adopted. Oh and by the way, I'm having dinner tonight with the sexiest man on the planet.* I closed my eyes a moment, tried to conjure up a picture of my husband. Only Dante appeared. I let out a long sigh. I didn't miss Teddy at all. My shoulders drooped with guilt, my stomach tightened in distress.

The emails had been easy. I sent a travelogue to Ted and copied it to our two boys. The note focused on my trip to Ripi and what I'd discovered. I made a copy for myself, hit send and started a second email asking Sam and Daniel about their overseas studies, if they were dating, all the usual "mom" stuff. I knew, from their weekly emails they were having a blast in

Australia. I also knew Ted was concerned they were concentrating more on the Australian outback and the twenty-four-hour night-club scene and not enough on their studies. I missed them terribly. The empty nest syndrome had hit me hard.

I logged off the computer. *I should not be going to dinner with Dante tonight. Mary is right. But I can handle myself. It's nothing.*

Sliding into a soft, pink summer robe, I grabbed a book and strolled to the kitchen for some fruit and cheese. I plopped the food into the basket on the kitchen counter, added a bottle of mineral water and my book, and circled up the stairway to the rooftop.

Curling my legs beneath me, I scrunched comfortably into the lounge chair, facing away from the finally-appearing sun. I wondered how Liz was doing on the back of a scooter, hugging Matteo close. I thought, too, about Mary's frequent visits to the Vatican. Mary had nothing good to say about the church. So what was going on with her?

And Ted...how painful was our separation for him? Or was he relieved; glad to briefly be rid of the tension between us? I knew my boys were aware of our unhappiness with one another, yet totally unaware...and fearful of my cancer. They refused to talk about it. Marriage troubles would hurt them, of course, and that was the last thing I wanted.

Picking up a clump of grapes, I plucked one at a time, chewing and thinking about my evening to come. I ruminated about my own motive for being with Dante. Did I really want to be alone with him? It was dangerous for me in my current state of sadness and insecurity as a woman. My eyes got heavy, and I drifted off to sleep.

"Hey, Jules." Mary's voice startled me. *She couldn't have gone to the Vatican and back in so little time.* I glanced at my watch: 2:30. I needed to think about what to wear for dinner.

Mary strolled over to the table next to the lounge and sat, sighing loudly. "So, you're really gonna be alone with the charming Dante tonight, huh?"

"Sure am, Mare." I shaded my eyes. "And did your visit to the Vatican comfort you today?"

"Yes." She picked up a piece of cheese, taking precise bites, to keep the morsel ever symmetrical.

"And what draws you there, really?"

"Nothing." She reached for a grape.

"Not going to do it for me," I said. "Something or someone is there that meets a need for you."

"Well, if you must know..." Mary paused. "Nope. I'm just not ready to talk about it yet. But I did call home with my calling card."

"And?" I leaned toward her.

"George is making good his threat." She fought to contain tears, but they fell anyway. "He's filing for a divorce and jeeringly told me I'd be homeless and penniless. I hate him."

I flung my feet to the floor and walked over to hug her. She pushed me away.

"Don't, Jules. I might break down."

"So what, Mary. Tell me." I sat at the table.

"What's to tell? He's leaving and threatening me with financial ruin." The mascara made sooty trails on her cheek. "But he doesn't know everything."

"What?"

"I've been hoarding money in a safe deposit box for years, including money from my mom."

"Good for you."

"Jules, when you live with someone like George, you're always in CIA mode. Always anticipating that day."

"I so can't identify."

"Of course, you can't," she snapped. "You don't know how good you have it." She tugged at her hair, twisting it tight between her fingers.

Until you walk in my shoes, I thought.

"Do you have enough money tucked away to survive?"

"I'll do just fine. Have to find a part time job. But that'll be good for me." She cast a rueful look at me. "I'll miss my house, though."

A soft knock on the roof-top door.

Gabby poked her head through, eyes bright. "Mind if I join you for a few minutes? Antonio and I just finished lunch, and he's gone back to his studio."

"Sit," said Mary, grateful for the interruption. "I want to ask you a question."

"Mary," I said sternly. "I don't think Gabby wants to share personal information."

"No, no I don't mind. Ask away." She waited.

"Why aren't you and Antonio married?" Mary sat straight in her chair and looked at Gabby.

"Because, my dears, he's already married." She spoke softly. A shadow crossed her face. "We've been together for five years. It's a familiar old tale. His wife won't divorce him. They separated ten years ago." She looked down, folded her hands. "A loveless marriage destroys a person, man or woman, deeply, and he had to get out." Gabby looked at me, then Mary. "You both understand the disharmony that can occur in a marriage."

Gabby stood and walked to the rail. Her hands clenched the metal. She turned to us.

"I love Antonio with all my heart." Her amber eyes glowed. "But I admit there is an underlying fear he could...slip away."

Mary and I sat silent.

"My personal history haunts me," Gabby confessed as she stared into the distance. "The man who raised me was aloof, very distant emotionally. He was a banker, the epitome of one's image of a banker with his precise manner and impeccable grooming. Banking was his true passion, his mistress. When he died, my mother seemed without grief, and soon after his death I learned why. She'd kept a secret, and that secret was that this man I'd called Papa for twenty years was not my real father."

"Horrible. It's a terrible situation all the way around." said Mary. "Sometimes a lie protects people and…"

I stared at her, but I asked Gabby, "What did you do?"

"Do? I couldn't do anything. I was confused and hurt, stunned, really." Gabby returned to her chair and sat down. "Mum went to her desk and produced a key. She unlocked a cubby drawer in the back of the writing space, reached inside, and withdrew a photo of my real father. It took my breath away. He stared back at me with the warmest eyes framed by dark curly hair and a smile full of love. Even in a portrait, the man radiated love."

"Did you ever meet him?" I asked.

Mary interrupted. "Did your father, um, the man who raised you, treat you well? Did he ever know you weren't his?"

"Papa never knew, according to Mum. But wouldn't you think he'd know?" Gabby turned to me. "And yes, I met my birth father here in Rome when I was twenty-five. Although he was introduced as a friend of the family." She smiled. "That's enough for now. Maybe tomorrow I'll show you some photos."

"How old are you, Gabby?" Mary asked.

"Forty. And yes, I've given my best years to a married man. And before Antonio..." she glanced down and paused. "Let's just say I don't choose well when it comes to men. A lack of trust."

Her cell phone rang.

Mary and I looked at each other. I was eager to hear more and Mary's widening eyes showed the same eagerness.

"Antonio needs me at the shop. *Ciao.*" She hesitated and looked into my eyes. "Be sure you know what you want, what you need, what you'll gain or lose. Dante can be...irresistible."

Gabby turned and strode to the door.

I glanced at Mary. "This feels like the middle of a movie. And you reacted in a very strange way when she said her mum lied about who her father was. How come?"

Mary glanced down. Her hands curled into fists. She said nothing.

"You need to deal with your past, Mary, just as I do. Or our hurts will destroy us." I gave her shoulder a gentle squeeze and returned to my room.

JOURNAL ENTRY

Okay, Ted. This journal seems to be more for you than for me. A cleansing of myself I guess. This man! I'm not feeling guilty so much as puzzled why I have this attraction for the man I met at the Café. It's strange…almost like being captivated by a mysterious Mafioso.

There's something about him that meets a need right now. I don't know. But I do know I should not put myself into a situation of compromise. My thought right now is we will have dinner, and I will enjoy knowing a true Italian and then it will be over.

He knows I'm married, Teddy. He has nothing to gain or lose. And he doesn't seem to be pushing me into anything. So I will be strong and not get into a situation I'll regret. If you ever read this, Teddy, you'd laugh. Well, maybe not. It's stupid, really. But I'm going to do dinner anyhow.

Maybe Mary's right. Maybe I'm being defiant. No, I am being defiant.

I truly need some help to understand what's happening to me. It's like I've become a stranger in a novel.

Chapter Eleven

Our conversation with Gabby had set me behind schedule. I rummaged through my armoire, regretting I'd packed so lightly. I finally settled on a soft broomstick skirt in black and a red silk camisole, complemented by black crystal chandelier earrings. I put the outfit on the bed. I chose black sandals with rhinestones scattered across the straps. The heels were probably too high for walking, but if these Roman women can walk in them, so can I.

Shower over, I wrapped myself in a robe. "Nice makeup, job, Jules. Hair looks great." I tousled my hair. Dressing in front of the mirror that hung on the back of the door, I wondered if the red and black were too bold.

My reflection mocked me. *What's the matter, Jules. Losing your nerve?*

I sprayed a whiff of Roma perfume on my shoulders, behind the knees, inside the wrist. The intercom buzzed just as I reached the living room.

"*Pronto,*" I said, heart racing.

"*Sono Dante. Permesso?*"

"*Si.*"

I hit the button that unlocked the main door.

Mary waltzed down from the roof garden. "I can smell your perfume all the way up the staircase." She took a big sniff then glanced at my clothes. "Red? You're wearing red?" She put her hands to her hips. "You're married."

"Didn't know that, Mare. Thanks for the reminder. And what's wrong with the color red?"

"Jules..."

A knock on the door.

"I'll get it," said Mary. Before she opened the door, she turned and said, "Red is the color of passion. I think it's inappropriate." She turned the knob and pulled the door open reluctantly.

Dante stood there, beige linen slacks topped by an open short-sleeved shirt of deep brown that heightened the intensity of his blue eyes. His hands held a bouquet of roses in red, violet, and yellow.

"For three beautiful women." He handed the flowers to Mary, kissing her cheek, turned to me and said, "*Belissima.*" No kiss.

"*Grazie*, Dante," I said.

Mary was speechless.

Dante winked at her. "See you later."

He took my hand and escorted me down the stairs, the other hand resting on the small of my back. We walked out onto the piazza and turned away from the clouded sun. The street was dappled with soft late-afternoon light. The remaining sun warmed my shoulders along with the heat from Dante's hand still on my back. My body stiffened.

The walk to the Spanish Steps took twenty minutes. We seldom spoke, strolling in a comfortable silence. The Steps glowed red in the nearing sunset.

"Climb the stairs or take the lift, Giulia?" God, he took my breath away, the sunrays catching the ends of his dark hair. The Steps were packed with people. I only wanted to watch Dante. He took my hand and kissed my fingertips. "Let's walk, *bella.* I will be the envy of every man here." He hooked my hand in his arm and escorted me up the stairs.

When we reached the summit, Dante led me to a wall overlooking the city. Rome glowed. I observed other couples entwined, kissing, and wanted it to be me. Pain fluttered across my stomach. It was a perfect setting for lovers, and I wanted to love like that again. The view from the top of the steps was so different from the morning Liz and I had been there.

"Come," said Dante, leading me away from the steps.

We entered the lobby of the Hassler Hotel. I'd read about it in Conde Naste, but being here seemed unreal. It was elegant, with melon, gold and beige tapestries accented by chairs covered in Venetian red velvet. My eyes were drawn to the deep orange and brown marble of the floor that dominated the room.

The hostess, a leggy brunette with enormous brown eyes, ushered us to the outside Palm Court Bar. "*Buona sera, Signore Capoferi.*" Her smile was a little too flirtatious when she said his name and her lips a little too thin as she nodded to me. Hmm?

Greenery and large bushes hid the chaos of the city cocooning us in beauty. Beds of red and yellow flowers surrounded us. The tables were dressed with crisp yellow linens.

Miss Brown-Eyes seated us at a table by the fountain, rainbows glittering in the water from the late afternoon rays. Dante brushed my shoulders with his fingertips. I was with a man about whom I knew nothing. And I not only didn't care, I wasn't afraid.

A waiter poured our wine into a crystal carafe, swirled it, and poured it into smaller carafes. With a gentle flick of the wrist, he filled our glasses.

Dante pulled a rose from the table centerpiece and placed it in front of me. We raised our glasses. *"Una bella signora, e una bella sera. Cin cin."*

We clinked our glasses and sipped the rich red wine.

While Dante held my gaze with his, I remembered Gabby's revelation about her and Antonio.

"Dante?"

"Si, cara."

"Tu hai una moglie?" I needed to know if he was married.

He looked at me carefully, and set down his glass.

"No, Giulia. Now, no. I have been single for many years." He reached across the table and rested his hand on mine. "I was married young. I have a son, grown. Why?"

"Because of a conversation with Gabriella." I looked at his hand and back at him again. "How old are you?" *Jules, what are you thinking?*

"Ho cinquanta cinque anni."

"Fifty-five. I would have guessed younger." His skin was flawless and bronzed, the perfect growth of beard casting a masculine shadow over his countenance.

"Now is what matters, Giulia. Right now. Tell me." He stroked my thumb. "Why are you running away?"

"Please, as you said, let's enjoy this time."

"Giulia, I like being here with you." His voice was a seductive whisper. My body tingled. He leaned back in his chair and began to speak of this city he loved. We talked about Italy, our love of history and art. It was an adult, stimulating, and engaging conversation. I'd been starved for this. For years. My husband's face appeared in my mind, and I remembered when we were like this. So long ago. I mentally shook off the image and glanced at my watch, noticing we'd talked for over an hour.

The wine, the company, the setting; everything was perfect. I tried again to visualize my American life. But Dante's face and voice clouded my memory.

"*Signore*, your table is ready." An elegantly dressed gentleman with dark eyes and a crown of thick gray hair pulled my chair out for me.

We took the elevator to the top of the hotel and walked into a golden glow of breathtaking beauty.

"I'm happy we're here." Dante squeezed my hand. "Next year they will close and change everything. I like the old world look."

A young man perfectly dressed welcomed Dante and ushered us to our booth tucked cozily in a corner. I took in the luxury and sheer beauty of this small restaurant. The intimacy and the soft-toned Venetian décor warmed me.

"Giulia, are you okay? *Va bene*." Dante looked at me, concerned.

"*Va bene,* Dante. This is overwhelming."

He took my hand and nodded to the waiter, who discreetly disappeared.

"Look, Giulia. Rome is here." He pointed far into the horizon. "St. Peter's Dome, to the left, the Monument of Vittorio Emanuele II, the Pantheon Dome."

He put his arm around my shoulder and leaned in. "And there is the Sant' Agnese Church built by Borromini at the Piazza Navona. And to the right of that," he paused and pulled my chin toward him, "is my apartment."

I sucked in a breath, hypnotized by his eyes. I inwardly shivered, imagining us together in his place.

The crimson sun had set, and ancient Rome came alive with dramatic lighting, almost as if someone had waved a wand dissolving the present day

Rome. I sat there, drinking in the sights. Then I looked at Dante. For a long moment our gazes held.

With a wave, Dante broke the gaze, calling our waiter. He handed us the menu. The food was described in Italian, French and English. Yet the words were so beautifully written:

Buffalo mozzarella lightly drizzled with Perugia's finest first press virgin olive oil, resting gently on a bed of brilliant red tomatoes; surrounded by fresh arugula..."

I felt a sinking in my stomach. Not only was I nervous being with Dante, I was overwhelmed by the menu and the prices. *Ted would hate this food. And right this moment, a hamburger felt safe and comforting.*

The menu presented exotic Italian gourmet dishes, most of them containing fish. I found no chicken or veal.

Dante smiled. *"Cara, recordi?* I know you not like fish." His laugh was deep, yet amused. "Let me order for us. You will like." He touched my fingertips then took a sip of wine. *Dear God, everything he does is sensuous. No more alcohol for you, kiddo.*

I'd had too many sips without food and felt dizzy. Dante looked every bit the Roman that he was. And I slipped into the intoxicating moment, wanting nothing more than to rest my head on his shoulder.

The waiter quietly arrived with a gleaming platter of antipasti, placed it on the table. Dante nodded. The waiter made a small bow and withdrew.

Dante looked at me. "Giulia, why are you sad?"

"Sad is not the right word. Resigned, maybe."

"*Non capisco.* You quit?" He guided my hand to his lips.

"*Incapace*, helpless, no way out of my situation." I splayed my hands and shrugged my shoulders. *"Capice?* I love my husband like one loves someone over a long period of time. But now, we're distant. He is *'chiuso'*, closed."

"Ah."

We ate silently for a few minutes. The waiter materialized, Dante nodded, and the antipasti plate was whisked away to be replaced by a plate of thinly sliced veal.

"Closed," Dante said.

I took a bite of the tender veal, savoring the lemon sauce.

"*Dimmi, Giulia.*"

"Tell you? What can I tell you? My personal life over the past four years has been sad. I needed to get away and think. And I wanted to learn about my grandfather. That has not gone well. Nothing has."

Annoyed with my whining, I reached for the wine and took a sip, then another. Dante took the glass from my hand.

"Four years? Your husband?"

"*Mio marito*...my husband couldn't deal with the events of my life. He shut me out, wanted everything to return to normal. And I understand that."

Dante took the fork from my hand, shifted in the booth, and I felt the warmth of his thigh against mine.

He ran his fingertips along my forearm. "You are okay?"

"I don't know for sure." My body gave an involuntary shudder. I felt fear again, not fear of Dante, but fear of my situation.

His voice stayed feather-light and tender. "I know people. When you need help, information, anything, I can help you. Now, *cara*, we forget sad things. Finish your food."

By the time dessert came, I realized I'd said far more about myself than I'd intended. *I mentally prayed to God. I needed to stop talking..*

"This is my favorite *dolce.*" Dante fed me a bit of the buffalo ricotta with white chocolate. "I hope you like." A smile lit his face, his voice filled with tenderness so sweet; I ached from the sheer pleasure of it.

"I need *caffé,* Dante."

"*Certo.*" He nodded to the waiter and ordered us *macchiato con panna.*

"*Che cosa*, Dante?"

"*Macchiato con panna* means stained with coffee. Whipped cream with a shot of espresso." He explained the drink to me, but his eyes...they locked with mine in deep intimacy.

A feeling of panic overtook me. "*Scusa*, Dante." I almost ran to the ladies' room. I walked into a golden marble room, saw a chair and sat down, trying to calm myself. I wanted to speak with someone. Mary. Mary or Gabby. I practiced the self-talk techniques I'd used during chemo.

Breath in, one, two, three, and out, one, two, three. You're okay. Be calm.

And gradually, I felt my body respond and relax.

What if Dante wanted more from me tonight than I was willing to give?

Then you don't give it, Jules.

But what if I want...

Stop it. Get back to Dante. You're an adult having an adult conversation. Finish dinner, thank him, and get back to your penthouse.

I strolled back to our table, trying not to weave. Dante looked at me, puzzled, like he knew something had changed.

"*Va bene?*"

"Si, Dante. I'm fine."

"I ordered you a fresh macchiato. You were gone so long." He paused. "Giulia, are you afraid?" He brought my hand to his lips. I said nothing. "Because you can trust me." His brows furrowed.

"Earlier, in the Palm Garden, Dante, when we were having a drink and talking about art and history, all the things we appreciate and enjoy; I felt so comfortable with you. Like I'd known you forever."

"And now?"

"I feel I spilled too much information."

"Spilled? *Non capisco.*" He raised his brows. "I asked, Giulia."

"I know nothing about you. I know only that I like being with you. And I shouldn't."

"*Perche?* Because you have a husband?" He leaned in and whispered, "I find you sad, a bit mysterious. Your husband is in America. You are in Rome. I would never let you go away for so long...if you were mine." He pushed a stray hair from my face.

He pulled the dessert between us, and fed me a spoonful of the berries.

He lifted his fork to his mouth and savored the taste, then sipped his espresso. The movement of his body, the rustling sound of his shirt, the soft scent of his cologne. I gazed with longing at his lips.

"To Rome, Dante," I said, and spooned the tantalizing cheese treat.

"To Rome, Giulia." He leaned over to kiss my cheek. "To finding Giulia."

Tomorrow. I'll think about it tomorrow. I sounded like Scarlett O'Hara...and had watched "Gone With the Wind" one too many times.

I gave him a rare unguarded smile.

Sated from dinner and two espressos, Dante and I left the Hassler.

The balmy night air of Rome wrapped around me like an old friend.

"Giulia, taxi?" Dante draped an arm over my shoulder. "Or would you prefer to walk?"

He was so close to me. I wanted to melt into him and let him care for me. But Ted kept circling in my mind. My faith, my vows that I didn't want to break. Our two sons. How would I explain this to them?

"Taxi, *per favore,* Dante." I tried not to look into his eyes. "A taxi."

I turned so his arm no longer held me. I touched the dark shadow of his face. *"Grazie, Dante, per una bella sera.* The evening, the dinner, you... everything perfect."

He kissed me, his lips sweet with the taste of wine, the pressure of his mouth light and gentle.

I heard a quiet sigh and knew it was me. Taking a deep breath, I turned my face away. I had to end this night.

"Taxi." Dante's voice was low and resigned as he asked the doorman to call for a cab.

We stood close to each other, his fingers entwined with mine, and waited for our ride. The silence lingered in the cab but it was comfortable, not strained.

The driver took us into the piazza and stopped. I couldn't see anything but the deep blue eyes of Dante illuminated by the lights of the fountain. He held out his hand to help me from the car, walked me to the door.

"Dormi bene, Giulia. Every moment with you tonight was magic for me."

He plunged his hands through my hair, cradled my head for a kiss.

I turned away. *"Buona notte*, Dante."

He walked to the waiting cab while I opened the door to my building, and closed it on the most intimate of nights.

JOURNAL ENTRY

I don't feel like writing a thing. If I put it on paper, the evening will become a memory too strong to forget. I'm wondering why he didn't press me further. Yet his demeanor – other than the kiss – was that of a perfect gentleman. Who am I kidding? I could have stopped him but didn't.

Teddy, I'm so sorry. I won't be alone with him again. He won't kiss me again.

But there is this mystery. Remember when we went to see "Phantom of the Opera?" How seductive Michael Crawford was? The women in the audience knew he was the bad guy. Yet we all fell under his spell. Well, he isn't a "bad" guy. He simply has the ability to cast a spell...with his eyes, his touch. Doesn't even need to say anything.

The dinner was amazing. The views of Rome. Why didn't you come to Italy with me? I begged you to come. What's the real reason other than work? I know something else kept you home. Have I missed something? I feel so alone, yet somehow soothed by being here.

Mary and Liz are great companions though...even with our different personalities and temperaments. I'm glad they're here.

I'm exhausted. I don't want to put anything else on this page. Good night, Teddy.

Chapter Twelve

Morning sun drifted through the open window, bringing with it the sounds of a new day in Rome. The chattering from the café below enclosed me in familiar comfort. Nine o'clock. My body felt like lead. I wanted to pretend last night never happened. That glorious, romantic night in the company of another man.

A loud knock on the door. "Hey, Julie. You gonna sleep all day? Get up!"

Mary. Good old Mary.

I muffled a yawn. "I'm awake."

"What?"

"I said, I'm awake. Come in."

Mary bounced into the room, dressed in her usual mix-and-match black. Her large brown eyes sparkled.

"Why are you so cheery today, Mare?"

"Well, I'm gonna tell you. But fix yourself up first." She sauntered to the door, turned and said, "Meet me on the rooftop. I have a surprise for you."

After my washing, brushing and combing ritual, I threw on a pair of black slacks and a black and white jersey top and trudged up the circular staircase to the roof.

The ten a.m. sun was blinding, the warmth hinting the day would be hot. Mary sat under the umbrella at the linen covered table.

"Wow!" I sat down next to her, impressed by the breakfast she'd prepared. She'd assembled thinly sliced cheese, salami, and an assortment of fruit.

"Thanks, Mare. This is lovely."

I breathed in the aroma of the latte and bit into a fresh roll filled with sweet cream.

"I went to the Campo di Fiori early this morning." She had an unfamiliar lilt in her voice. *"Mangi, mangi.* I have to tell you about last night."

It surprised me Mary wasn't grilling me about my evening with Dante. I bit into a peach slice. The juice dribbled down my chin. Mary leaned over with a napkin and wiped my face.

"Can you not drip when you eat? Now, listen to this."

"Okay," I said, muttering 'bossy' under my breath.

"Last night I sat up here, sipping my *limoncello,* staring out at this magical city and wondering where my life was headed." Mary paused for a sip of coffee. "Gabby came up. She joined me for a drink. And then, Jules, she said something so strange. She looked at me and told me we had a lot in common."

"Really?" I popped a grape in my mouth and leaned forward.

"Yeah. It was remarkable. She came right out and asked me why I was staying in my marriage." She stopped. "Did you say anything to her, Jules? About me and George?"

"No. Not even in my e-mails before we came here. I told her a lot about me. Regarding us, only that we were all studying Italian and wanted to research our families. So, what'd she say?"

"Well you know how closed I am." Mary splayed her hands. "But that Gabby had me singing like a canary. Before I knew it, I was spilling my guts. And do you know what she said?"

"Not unless you tell me, Mare. Hurry up."

"Gabby looked me in the eyes and said, 'There are worse things than being alone. And one of those things is the pain of having a husband who makes you feel you never measure up. Jules, it's where we all are. You, me, Liz. We don't love ourselves, respect who we are."

"Not quite following you. Furthermore, I'm not afraid to be alone."

"Yes, you are. Because, dear Jules, if you weren't afraid, you wouldn't be having an emotional fling with a total stranger." Her eyes were clear, her tone firm. "Look, Jules, we all need time to heal and rediscover who we are."

She tapped the table with her spoon. "Take our gorgeous Liz. She was so wounded by that jackass of a husband. He betrayed her in the worst way, and she thinks another man will heal her. NOT."

"Hold on a minute, Mare. Each situation is totally different. We have nothing in common except our age, our..."

"Stop. Let me finish. I'm staying in an abusive relationship because I'm afraid to go it alone. You don't know the half of my story. But you, you are..."

I tried to interrupt again, but she held her hand out and kept right on speaking.

"You've had a good marriage, you've hit a deep, bumpy valley, and you're running. To a man you think will give you what your husband can't."

She paused.

I simmered.

"You need to find out what you want and make those changes. Because if you don't, Ted won't have a chance..." she paused, leaning in close..."and neither will you." In a rare show of gentleness, she reached over and stroked my arm. It alarmed me because it was so "un-Mary-like."

"You have the stability we all want, Jules. Change yourself, and Ted will change."

"But..."

"Hear me out. I've paid a price for living with evil rather than risking the unknown. But you're risking everything that's good."

Mary squinted and pursed her lip. "What DID happen last night with you and Dante?"

"Nothing."

"But you wanted something to happen, didn't you?"

"We were talking about you, Mare."

"Don't change the subject, Jules. I already told you I spent a long evening with Gabby. Back to you."

"I don't want to talk about it." I clasped my hands and looked down. "It was just dinner with a friend. I need to go to my room and make a phone call." I walked to the stairwell leading down to the penthouse. Halfway down, it dawned on me that Liz must be alone with Matteo. I climbed back up, peeked my head out the door and said, "Mare, is Liz okay?"

"She's surrounded by people. She's fine." She waved me off, her jaw tight. I knew she was angry that I'd cut her off.

I plodded to my room, confused, angry. The phone loomed large and black on the nightstand. It would be a good time to call Ted.

My hand trembled pushing the numbers. *What am I going to say to him?*

By the fourth ring, my stomach had tightened into a large knot. His brother answered the phone.

"Hi, Bryan. It's Jules. Ted available?"

I waited, tense, for Ted to answer the phone. His voice was curt.

"Hey, Jules."

"Hi, honey. You enjoying the fam?"

"Weather's awful. Been raining the entire time. Weather good for you in Rome?"

"Sure. It's nice. I'm really having a good time."

Silence. *I grasped for words, conversation.*

"Ted, you said you wanted the old Julie back. I don't think I can ever be the 'old' Julie. Maybe a better Julie?"

"Obviously, Jules, old and familiar didn't work for us." He paused, and I heard him take a deep breath. "I've been somewhat of a jerk through all of this, too. At least that's what my sister-in-law's been telling me."

"I love Rome, Ted. I wish I could share it with you."

"I told you to go. You went with my blessing and I'm happy you love it, Babe. I'm here, you're there." Silence. "Oh, wait. Are you the old or the new Julie at the moment."

He called me Babe. Again. It'd been a long time. It helped me overlook his sarcasm.

"Can we fix 'us'?" I waited for his answer.

"I don't know. I like comfortable. Not keen on dealing with a new Julie who," he cleared his throat, "might find me boring." He laughed, but it was a nervous laugh.

"Boring?"

"Yes. According to my family, you'll find me boring after Italy."

"Tell your friggin' family to butt out."

"Yeah, sure. I'll tell them that." He laughed again.

"Jules, we're getting ready to eat. Call me in a few days. I'm flying home midweek. Just wait and call me at home."

"Okay. Ted?"

"Yes?"

"I love you."

"Me, too."

I placed the phone on the receiver, fell back on the bed and curled into a ball. What was I thinking tryng to have a heart-to-heart conversation while he was away from home. Mary's right. I'm the one who needs to change.

I glanced at my watch. Almost noon. Time for wine. I marched out of my room to the kitchen, gathered some glasses and the yellow pitcher of our homemade sangria and climbed to the rooftop to rejoin Mary.

The Roman sun warmed me. I plopped into the lounge chair.

"I'm sorry I walked away so abruptly. I needed to call Ted."

"Ha! I got to ya, didn't I?"

I answered with a silent glare.

Two glasses of wine later, Mary and I were into another intense conversation.

"So where was the dreamy Antonio all the time you and Gabby were talking?"

"Gabby said he was in his studio sketching. They had a fight. I guess he does his best art when he's angry."

"What'd they fight about?"

"His wife."

"Gabby knew he was married when she got involved with him."

"But she's doing exactly what her mum did." She paused. "Remember? Her mum was unhappy in her marriage and Gabby resulted from the affair."

"So they had a fight and came home and left Liz alone with Matteo."

Mary stood and walked to the fence at the edge of the rooftop garden. "Gabby assured me Liz will be okay. Evidently Matteo's family is loaded and his family villa is full of people this weekend. And get this."

"What?" I joined her among the potted fichus trees and trailing purple wisteria.

"I think Gabby is in love with Matteo. And he with her."

"Huh?"

"She glowed whenever his name was mentioned. I think she loves Antonio too. But she knows he'll never divorce his wife because of his family." She put her hands on her hips. "It's a mess. But I think she's rethinking things."

"Really? How?"

"Believe it or not, we American women have influenced her. I think she's giving Mr. Gorgeous-Hard Body-Lover the boot...or at least an ultimatum."

"Wow." Gabby, the risk-taker, was changing. Wanting more stability.

"When will Liz be back?"

"Later today."

"Then I suggest we wait for her and spend an evening sorting some things out."

"What about Dante?" Mary's tone carried a definite edge.

"Dante is a most incredible man."

"What do you know about him?"

"I know he's been divorced for many years, he has a grown son, and...."

"No, Jules. Who IS he? What kind of a man? What does he do for a living? Where is he from? What are his values?"

"I'm satisfied, at this point, with what I know about him. Now let's change the subject." I gave her a look. "By the way, can Gabby contact Liz?"

"I imagine so. I'll go call her. Why?"

"I just want to know when she's getting home." I watched Mary head for the door leading down into the penthouse. I walked to the lounge chair and sank into the soft cushions, reached out and pulled the umbrella closer to shade me from the sun.

I'd tried to be nice to Ted on the phone. What did he mean by 'comfortable?' The status quo wasn't going to work for me anymore. I wanted, no needed, a relationship where two people work hard to keep things fresh...maybe not the excitement of twenty-five years ago but not comfortable. Yet, maybe at his age, he needs comfortable.

Dante's intense gaze floated into my mind. I remembered the taste and feel of his kiss. Exciting, not comfortable. *He's not your reality, either, Jules.*

"Jules," Mary called. "Gabby said Liz'll be back in about an hour."

Mary plopped beside me in the other lounge chair. "I went down to Gabby's apartment. I guess she and Antonio have 'made up.' He had his hands all over her, and she had that dreamy look in her eyes."

"What about her and Matteo. I'm confused."

"Well, sometimes the addiction to a person isn't so easy to end. I know that when I had..." She stopped cold.

"Mare, what were you going to say?" I watched her. She wasn't going to talk. But it confirmed what I'd been suspecting. There was a secret of gigantic proportions in her past. And Gabby knew it all.

"Nothing, Jules." But her face had blanched. "Hey, everything's closed today except for churches and a few restaurants. Want to take a walk along the river?"

"I'll pass for now. It's too hot." I flung my feet to the floor. "I'll just go to my room and read for awhile. And do some journaling."

Mary stayed put. "I'll see you later. I don't want to walk by myself." She closed her eyes, dismissing me.

I meandered to my room, reveling in its brightness, picked up the journal from my desk and crawled onto my chair. Before my pen stroked the page, I thought of Dante, Ted, myself. My hand touched the side of my breast. The lump seemed smaller. Probably just a swollen node, like I'd experienced before. I had to find a way to stop obsessing about the cancer returning.

I inhaled deeply, started a slow exhale and began to write.

So much has happened. Before Rome, I thought my heart would break just thinking about a twenty-five year marriage gone stale. Before Rome, I'd never thought I'd be attracted to another man. Life takes strange turns. I'm afraid to write the truth.

My husband continues to puzzle me. I feel distant and unconnected. Yet he admitted there was fault on his part, too. A huge step for him.

I miss my boys. But they are too full of life and dreams to be concerned with my fears.

Fifty. And I don't have my act together. I've survived so many things in the past two years, including facing my own mortality. Yet I struggle to find myself.

Rome has a life of its own. I love the frenetic pace, the constant shoulder shrugging and the "whatever' attitude. I love the way they do family; their togetherness at dinner, their strange concept of time. But I'm just a visitor. It's not my reality. I'm beginning to learn from Roman ways, though.

I've faced temptation for the first time in my married life. I wonder if Ted has ever wanted another woman. But then, he's a man. Of course he has.

I left the journal open beside me, placed my feet on the ottoman and leaned into the chair, enjoying the soft white and blue room, organza curtains moving gently in the breeze.

Had Ted ever been tempted? The thought stuck in my head and quickly meandered to my stomach, leaving me anxious and sad. I'd never for a moment thought about that scenario. He's a man. Of course he'd been tempted.

GABRIELLA

Chapter Thirteen

Gabby stared out the window of the bedroom, her body damp. Antonio's body was tightly curled around her, his arms heavy with sleep, his breathing steady. She used to feel comfortable with him next to her. But each day she spent with the American women, she realized a disappointment in herself, following in her mother's footsteps, wasting precious years she could have spent in a normal relationship. She yearned for children.

Tears streamed onto the pillow, falling in silence.

Seeing Matteo with Liz felt like being slapped. But when she saw the raw look of love in his eyes, she knew Matteo still loved her... even while holding the hand of the exotic redhead. She hoped.

Gabby lifted Antonio's arm and slipped off the bed, careful not to wake him. She walked to the bathroom and turned on the shower, letting the water stream hot. She washed the scent of Antonio away and cried.

One man loves me who's free to love; I love another who's not free.

Toweling her body dry, she looked in the mirror. The anguish in her eyes troubled her. She walked quietly back to her room to dress. A movement from the bed caused her stomach to tighten.

"Hmmm, Gabby. You're so beautiful. Come, *bella.*"

"No, Antonio. I just showered and have to finish my office work. I'll see you later."

"I need a shower, too." He took her hand and pulled her close.

"No. Antonio."

But he was in no mood to take no for an answer.

The water of the shower mixed with her tears. Antonio never even noticed. He took her tenderly, and all thoughts of Matteo vanished.

Chapter Fourteen

I heard Liz before I saw her. Matteo's *motorini* roared across the piazza breaking the calm of the late afternoon. I'd drifted into a light sleep and uncurled my body. The journal lay open, the repository of my emotional struggles. I walked to the window to see Liz's hair flying beneath her helmet.

"Ciao, *bella.*" Matteo's voice echoed to my window. He leaned over to kiss Liz goodbye. It surprised me he didn't come in. He removed his gloves and raked his hands through his curls, white hair gleaming in the sun. With each movement his muscles rippled.

Liz gave him a flirtatious look and said something to him as she unlocked the door. Matteo threw his head back in laughter.

I listened for Liz but watched Matteo. He glanced up to Gabby's window, and quickly bowed his head. Covering his head with the helmet, he jumped on the cycle and jetted away from the penthouse, away from Liz, and away from Gabby.

We needed girl time. I was relieved Liz was back safe and sound from her weekend at the sea with Matteo. I hoped.

"Hey, Red." I hugged her as soon as she walked in the door.

"Jules, you would not believe my weekend. Oh my gosh. He's rich. And...."

"Stop. I want to hear everything. But first, I'll fix a snack."

I went to the kitchen cupboard and gathered plates and cups. Pulling food from the refrigerator, I thought about all the changes in our lives during our first week in Rome.

Gabby's story seemed to have opened the floodgates of secrets from all of us. Strange.

"Hey, what's the big powwow for?" Mary's entrance always heightened drama.

"I just thought that since we've all been doing something different, we should have a light dinner on the roof, watch the sunset, and talk."

"And I suppose you want ME to fix the food," Mary said, eyebrows arched.

"I'll fix everything, Mare."

"No. I'll do it." She grabbed a knife from the drawer. "I like things cut neatly."

"And you're inferring I'm not the perfect preparer?"

"Hey, guys." Liz meekly interrupted. "Let's all do a part of the meal. I'll make some home-made sangria. Jules, you take care of dishes and glasses. Mare, you cut what needs to be cut."

"Bossy women," I muttered under my breath.

I pulled out olives and oil, grapes, already neatly sliced salami and popped a few olives in my mouth. I swirled the flavor of the juice. It calmed me. I went to the pantry and found an unopened box of shortbread cookies for dessert. Surely I could arrange these to please Liz and Mary.

"See you at the top," I said, carrying the tray of goodies up the precarious staircase.

Thirty minutes later, we had assembled a lovely and simple dinner, each of us sipping sangria and watching the sun start its glow over the city. The candles cast long shadows over the food. The setting was complete.

We kept the house phone on the table in case someone needed to find us.

"This is perfect." Mary's smile was deep with satisfaction and wine. "So Liz, what was the weekend like?"

"Well, first of all, I don't like helmets." She tossed her wild hair. "They mat your hair to your head and it gets all sweaty. And then there's the wind tangling the loose hair, making it impossible to comb." She sighed.

"Ooookkkaaay." Mary's voice dripped with sarcasm. "Let's move on to the actual weekend. You know, beyond the bad hair experience."

"For instance," I asked. "Was it exciting to be with Matteo?"

"I was scared out of my freaking mind." Liz slapped her hand on the table. "I clung to Matteo for dear life, afraid I'd die on the *autostrada.*" Liz grinned.

I said, "Okay, so we're at his country place on the ocean somewhere north of Rome and...."

"And," said Liz, "you can imagine how mortified I felt meeting his family and friends looking like a wet-head. I asked him immediately where the bathroom was, feigning an emergency." She swirled the liquid in her glass. "I repaired my hair and makeup and managed to look quite presentable. My stomach was in knots, but I pretended to be calm." She reached for a piece of salami.

"I'm sure it was difficult, Liz." I patted her hand. "Now what the heck did you do for two days with Matteo? Focus." I rolled my eyes at Mary.

"Okay." She smiled shyly. "The first day was a rush of activity, everyone speaking Italian, me catching a phrase here and there. I did a lot of smiling and laughing." She looked at me, her face showing the stress of language immersion. "If Gabby hadn't been there, I don't know." Liz shook her head. "Matteo held my hand and tried to include me and keep me with him. But I noticed him looking at Gabby a lot." A frown shadowed her pretty face. "I think he likes her."

"What about the house?" Mary asked.

"The house was old but elegant. I was too preoccupied trying to keep names and faces straight, let alone the language problem. I thought it would be more like, you know, time alone with this fascinating man." Liz sighed.

"You're disappointed, aren't you?" I asked.

"Well, it was fun, and the patio dinner at night facing the ocean was romantic. But then tension started between Gabby and Antonio." Liz yawned and reached for a grape. After a few moments of silence, she said, "The next morning, Gabby and Antonio had already left for Rome. Something about a fight."

"Yeah," Mary said. "She told me they'd had a whopper."

"Matteo was moody all day, and I couldn't wait to get back here." Her eyes widened. "What's wrong with me? I can't seem to choose men wisely."

I pushed my chair back and walked over to Liz. "It's okay. All of us are here to learn and change, and to focus on what we need and want and are willing to—I don't know—fight for?" I hugged her.

"Okay, so your weekend was a bust." Mary turned to me. "Now, Jules, tell Liz about your date with Dante."

"Crap, Mary. You can be so intrusive." I nodded toward Liz. "And it wasn't a date."

"Sorry, Liz," Mary mumbled.

I wanted to slap someone. Instead, I walked over to the wisteria, jerked a clump of bright purple flowers off the vine, and crumbled them in my fist. A sweet perfume exploded. I breathed in deeply and returned to the table.

"So, Liz, Dante took me to a delightful restaurant that overlooked all of Rome. We had a nice time and talked and talked."

"Curious, Jules," said Mary. "At the end of the evening, who knew the most – you about him or him about you?"

"Huh?"

"Tell Liz what you know about him."

"Mary, you're are seriously ticking me off." I paced back and forth in front of them, fortified with twice as much wine as I usually consume. "Dante is rich, divorced, has a grown son, inherited some kind of property business, has a home near Venice, an apartment in Rome, and is the most delicious, handsome, romantic man I've ever met in my life."

I stopped, placed both hands on the table. "And yes, he tempts me. Especially after he kissed me."

Mary and Liz sat there, mouths agape.

"And do you know why I didn't give in...YET? Because I'm afraid he'll be repulsed by my body, just like Ted was. And my breasts are pretty damn awesome, created by Dr. Edwards, creator of Boobs, Incorporated, a subsidiary of Breast Cancer Victims, Inc."

"Oh, Jules..." Liz began.

"Nope, I'm just getting started." I walked back to my chair. "Here's the thing. We accumulate pain over the years and stack it in piles and argue about one's pain being worse than another's. Then, we reach midlife and women are never prepared for it. Men just deny it along with their feelings."

"Julie, chill." Liz patted the chair next to her. "Sit. You're scaring me. Are you okay?"

"I'm just fine. See, last night Dante led. He was in charge, sure of himself. But, he didn't diminish me."

Mary's face brightened. "Now THAT I understand. The diminishing thing."

"Ted has always led me. But when I had to fight for my life, go through the indignity of loss with this cancer, I didn't want him to lead. That created conflict. After the cancer, I craved becoming my own person. I wanted to change." My face felt damp with my tears. "Right or wrong, I felt like he was trying to erase me. I'd sprout my wings in one direction, and he'd pull me in another. And we should have been growing together, not making our lives a contest."

I buried my face in my hands. "I want to be in control of my life. But trust is the issue. Why the hell do I trust a stranger when I need to trust my husband?"

I walked to the lounge chair and collapsed in a heap. The sun was disappearing from view, leaving a red sky. It was breathtaking. I could only stare.

The phone rang.

Mary answered it. *"Pronto, chi e'?* Mary's face revealed nothing. "Sure, bring it up, Gabby."

"So, Jules, evidently a package is being delivered to you. Gabby will be up in a minute."

Liz didn't move other than touching her cheeks...her indication that her face had gone numb from too much wine.

"Let's have some *limoncello* and a good time." I struggled to swing my legs to the side and managed to get out of the lounge. "Be right back." I carefully descended the round staircase to the kitchen, loaded another tray with the frozen liqueur, four little icy glasses from the freezer and climbed the stairs. I was halfway up when I heard Gabby open the front door. She was holding a tray.

"I'll carry the drinks," said Gabby. "Here's your package."

Holding tightly to the thick envelope, I followed Gabby to the rooftop. There was no identifying writing except for my name. Puzzled, I opened it and pulled out the contents. Medical records. Consulting records. Surgery results. A piece of yellow paper fell to the floor. I leaned down to pick it up.

"Cara, Giulia, I have gathered all information and have sent it to a specialist. I want you to not fear this cancer. I will take care of everything. Nothing, nothing can detract from the beauty of you. Nothing. Ci penso io. Dante

I needed to sit. I absently twirled the dark strands of my hair between my fingers.

Gabby poured the limoncello into the small glasses and sat down, cross-legged, on the small piece of carpet next to the table. "What's wrong, Julie?"

I handed her my drink. "Here, Gabby. You drink mine. I need a clear head."

Mary drummed her fingernails on the table. "What's in the package, Jules?"

"Medical records. Everything about my cancer. Everything. How could he get this information?"

Gabby got up, pulled a lounge next to the table and, with a steady tone, said, "Julie, you need to trust Dante. He would never ever hurt anyone." She paused, tucking her hair behind her ears. "He's a powerful man with connections."

"All over the world?"

Gabby nodded at me then glanced at Mary and Liz. "And you know how easy information is shared on the Internet?"

"I know," said Mary, a frown on her face. "But medical records."

She turned to me. "What's the note say?"

"Nothing important. Dante just wrote, '*Ci penso io.*' Which simply means he'll think of everything."

"Oh, no, you don't." Mary stood up and came over to grab the note.

"It's none of your business," I said, folding the paper and slipping it into the pocket of my slacks.

"*Non hai paura.*" Gabby patted my arm.

But I was worried.

I noticed Liz staring at Gabby. "What's wrong, Liz?"

She tapped her cheek. "Might as well say it while I'm drunk." She looked straight at Gabby's eyes. "What do you want, Gabby? Antonio or Matteo? Why is it you need to keep two men in love with you?"

Gabby's eyebrows shot up. "I suppose you deserve details," she said, forcing a tight smile. "I'm sorry I ruined your weekend."

Liz looked away. "Just tell me if I'm wasting my time with Matteo." Her face flushed as she downed the to-be-sipped limoncello. She gasped. "I mean, what's going on?"

I threw Liz a look, hoping she wouldn't take this conversation any further.

"I love Antonio," whispered Gabby. "He's the classic Renaissance man, speaks five languages, he's charming, and he has the heart and temperament of an artist."

"And he's married," interrupted Mary. "And where does this 'wife' live, and why isn't he divorced?"

"Have you ever heard the expression, *mammoni*?" Gabby's eyes sparked with anger. "Antonio is a mama's boy. Lots of Italian men are. Mama does for them, spoils them, controls them. Antonio's mama still washes and irons his clothes. Even his underwear, for goodness sake."

"But the wife?" Mary was like a dog with a bone.

"His wife is living with another man. He happens to be a high ranking *carrabiniere.* You don't mess with them."

"The carra what?"

"You've studied this, Mare," I said. "They're more powerful than the police and walk around with the Uzis. We're always asking directions from them."

Mary gulped her limoncello and poured more. "Still not getting this." She leaned forward, placing her chin in her hands. "'Splain." Silence. "I'm waiting."

"Antonio and Stefania had a child. He's ten now." Her tone took on an edge. "Stefania won't let Antonio's mama see the child if he divorces her. And, in Italy, the mother of the child almost always wins. The woman is unstable and moves from man to man. But Antonio's mama is afraid of her."

Mary stood, hands on hips, and announced, "This is all just so much bull. Why? Don't grandparents have rights here?" She pointed her finger at Gabby, her voice bouncing across the rooftop. "Get a life, Gabby. We all need to decide what we want and go for it." She sat down, took another sip of her drink, and drummed her fingers.

Liz twirled her hair. "Where does Matteo fit in the picture? I mean, I just met him, but..." Her eyes pooled with tears.

"I met Matteo when I came to Rome. He's older than I am. He restored most of the furniture in the building for me, antiques from my dad's estate. He was a friend of my father's over the years and his father before him."

Gabby walked to the arbor, shading her from our view. "Antonio opened his art store a few years ago. I knew Matteo cared for me, but Antonio took my heart at first sight."

Gabriella walked back and sat on the lounge, hugging her knees to her chin, her hands curled into fists.

"I didn't want this to happen. One night I stayed until Antonio was ready to close the store. His mama wasn't there that night. If she had been, things might be different." She sighed. "He touched my arm and asked if I wanted to get a drink. It was eleven at night on a Friday. We walked by every bar and café on the way to my place." She stopped for a moment, remembering. "He draped his arm around me. It gives me chills just thinking about the feel of his breath against my neck"

I sat, transfixed, as she spoke.

"I led him to my apartment. When I shut the door, he whispered that he'd been watching me for weeks, wanting me."

"Oh," Liz said softly. "So you love him?"

"Yes, I love him. I could be with him for hours and feel content." She looked at us through tear-filled eyes. "But I want all of him. All of him. And I hate that he's married. I'm doing exactly what my mum did." She looked at Liz. "I was trying to make Antonio jealous this weekend. I'm sorry."

"So," said Mary. "You're in an unhealthy relationship like the rest of us. Well, like me. Well, not LIKE me, but you don't have what you want."

"You're not making sense, Mare." I turned back to Gabby. "I think the question is, Gabby, do you have the courage to do what needs to be done so you can have Antonio all to yourself?"

"Someone talking about me?"

We all sucked in our breath as Antonio walked toward us. He was barefoot, wearing only his jeans, walking with his usual confident swagger, large brown eyes focused on Gabby. He sat down and put his arm around her, rubbing her arm, while we stared at him.

"*Ciao,* Antonio," I said. "We've all had a bit much to drink. Care to join us?"

"No, *grazie.* I just came to find my Gabby. *Tutti bene?*"

"Everything's fine, Antonio." Gabby gazed at him, heart in her eyes.

"Come to bed, Gabby. It's late." His fingers tousled her hair as he leaned in for a kiss. His impatience to be alone with her was palapable.

"*Ci vediamo domani,*" said Gabby, her voice strained.

After they left, we sat, stunned by the raw passion the two shared, the complications caused by his marital status.

"Well, I have one thing to say," Mary said, taking another shot of her drink. "I've discovered I'm sexually frustrated."

"After that scenario, aren't we all?" I asked.

"Maybe, just maybe, I have a chance with Matteo." Liz spoke softly, a dreamy look on her face.

"I'm going to bed." I began gathering the drinks.

"I'm not done yet." Mary smacked my fingers.

"Okay, whatever." I turned abruptly and headed to my room. I clutched the packet containing all the information Dante had sent and tried not to think about anything.

I dressed for bed and slid between the sheets, the note from Dante clutched in my hand, waves of guilt washing over me. I lifted my journal from the night stand and began to write, hands trembling.

JOURNAL ENTRY

Talk about being confused. I can't even comprehend how someone can get all of my medical information. Or why they would want to. Or how someone could break the law to get them. Was Dante some kind of powerful Mafia figure? Gabby says no to that. But good grief.

Teddy, he had everything. He assures me I'm okay.

I've heard that anyone can find out anything about a person in this computer age. I don't know if I should pound my fists in anger and call my doctor to see what happened or to simply be thankful for all the secret details about my physical health.

And the drama with Gabby and Matteo and Liz…it's all piling on. All I want to do is sleep and forget about everything. I'm taking an Ambien tonight.

I want a dreamless sleep.

Chapter Fifteen

A light musky scent lingered on the crumpled yellow note on the corner of my desk. I smiled, remembering what it said.

"I'll think of everything," he'd written. *I immediately felt stupid. After all, Ted has always taken care of me. Yet, this stranger makes me smile. Stupid, stupid, stupid.*

It was almost eight. My head ached from last night; my heart, from guilt.

I peeked through the curtains onto the piazza below. It was Monday, our second week here. I noticed a growing comfort in the rhythms of my Roman life...the morning café, trips to the market, knowing the merchants, feeling a familiarity with waiters, the comfort of a gelato. Despite my headache, I felt happy.

Yet my life at home circled me. At home, I'd be working on theses and papers for my grad students. . .deadlines. Procrastination seemed to be an art form with students. And their pressures became mine. Maybe that's why I felt happy. Relieved from stress.

I left a note for the girls, went to the café for my normal morning routine. I loved the alone time. . .although the revelation of Mary and Liz's problems had gone a long way in bonding us beyond our shallow Italian language and ancestry.

The first thing I noted was the absence of my waiter. His replacement, a small rotund man with an infectious smile, informed me it was Carmello's day off. The second interruption of my Roman rhythm – no *cornettas con crema*. With a long sigh, I noticed the third thing missing...Dante. Monday in Italy seemed empty due to the closure of stores and businesses. . .at least until noon. But that was the Roman routine. I could resist or adjust.

I fished my notepad and pen from my purse, and was scribbling a few thoughts about Rome and Italy in general when I felt a slice of warm sun. After a few minutes of journaling, I made an attempt to read La *Stampa,* getting bits and pieces of Italian news. I looked up, saw the regulars had come and gone. Still I stayed, enjoying the serenity. I glanced at my watch and noted an hour had passed. Suddenly, from the corner of my eye, I saw a large manila envelope slide into view.

I looked up into the sea-colored eyes of Dante. The shadow of his beard appeared darker than usual, and I sensed a shift in his mood.

He didn't smile. Just held my eyes with his until I had to look away to catch my breath.

"Permesso?"

"Certo," I said, patting the chair next to me.

Dante leaned back in his chair, hands behind his head in that sensuous power position, and smiled, showing off his to-die-for dimples.

"L'informazione," he said, placing his strong hand on the envelope. *"Facile."*

"Information about what?"

"Your family. *Ho trovato la famiglia.*" He leaned in, his breath sweet and familiar. "The family who adopted your grandfather. *Tuo nonno.*"

"But how? No one would take the time to help me when I visited the town."

"One phone call." He leaned back again, studying me. "To the right person."

The waiter took his order, scurried back into the café, and reappeared a few minutes later with an espresso for Dante.

I watched him drink it in one gulp, his face quiet and contemplative, his skin bronze against the navy blue of his shirt.

I touched his arm. "Thank you, Dante. I've been searching for this news about my grandfather for years."

"Open it."

I lifted the flap, hesitated, and pulled out the contents. Puzzled by this family secret, I yearned to check what Dante had found with my research.

Why was he doing this for me? Finding details about my medical condition? Now my family? And, more important, how?

"Giulia, let's have an adventure today. You and your friends." He took my hand in his. "Tivoli. We'll go to Tivoli," he said, stroking my arm. "Let me call your friends."

"Well, I..."

He dialed. I waited anxiously, wanting to be alone with him while hoping my friends would jump at the chance to see Tivoli.

He tossed me a rare smile. *"Non c'e problema.* Mary said they'll be ready in thirty minutes."

"I'm not prepared for a day trip, Dante." I stood up, clutching the envelope. "I need to change clothes and grab my purse. I'll come down with Mary and Liz."

"I'll be here." He pulled his sunglasses from his head, and buried his face in the newspaper.

I shivered inside, took a deep breath, walked across to my door, and climbed to the penthouse feeling light, like I was floating.

Mary met me with a wide grin. "Tivoli. Wow."

"What is Tivoli?" Liz asked. "Are there shops? Please tell me it's not just museums."

"Tivoli is a small town overlooking Rome. The Pope has a villa there and the villa of an ancient emperor is there. The gardens of Tivoli, I hear, are spectacular." I took a breath. "It's one of the places on our list of things to do and impossible to get to without a guide."

Here I was, using Dante again. Forgetting all the questions and doubts. But Tivoli? With Mary and Liz with me? Really, Jules, what could happen?

"I need to get to the Vatican today." Mary stood watching me. "What time will we be back?"

"I don't know, Mare. And if the Vatican is that important, you can stay here." I turned to my room, miffed. *What on earth? She must be seeing someone at St. Peter's.*

"Oh, I'll go. Just wanted to know what time we'd be back is all." She sounded sad.

"Maybe tomorrow we can go to the Vatican together?" I said. Mary looked away with no response.

"Dante said it will be cooler in Tivoli," I said. "So I'm taking a sweater, just in case." I disappeared into my room, fixed my hair and makeup, put on comfortable sandals, and tried to suppress the anxious feeling in my stomach.

It's just a day of sightseeing. I'm not doing anything wrong.

❦

We strolled through the Campo di Fiori where the vendors displayed rows of colorful, in-season vegetables and fruits. Dante led us down an alley to a car that waited for him. A young leggy brunette handed him the keys to the sleek charcoal gray Mercedes, and walked away without so much as a nod to me and my friends.

"Who was that?" asked Mary. "Wasn't very friendly."

"She works in my office. She's young." Dante shrugged and opened the car doors.

Sliding into the front seat, I sank into the leather. The car carried a soft scent of Dante's cologne. Mary and Liz struggled into the back seat, fitting their enormous purses between them, jammed with enough stuff for a weekend trip.

The fire of the sun on this steamy September day had warmed the leather seats. Dante opened his door and handed me four bottles of cold water. He drove confidently through the midday traffic of Rome, his large gold ring glistening as he eased the car through its gears. I watched his hand with a strange fascination, quietly aroused.

Dante didn't speak. His profile, sober and determined, held my focus as he expertly weaved the graceful gray car to the main highway that would take us to Tivoli. Mary and Liz's chatter sounded like a locomotive bearing down on a lone soul stranded on a railroad track. I wanted to hear the sound of Dante's breathing, his voice.

The drive took forty-five minutes through crowded streets to rolling hills, beige from summer sun. As Tivoli loomed on the hilly horizon, green foliage appeared. The temperature dropped.

"It's cooler here, I promise." Dante reached across and touched my arm. It was an intimate stroke, soft and subtle. I was grateful for Mary and Liz in the back seat.

We parked on a tree-lined grassy lot reserved for Villa D'Este, an elegant estate of faded yellow, perched on a hill. Dante paid the attendant and led us to the entrance.

Liz tapped Dante on the shoulder. "Please, let me buy the tickets."

"No," he said, pulling out his wallet. He gave her a flashy smile as if amused by her offer. I felt a twinge of jealousy. "Today I am a tour guide. *Andiamo.*" He led us through a row of inexpensive souvenir shops with dusty made-in-China replicas of every famous Roman landmark. We followed him to a drab beige hut with a lopsided sign that said "Tickets for Sale."

"Buon giorno." Dante greeted the petite woman of undetermined age cloistered inside. *"Quattro biglietti, per favore."*

"Si." She counted the tickets. *"Uno, due, tre, quattro. Prego."*

"Grazie." Dante took the tickets and walked quickly to the entrance, urging us to hurry. He nodded to the left. A tour guide with a large umbrella signaled at least thirty Japanese tourists to move. He stood in front of the guide, blocking him, and we scurried inside.

"Wow," said Mary, almost disappearing among the other tourists already crunched into the large foyer. The frescos on the wall were brilliant and clear even though painted in the fifteenth century.

"Hurry," urged Dante. "We'll see the inside later. I want to beat the crowds."

Dante was in control. He turned from sexy and gorgeous to an all-business-CEO of Villa d'Este and its lush gardens. The three of us followed him without question, even Mary.

We stood on the patio overlooking breathtaking gardens and fountains, contemplating the heat of the city from the cool precipice of the villa.

"There's Rome. It's about twenty miles from here." With a sigh, Dante pointed to the steaming city. Giant cascades of water splashed into quiet shady pools.

"The opening scenes from Three Coins in a Fountain were filmed here." Dante led us to the narrow and steeply descending stairs and slopes giving way to panoramic views and gushing fountains.

He pointed to the bottom of the gardens.

Mary studied the steep incline, looked at me, hands on hips. "Okay, so is there a lift to get us back to the top? No? You're planning to kill me, aren't you? Admit it. You want me to die in Rome climbing things. Stairs, slopes, hills, streets, buildings...I'm going to have a heart attack."

"Mary, we're not in flat country. This is a garden built on a mountain. You don't put lifts in a fifteenth century villa."

"Come on, Mary," Liz said, taking her arm. "Just get to the bottom and we can take our time to the top." And off they went, Mary hustling to keep up with Liz's elegant long legs.

I started to follow. A firm hand grabbed my elbow.

"Let them go, Giulia." He took my hand and ushered me in the opposite direction down a threadlike path through a grove of pine trees.

My heart thumped. We came to a cloister of flowers and a cave. A stone bench perched by the side of a waterfall, the sun filtered by an arbor of wisteria.

"Giulia." He traced his fingers across my neck, my chin, my lips. He tilted my head with his hands and kissed me. The falling water splashed a mist around us. The kiss lingered, soft and sensual. Suddenly there wasn't enough air in Italy. My arms wound around his neck, my fingers playing with the thick tendrils of hair damp on his neck. I'd crossed a line between desire and temptation. *Jules, STOP.*

Dante pulled away, eyes fixed on me, a muscle in his jaw twitching. He drew my head against his chest, and I listened to the drumming of his heart.

The prattling of a tour guide snapped us apart. We turned to see dark eyes gaping at us.

I drew a deep breath, my heart resonating, as I rested my head on Dante's shoulder. We stood against each other, listening to the droning of the guide and the chatter of a foreign tongue, breathing in unison, wanting the world to go away.

I want to do this. I'm so scared. How can I not do this?

"Giulia, don't cry." Dante wiped away a tear, looking at me with tenderness.

"I'm sorry, Dante."

"For what?" He swept the damp hair from my face. "I know you're not free. Come. Let's find your friends." He drew me to him and whispered, "I can help you. I want to show you love, to help you feel like a woman again."

No. Not this way.

He turned me toward the path. "Come, Giulia."

I saw a flash of red hair by the main fountain. Liz.

"There they are." Dante waved.

We walked briskly down the winding path through a myriad of fountains. Dante led, I followed. And at that moment, I realized I was using Dante. Depending on him. Reacting opposite of an independent woman.

I watched him walk. Clothed, the man was lethally handsome. Something about him today, though, showed a lot of raw power. I felt uneasy, conflicted.

Mary looked up and waved.

I hurried to them.

"Isn't this amazing?" Liz sounded breathy.

"Yeah," said Mary, "and there isn't a store in sight, Red."

Mary turned to me. I couldn't even imagine what I signaled to her.

She touched the back of my hair. "You're wet. Where were you?" She sniffed. "I smell cologne."

Dante took Mary by the arm. "Thank you. It's mine." He artfully distracted them with details on how the fountains worked. "This way," he said, nudging Mary's elbow, and moved off to the left. I followed, begging my heart to stop pounding. Dante's cologne had bled onto my clothing and screamed "guilty" to anyone within a foot of me.

"Ma va!" He flung his hand to the top of the gardens in the direction of the gaggle of tour groups clustered around the entrance. His bright eyes clouded with annoyance.

Coiled power emanated from him.

"Andiamo." Dante waved us on, and we chugged up the slopes.

Mary glared at me, muttering about another hill to climb. "After the penthouse stairs...with no lift, I'm not certain I can scamper up anything else on this trip." She heaved a breath.

Dante laughed. "*Signore*, take your time. We stop for lunch at the little café. The views are spectacular."

He pulled his sunglasses from his face, looking at me with a hint of intimacy, and continued up the slope, leaving all of us behind.

"Wish Matteo were here," sighed Liz. "There are so many nooks and crannies, and it's romantic."

"And I'm sure Dante and Jules found them all." Mary glowered. "Where were you hiding out? And don't play innocent. Dante's scent is sticking to your skin. And your bright lipstick has vanished." She stopped and pointed at me. "You're in big trouble."

"Is there a problem?" Dante stood by a fountain, shaded by trees.

"No, Dante. *Non c'e problema.* We'll catch up to you at the café." I wanted to smack Mary. Instead, I threw a wide smile to Dante, blew him a kiss, and put my head down.

"Look, it's not like we slept together." I kept talking to the pavement. "I mean, yes, he kissed me. But it was just a moment. And he was a perfect gentleman."

"Oh my gosh! Listen to you." Mary grabbed my shoulder to stop me. "His kissing you is not the act of a gentleman with a married woman."

"Bug off, Mare." *In my heart, I knew she was right. But something puzzled me. I couldn't shake the feeling that Dante knew everything about me...had known before we even met.* I thumped my forehead, trying to knock some sense into myself.

Liz quietly interrupted us. "Hey. Whatever happened to 'What happens in Italy, stays in Italy?'"

I tossed her a grateful look. "Liz is right. We're fifty freakin' years old. Old enough to know better, old enough to practice self-control." I planted my feet apart, hands on hips and glowered at Mary.

"Do you think I'm stupid?" My heart beat steadily. "I know what I'm doing. And I know I feel beautiful when I'm with Dante."

Mary's dark eyes flashed. "So now you're needy?" She drew up her slender five-foot frame and glared at me. "Make choices based on facts, not emotion. And have you ever asked Dante what he wants? For you or for himself?"

She hefted her bulging purse high on her shoulder and clenched her teeth. "I will not let you make the biggest mistake of your life." Her finger stabbed me in the chest. "I mean it. Deal with Ted first. Clean that up and make a wise decision. Then, and only then, do you have the right to even think about another man."

"Thank you, Dr. Laura," I said. "You can hang up and move on to the next caller now. And do you have another man, Mary? What about the Vatican obsession? I'm doubting it's confession for the soul that's taken you there so often." My face felt hot and sweaty.

"You both come with me tomorrow." Mary reached up and 'fixed me' by pushing the damp hair from my forehead. "I have nothing to hide."

The defensive tone of her voice screamed she was hiding something.

Liz nudged me and pointed to the top of the path. Dante stood there in the sun, arms crossed, watching us.

"Let's go." I turned and started back up the hill.

We stood in silence next to Dante. He ignored the tension. "I have a table ready." He ushered us to a ledge with a fountain and breathtaking view of the Eternal City, a thick and steamy haze hanging over it like a canopy.

The circular table was covered in a soft green cloth. Four glasses filled with ice tea and a large bottle of water stood in the center.

"I thought you might be thirsty from the climb." He sat down across from me, his eyes covered by his dark glasses, his body language unreadable.

Lunch was light, a simple salad and good bread. Dante wanted to be on the road early to avoid rush hour.

Liz and Mary thanked Dante for lunch. We'd declined any wine.

"I take you on a tour through the villa itself and then back to Rome." Dante guided us to the back entrance of the villa. He told us about the history of this striking country house, built as a Pope's summer home.

He was all business, yet charming and engaging...interesting enough to hold the attentions of Liz the Shopper and Mary the Skeptic. His blue eyes ran cool inside the dark structure, adding to his wild beauty. His features hid all signs of being approachable. And I found myself drawn even more to this mysterious man. I blinked hard, trying to bring Teddy's face into focus. His kind brown eyes, rugged face, ready smile. I couldn't seem to hold the image. Dante seemed dangerous, Ted comfortable and familiar.

I'm okay. The attraction's over. My body relaxed and I heaved a sigh of relief.

Chapter Sixteen

The drive back to Rome held a pregnant silence. I glanced into the visor and saw that Liz and Mary's eyes were closed. Dante had a death grip on the steering wheel, cheek muscles twitching, eyes concentrating on the winding road.

The poignant aria of Nessun Dorma played softly on the CD, ironic because everyone seemed to be sleeping.

Leaning my head back against the pliant leather headrest, I watched him, our sunglasses a barrier to our thoughts. With Dante I'd often experienced fully 'the eyes are the windows to the soul.' My emotions went on a rollercoaster ride, my mind too full of questions I couldn't answer.

It seemed Dante has pushed aside the day, his mind on other things. My gut instinct told me he'd drop us at our door and leave, with me wondering what the kiss at Tivoli meant, the feel of his hard body, the raw intimacy. It was as though he had an on-off switch to his emotions. And it was disturbing.

"Giulia." Dante's right hand left the steering wheel and found mine; heating my body as though he could read my thoughts. I looked at him, but he said nothing.

"Holy buckets." Mary said. "Look at this traffic jam."

"*Ma dai.* I don't believe," said Dante, fist pounding the wheel, his free hand dialing his phone. "*Che cosa?* Why aren't we moving?" he asked the invisible person at the other end. He listened, pounded some more, snapped the cell phone shut and crossed himself. *"Mannagia."*

"*Mi dispiace.* Sorry, but the Pope has decided to visit *la chiesa* di *Santa Maria Maggiore*. Half the streets are blocked for his safety." He turned his head to Mary and Liz. "A long wait. I try for another way. But I think we must stop for coffee." He leaned his head out the window, said, *"Scusa,"* and maneuvered the car across five lanes of traffic. He turned onto the narrowest of streets paved with cobblestones and potholes.

The car bounced along a street lined with part of the original aqueduct, speeding like a bullet with Dante pointing out the many homeless people setting up camp under the arches. He pulled onto a tree-shaded street amazingly void of traffic, careened around a few corners, pulled into a group of autos and motorinis parked helter-skelter and slammed to a stop in the midst of them.

"Arriviamo," he said, opening our doors. He sounded annoyed. Dante stood by his car, pulled his sunglasses to the top of his head, and watched. A slim-suited man, a sliver of cigarette dangling from his mouth, noticed him and waved Dante to a table on the sidewalk to the left of this tiny coffee bar. He rushed to add more chairs to accommodate the four of us. The bar was quaint, an arch of marble outlining the red painted door. The tables were covered in red cloths.

"Prego," said the waiter, taking a slow drag on his cig.

"Grazie," said Dante, motioning for us to sit. "Four waters, two flat, two sparkling. An iced tea, two caps and one machiatto." He rattled the order, remembering what we preferred to drink, all without any sign of politeness.

"Beh! Il Papa?" The waiter waved his cigarette-laden hand.

"Si," said Dante. *"Molto traffico."*

Mary looked at the waiter, Dante, and then me. "What was that all about? Doesn't anyone like the Pope?"

"No, no, Mary." Dante half smiled. "But when he moves about the city, it's always an inconvenience."

"You seem to be in a hurry. Are you?" Mary asked.

"Ah, it shows. I'm sorry." Dante leaned back in a relaxed position and smiled. "I just have some business to take care of and need to check my computer." He glanced at his expensive Tissot watch. "It'll wait."

The waiter presented us with our drinks and a little dish filled with biscotti. *"Prego,"* he said.

"*Grazie*," Dante nodded and handed him some euro. End of scintillating conversation.

"I must go out of town for business. Two days." Dante looked at me as he spoke. "When I come back, I arrange a trip to the Isle of Capri. A long day or we can stay the night." He glanced at Mary and Liz.

"Don't be kidding with me," said Mary. "I've always wanted to go there."

I thought for a moment her body would bounce out of her chair. I'd never seen her so excited.

"Liz?" Dante reached across the table and touched her hand.

"Sure, Dante." Liz flipped her hair as only she could flip. "I'm game for anything."

"Oh, and Matteo, Gabby and Antonio will join us." He paused, circling the rim of his shirt collar with his finger, showing an unusual trace of discomfort.

He glanced at his watch again and downed his drink.

He really needed to be somewhere. I wondered if he'd lied about being married. But then, what did it matter? I was married.

"*Andiamo*," said Dante, pushing back his chair. We piled into the Mercedes and sailed through the streets on this western side of the city, and coming again to a standstill by the Borghese Gardens. We traveled down the elegant tree-lined Via Veneto and arrived at the Piazza Farnese. It was seven, and the piazza was tranquil. Monday nights, the Romans stayed home.

Dante took a key and opened the door to our building. *He had a key?*

"Oh, man. Stairs," groaned Mary. We filed up the steps until we reached the door of our penthouse.

We savored the air conditioned penthouse. Mary and Liz said goodbye to Dante, thanked him for the day and disappeared into their rooms.

"Giulia," Dante said, reaching for my hand. He kissed the tips of my fingers. Inside, I melted like a Swiss chocolate bar. "I'll call you on Wednesday to let you know the day we'll go to Capri by boat." He took my shoulders, pulled me to him, and kissed me softly, the faint taste of coffee on his lips. He turned and walked out the door.

JOURNAL - ROME

Tivoli was amazing, Ted. The day rushed by with new sights and sounds and the excitement of exploring history and another part of Rome.

I'm trying to remind myself to destroy this journal before I come home. But Teddy, we used to have this wonderful exciting tension between us. Everywhere we've gone together for years, even with the boys, our excitement roared to life with each adventure, along with a bond between us.

I've been thinking a lot about the last few years before I was diagnosed. Several things come to mind. For instance, your complete resistance to our last vacation. You fought me every day on the details, where to go, how long to stay, how much money to spend. You groused about insurance and losing work time and worried incessantly about the business. And it wasn't just you being practical. There was a frustration and anger there. And sometimes even a look of fear crossed your face.

When we finally agreed to take another cruise instead of a road trip, I was thrilled. I looked forward to staying up late and dancing together, followed by long chats on our balcony, remembering the joy of the day. Instead, you avoided dancing and turned in early to bed. It's coming back in detail to me right now. You were fatigued. And I was having so much fun I never noticed.

My heart is racing right now wondering if you're okay. I've asked you a couple of times. Your answer is always, "I plan on living until I'm at least a hundred." Followed by a laugh.

Dear God, I'm going through all my stuff and menopause to boot, and not even thinking about you and your health. And to top it all off with a huge blast of unreality, I am finding myself drawn more and more to Dante. But I love you, Teddy. You're my rock.

GABRIELLA

Chapter Seventeen

Dante knocked on Gabby's door.

She opened it, saw his face and said, "You've fallen for her, haven't you? Didn't I warn you?

"No," said Dante, lips tight. "I'm fine. *Tutto bene.*" He caught a glimpse of flowers.

"They're for Jules. From her husband."

A frown shadowed his face.

"By the way, Dante, have you told her about us yet?"

"No."

"But you promised. I've told them most of the story. Can't you do this for me? I don't like keeping things from my guests. Especially since you're so smitten with one of them. Who happens to be very married."

"Antonio is also married."

"Guess we're not too wise in love." She studied his face. "Dante, tell her."

"When we go to Capri. By the way, did you make the arrangement for the train?"

Gabby touched his arm. "You know I'll do anything for you. I have the tickets for the boat, Roberto is available, and the accommodations are booked." She gave him a reassuring hug. "I have to deliver these flowers now." She gazed at his serious face and saw his blue eyes cloud to a stormy gray.

"Mine will be more beautiful." He kissed Gabby on the cheek and left.

Gabby gathered the bouquet, climbed to the Penthouse door, and knocked.

When Julie answered, Gabby handed her the flowers. "These are for you."

"Who sent me flowers? They're beautiful, incredible."

Gabby watched Julie set them on the coffee table in front of the couch, observing a tremble in her hands as she opened the note.

Julie's face paled to parchment.

Chapter Eighteen

In the middle of the dark mahogany coffee table sat an arrangement of silver-violet roses just beyond the budding size. Iridescent ribbons of silver and lavender were tied to the base.

I paused for a moment, trying to catch my breath. With deliberate steps, I walked to the couch, sat down, and hugged my knees to my chest, my gaze fixed on the elegant bouquet.

"What the heck?" Mary stopped in her tracks at the flowers. "I thought I heard a knock." She turned to me, her lips in a stiff, straight line. "This has gone too far, Jules."

"Stai zita."

"Don't tell me to shut up."

"Mary, the flowers are from Ted."

Mary's mouth opened wide.

Gripping the gift card in one hand, I used the other to swipe away tears. I read the card again.

Jules, I hate wasting money on things that die. But just wanted you to know I was thinking about you. And flowers were something I could give that I knew you'd like. Ted

"See what a standup guy he is?" Mary almost beamed.

"Yeah, well read the romantic card he sent with the flowers. And leave me alone." I flung the card at her, pushed myself from the couch, and stomped all the way to my room.

I was behaving like a two-year old with my friend, guilt pushing me. I wanted it all, the romance, the perfect marriage, all wrapped up in a nice package.

The computer in the corner took on the image of an ugly alien. The beauty of the blue and white room retreated. The screen dared me to write an email. I sat cross-legged on the chair, entered my password, and waited.

When I clicked on AOL, I heard the familiar voice. "You've Got Mail." I skimmed down until I found one from Ted. It was dated four days ago. Opening it, I found a clipped but typical Ted letter.

"Jules, miss you. Gang went to Mama Gina's for dinner. Wish you were here. Love...."

The second one, dated two days ago read, "Did the flowers arrive? I know they mean something to you. Me."

My head dropped into my hands. *"Dear God, what am I going to do? Ted isn't going to change, I've changed so much, and guilt is eating me alive."* I looked at the ceiling where the painted angel hovered. "What?"

I glanced toward the door to make sure no one was listening to my conversation with the ceiling.

I flicked the respond icon and wrote:

"Ted, I'm glad you're missing me. The flowers are absolutely perfect. I think of you every time I look at them."

I paused. "Damn! I can't tell him the truth. I don't think of him." I struggled to write more. I knew if Dante weren't hovering in my mind...but he was. My problem.

"Hey, we'll have a long talk when I get home. In the meantime, enjoy the quiet. Rome is changing me. It's strange. And wondrous. Catch my kiss, Jules."

I hit send, immediately felt cruel and ungrateful. "Ted, my dear Ted. You're trying, but I don't know if it's enough." I remembered his humor, faded now. It was what had attracted me the most. Was I the one who'd erased it off our foundation?

I heard a light tap on the door.

Liz peeked in. "Hi, Jules. I saw the flowers. They're incredible. And from Ted?"

"Yeah. I can count on one hand the number of times he's sent me flowers. I don't know if he's reaching out, wishing he were here, or just being wonderful."

"You must be confused right now. Flowers from Ted, Dante..." She raked her fingers through her long hair.

"I'm ready for a quiet dinner. How about you?" She winked at me. "I'm going to the butcher shop, wine shop, and fruit vendor to buy all our favorites." Liz smiled and added softly, "It'll be a good change for all of us. A relaxing evening on the rooftop overlooking Rome."

I reached for my purse.

"Nope, this is on me." She marched out the door.

I sat in my hushed room. I remembered my husband's touch, his kisses. Seared into my mind, however, was my reality versus my fantasy.

After Liz left, I walked into the library off the parlor in search of distraction. I found Nicholas Sparks' The Notebook translated into Italian. An hour later, after looking up every fifth word, I twisted my body from the hard desk chair and muttered, *"Stupida."* The front buzzer answered me.

Mary yelled, "I've got it." When she opened the door, Liz was standing there with wild hair, her arms in a death clutch on several bags.

"Aiutami," Liz said weakly, asking for help.

I grabbed two bags, one full of fresh bread and the other full of grapes. Mary followed me with the wine and cheese. Liz trailed behind, lugging bottled water and assorted cold meats.

We stood around the kitchen table, emptying the bags, salivating over the aromas.

"I'm so tired from today," I said, cutting the bread and cheese.

"You're tired because your emotions are in overdrive." Mary walked to the cupboard and removed a bright yellow plate. "I'll cut the fruit." She turned to Liz. "You forgot the tomatoes?"

"The tomatoes are down at Gabby's." Liz's face colored slightly. "She has something for you, Jules. Said she'd bring everything up in a few. She heard me come upstairs, I guess." Liz gave Mary a shut-up look. "I'll arrange the meat."

We busied ourselves with cutting, opening wine, and gathering dishes. In silence. I felt tension but didn't know the cause. Didn't want to.

The buzzer announced Gabby. "I've brought fresh tomatoes and a lovely bouquet." She breezed into the kitchen, both hands full, damp tendrils around her face. She held an enormous vase of wild flowers in every color imaginable.

I ran to grab the plate of tomatoes, cut and ready to eat.

"Take them, Julie. They're for you."

The vase was a foot tall, deep red cut crystal. A white card dangled from the red satin ribbons that wrapped around the vase.

"Pensi di me. A sabato, Dante"

Everyone but Gabby held their breath.

"What's it say on the card, Jules?" Liz's voice was a whisper.

"Think of me. Until Saturday, Dante." My hands trembled.

"I'll take those, Julie." Gabby walked to the table, saw the other bouquet, turned, and put them on the buffet next to the front door.

"Now," said Gabby, walking back to the kitchen. "Let's get everything up to the roof for dinner." She walked straight to a cupboard, pulled out some screen covers, and led the way.

None of us spoke as we navigated the circular staircase to the rooftop. The sun dropped behind a cloud, giving us welcome shade. Two trips later, we had everything in place.

"Antonio is dining with his mama tonight." Gabby smiled brightly. "I'm inviting myself to dinner."

"We're delighted, Gabby." I gave her a genuine smile.

No one spoke of the flowers.

Gabby reached for the wine, a deep red chianti, and filled our glasses.

"Cin, cin," we said in unison.

We drank, devoured the food, drank more wine, polished off the second bottle and sent Gabby to her place for more. She returned with wine and *limoncello*. I was determined to stick with water.

"So, now, why don't we talk about this elephant on the rooftop?" said Gabby, sipping her wine, amber eyes glistening.

"What elephant?"

"Dante, the flowers, your dilemma, Rome, your future." Gabby waved her wine glass. "Talk to us."

"Yeah," said Mary. "Talk."

"You," said Gabby, holding her glass toward Mary's face, "*Silenzio.*" She turned to me. "Just talk, sweetie. We'll listen."

I closed my eyes and leaned my head against the back of the lounge chair. No one spoke. They waited with an endurance known only to women. I opened my eyes and stared at the faded twilight over the skyline of Rome.

"My marriage started to drift when the boys left for college. I felt like I had nothing to do. The sports, high school activities, and their friends...that was my life. Ted worked twenty-four/seven selling commercial real estate. We were busy. Life was great. Then, it all started to fall apart with a phone call. After that, things piled up."

"I empathize," said Gabby.

Liz pursed her lips. "Everything seems to come in sets of three."

"You're right, Liz. My sister-in-law called to say my brother had dropped dead of a heart attack. My Dad was diagnosed with cancer. Two years later, I buried him. Then the final straw, my diagnosis with breast cancer."

"Jules, I didn't even know you had a brother." Liz's voice resonated with soft concern.

"I wasn't inclined to share my bizarre life while conjugating Italian verbs." I gave them a wan smile.

"I can't explain it. Downstairs, in our penthouse, sit two vases filled with flowers. Ted's flowers represent what's safe and predictable, a twenty-five year marriage with a good man. Roses show he's trying." I took the tissue Mary offered.

"Dante's flowers represent passion, adventure, a dare." I dabbed at my eyes and looked at them all. "I feel like freakin' Shirley Valentine in that crazy Brit movie where she ran away to Greece and felt the earth move. I've lived my whole life being and doing what's right...traveling the flat and fruited plains. I want an exciting rollercoaster ride for the second half of my life. I think." I grinned, felt my face flush. What I'd said was foolish and I regretted it immediately. In reality, I was fearful of roller coasters and beginning to understand that deep within me, I wanted a simpler life.

"Well," said Mary, "I've had enough up's and down's. I want a nice straight road."

"Up's and down's are not the image I meant by a rollercoaster. I'm trying to convey excitement, never knowing what's around the corner. Not mountain tops and valleys."

I stood, and walked to the edge of the roof garden, and gazed down at the piazza below. I turned slowly. "What do I do? I need a sign."

JOURNAL - ROME

What a strange evening. What a dilemma indeed with the flowers. All I have to say tonight is I wish I could edit my life. I mean…life is not a journey to the grave with the intention of arriving in a pretty well-preserved body, but rather to skid in broadside, thoroughly used up...and loudly yelling, "Wow, what a ride."

I wanted to edit the last five years and never get off the rollercoaster of excitement. And, as you grow older, it seems to be more difficult. I'm selfish and insensitive. I think about the fact that Ted is slowing down. But his vitality shouldn't be dying out yet. There must be something wrong.

I need to get over myself. I can't edit real life. But I certainly can make changes to myself. Teddy. I hope you're okay.

GABRIELLA

Chapter Nineteen

The morning dawned gloomy and chilly by Rome standards. Battleship gray clouds appeared, encompassing the buildings surrounding the piazza.

Gabby stretched, re-curled her body into a tight ball, and thought of the previous night. She'd loved the conversation with the American women, appreciated being a part of their lives. At the same time, she felt sad.

Antonio had interrupted them. He'd appeared, with his dark unruly hair and bitter chocolate eyes, looking good enough to eat. Although amused by their reaction to him, she hated herself for leaving with Antonio. She wished she'd just waved him off to bed. But then, she wouldn't have experienced their intense passion.

"Gabby," said Antonio, nuzzling her neck. He gathered her close to him. "You're tense, *cara. Che cosa?*

"I was just thinking how much fun I had with the American women last night."

"Please, Gabby." He turned her body to his. *"Ti voglio, caramia."*

Gabby returned his gaze, not smiling. "I know you love me, Antonio. But I want more. I want intimacy and security beyond this apartment." She sat up, holding the sheet to shield her naked body. She glanced nervously at Antonio. "I want marriage. All of you." Anger, long held back, started to simmer within her. "This isn't enough."

"Damn American women." Antonio scowled and scrambled out of bed. "Don't try to be like them, Gabby. Be who you are."

"What am I? Stupid? Always number two in everyone's life?" She glared at him.

"I don't need this," said Antonio, grabbing his jeans. He walked into the bathroom and slammed the door.

"That's the way to handle things. Walk away. That's what a man does, isn't it?" she shouted. She took long angry strides to the wardrobe, threw on a robe, and marched to the kitchen.

"I'm tired of complications. I want comfortable." She made espresso, roughly handling the machine. When the coffee was ready, she sank into the white kitchen chair and looked out the window onto the Campo di Fiori.

"Just walk away, Antonio." Salty tears trickled down her face and wet her lips.

She heard footsteps in the apartment above and knew the three women were preparing for whatever the day brought them. She sighed, admiring their apparent independence.

Chapter Twenty

Mary, Liz and I had just entered the main street leading to St. Peter's. The church's golden dome gleamed in the afternoon heat and dominated the square. The streets were packed with tourists in colorful, casual wear and an ample sprinkling of priests and nuns in their stark black and white attire.

"Mary, slow down." Liz released an exasperated sigh. "I can't even window shop at this speed."

"Hey, Red," said Mary. "Have you noticed the shops? Lots of black shoes, black skirts, black habits, beads, and belts made of rope." She waved her hands and pointed to the religious icon store to our right. "In case you hadn't noticed, we're in Vatican City. They cater to the clergy. No Prada here, Red." Mary arched her neck high, looking for something. A soft, "Ah," drifted from her lips.

Tucked in a corner alley stood a small café with "D'Angelo" etched in gold leaf on the door and window. A small man with a melancholy expression and gentle eyes leaned against the door. His dark hair was slicked back. He drew a pack of cigarettes from the pocket of his crisp white shirt and, with a deliberate movement, tapped out a slim brown Italian cigarette. He walked to one of the outdoor tables covered in maroon linens, flipped open a pack of matches, and readied his smoke. He drew on the cigarette, inhaling deeply, his expression faintly resigned.

I drew my gaze from him to Mary. Her eyes widened when she saw him. We waited for a gaggle of tourists to pass. When a hole opened in the crowd, he saw her.

"*Maria, ciao!*" He exhaled, holding the smoke between his thumb and forefinger, and walked toward us.

"*Ciao, Stefano.*" Mary held her face up as he leaned in to kiss her cheek. "*Come va?*"

"*Bene.* Now, I'm good," he answered.

Mary looked relaxed, and soft.

She turned to us. "This is Julie and Liz."

"Ah, the famous *le donne.* Heard all about you guys. Call me Steve." He waved to a table. "Please. Sit." He held Mary's chair, his face breaking into a brilliant smile when he gazed at her.

Mary asked, "How are mama and papa' today?"

"Stubborn as ever. *Beh!*" He inhaled and blew the smoke to the side, holding his cigarette down.

Mary hated smoking. Hmmm. This was very strange.

I noticed a sliver of a scar across his cheekbone. It gave him an edgy mysterious look. He wasn't handsome, not in the classic sense. But he had a kind face, and a seemingly gentle spirit.

"So, Stefano, uh, Steve. This is a lovely coffee bar."

"Yeah. Problem is, I'm working it because of my folks. I own a restaurant in Brooklyn." He pushed some hair behind his ear.

Mary talked to me, but she looked at him. "He's here because his parents are struggling to keep the store. Like a good son, he came from Brooklyn to help them."

"And, like good parents," he said as he looked up and locked his hands in prayer mode, "they're driving me crazy." His brown eyes gleamed. "You'll see when you meet them. First papa' will come out and flirt with all of you, missing teeth be damned. Mama will follow and fuss over you while giving pa punches in the arm." He winked at Mary. "Poor guy's on blood thinner for his heart. One day mama's going to hit him, and he's going to hemorrhage right into someone's coffee."

Mary's gentle laugh startled me. Liz raised her eyebrows at me in equal surprise.

"Is this the Vatican attraction, Mare?"

"It's just a place I found with good coffee. You know, like we go to the same place every day by the penthouse."

"Buon giorno!" The cheery greeting came from a short old man in a stained white apron covering a worn pair of trousers and a yellowed shirt. A gust of wind would have tumbled him to the ground.

"Papa', viene qua." Stefano motioned his father to join us.

He approached the table, winking at us. *"Bellissime! Belissime!"* He grinned widely and waited.

Stefano laughed. "He no speaka da English."

I found his laugh infectious. "What's his name?"

"Signore D'Angelo. He's old fashioned. At his age, he still requires formal address, as does mama."

I extended my hand to him. *"Sono Giulia. Buon Giorno, Signore D'Angelo."* He took my hand and kissed it softly.

"Carmellooooo." The voice was raspy for a woman, probably from years of smoking. *"Dov'e?"*

"Mama," said Stefano, looking toward the doorway, annoyed.

There stood the stereotypical mature Italian woman, graying hair pulled back from her round face in a severe bun so tight her eyes bulged. Her body was equally round. An ample bosom covered what had been a waist. Her dress shouted Italian movie wardrobe...black, simple, unadorned. Straight away, she conveyed that she was the boss.

"Buon giorno," she said. She turned her attention to her husband. "Carmello?"

Carmello rolled his eyes, looked pleadingly at his son, and then followed mama back into the shop.

"Well, ladies," said Stefano, frustration etched into his face, "now you know my problem. Five minutes, two *buon giornos,* and it's obvious, *si?"*

I looked at Stefano, curious. "Your parents seem to be in good health and have lots of energy."

"This year my father turns eighty-six and my mother, eighty." He took a deep breath and scrambled to light another cigarette. "They can't do this anymore. They think they can." He shrugged. "It's all they know." He looked at the window of the coffee shop. "My biggest fear is that they'll kill each other."

"Stefano." Mary put her hand on his. "Haven't they always been this way?"

"Yeah. They show their love by haranguing each other." He drew in the nicotine and blew it skyward. "But I'm the youngest of six, and single. And I'd like my life back, thank you very much." He sighed. "Mary has listened to me since she stopped for coffee after her first visit to the Vatican." Stefano cradled her cheek in his palm. "She has the patience of Job."

I looked at Liz. She looked at me. We both burst out laughing.

"The patience of Job. That's our Mary," I said, struggling to keep from giggling.

"What?" Mary said.

Stefano excused himself. "I need ta see what's taking 'em so long." He rushed to the door. "Mama! *Dov'e?*"

She answered with a stream of gravelly Italian.

Mary smiled. "Always yelling. Doesn't mean a thing."

"She sounds angry," I said.

"Hey, I live with a man who hasn't shown any emotion or paid attention to me for years. He comes home, turns on the television, and waits for me to serve him dinner. He eats in silence, watches TV in silence. He never communicated with the kids." Mary's eyes sparkled. "Don't you get it? They all love each other."

"Mary, you're glowing." Liz paused. "You have a crush on him, don't you?" She sat back against her chair in one elegant move. "You do! I can see it."

"Hey, he's nice. I enjoy coming here. Besides, he's too young for me. And I'm going through a divorce."

"Wait a minute, Mare." I explored her face, curious. "Have you heard more from George?"

"Yup. He sent me another email, basically saying he's moving on, I'm a loser, and will be nothing but a poor displaced housewife." She grinned. "Ask me if I care?"

"But Mare..."

"But, nothing. After Red told us about her experience, I've become a bit brave. In fact, take a look at this." She plucked something from the wallet in her purse and slid a business card toward us.

"Anthony DeLucca, Attorney-at-Law?" I re-read it. "Attorney?"

Liz popped up from her seat and ran around to Mary, giving her a huge hug. "You did it? You hired a killer attorney?"

Mary's face reddened. "Yeah. So what?"

"So what?" I picked up the card again. "This guy's from Brooklyn. Mary, a Brooklyn lawyer can't represent you."

"Gimme that." Mary grabbed the card and turned it over. On the back was another name. A Joseph DeLucca, with a Newport Beach address.

"A cousin of Stefano, no doubt?" I asked. I was enormously pleased to see Mary show some backbone when it counted.

"What's so amusing, girls?" Stefano strolled to our table, looking calmer.

"Nothing," said Mary. "And your parents?"

He slid his hand through his hair. "Food. It's always about the food. Mama's upset because she didn't know there'd be special guests here at lunchtime." He rolled his eyes. "She's throwing together some pasta and her famous sauce as we speak." He cast a grin toward Mary. "*Scusami.* I have other guests, and the guy who's supposed to be here to help is late as usual. I'm going to fire his ass. Oops. Sorry, ladies."

"No problem," I said as I laughed. "We've all heard worse."

The minute his slim backside disappeared into the café, we grilled Mary.

"How old is he?" I asked.

Mary mumbled a number.

"Can't hear you. Repeat, please," I said, nudging her arm and holding my other hand to my ear.

"Stefano's only forty-two. He's a baby. Never been married. The good child, the fun uncle to his huge assortment of nieces and nephews. A great cook."

Liz crossed her arms, giving Mary a scrutinizing look. "And you come here just about every day, because...."

"Yeah?" I pushed back my chair, crossed my legs, and waited.

"Okay, Jules. It's nothing. I'm just enjoying his company, the way you enjoy Dante's, and the way Red enjoys Matteo."

"No physical attraction?" I asked.

"Sorry to disappoint you. But I'm just enjoying a comfortable relationship with a perfect stranger."

"Relationship? You're having a relationship with him?" I asked, grinning.

"Oh, knock it off. I like his company, I love the way he cares for his parents. I feel normal with him." She peered into my eyes. "And we have not kissed because I am still married, Jules." Her voice was biting.

"This is about you, Mare. Not me." I opened my mouth to ask another question, but a plate full of pasta with tantalizing aromas of garlic and tomato sauce wafted to my nose.

"*Mangiate!*" Mama ordered us to eat.

We looked at the pasta and groaned.

"*Mangi, mangi,* girls. There's more to come." Stefano's grin was impish. "You never want to upset an Italian mama who's fixed a meal."

Papa' arrived with a tray of still-warm bread. "*Buon appetito.*" He stood next to the table, beamed as usual, then smiled at his wife, a look of pride on his lined face.

They loved each other. After all these years, fights, hardships, yelling, long hours of work, and raising kids...they still loved each other. It was beautiful.

I thought about Ted. Maybe comfortable was a good thing. But the high level of passion I felt when I was with Dante was more than intoxicating. It was addictive. Something I'd never experienced before. I knew it was wrong. I also knew comfortable came after years of trust and acceptance.

"Jules, hello. What do you want to drink? Red or white?" Mary waved her hand in front of my face.

"Water, please." I smiled at *Signora* D'Angelo.

She shrugged and waddled back to the café.

The crowd passing us on their way to explore St. Peter's had grown. We laughed ourselves silly listening to their complaints.

"I need to sit down," said a plump gray-haired man laden with a huge camera and backpack.

"Sam, the program says we sit at four." The wife's fanny pack bulged, sweat dripped down her face. "Quit complaining."

"But I have to pee," he groaned, following the line.

A tall, lanky young man pushed his way through the people, slowly tying an apron around his waist. *"Mi dispiace, Stefano."* He swept a lock of dark brown hair from his equally dark eyes, looking sheepish.

"Finalmente, Eugenio. Beh! Vai." Stefano waved him to the door. He held his hands in a position of prayer and glanced upward again. *"Mannaggia. Sempre in ritardo.* Never on time. And telling me he's sorry doesn't cut it."

Stefano, suddenly stern, ordered the young man to get to work. "No more chances for him," he said, watching Eugenio scamper into the café.

Stefano sank into the seat next to Mary, frustration emanating from his face. He started to slide his arm around her shoulders.

Mary edged away as though uncomfortable with the intimacy of the gesture.

"Sorry." Stefano rolled his eyes. "It's just, 'dat kid is driving me nuts. Then the folks get upset when he's late. Mama starts to yell. It's a cycle."

We all nodded, savoring the rich marinara sauce and enjoying every bite.

"So what are your plans for the weekend, ladies?" He glanced at Mary.

"We're going to Capri with some friends. Want to come?" I asked.

Mary put her hand up in protest and glared at me. "He's too busy with his parents."

I enjoyed Mary's reaction to my bold invitation.

"Hmmm, it's tempting." He tossed Mary a quick look. "The café is closed from Saturday noon until Monday noon."

"It's okay, Stefano." Mary's voice was gentle, but her glance toward me displayed an if-looks-could-kill expression.

"No, no. Let me think," he said, face thoughtful.

"Come on, Stefano." Liz leaned in. "Mary would love your company, and it would give us time to get better acquainted."

"Imbecile." They heard Papa' yelling at the top of his voice from the kitchen.

Eugenio scampered out the door, looking frightened. He untied his apron and threw it on the table in front of Stefano. *"Finito."* He walked away.

"Wait. Eugenio, what happened?"

He paused and faced Stefano, his hands raised in frustration. "They not want me. *E' difficile."*

"Come back on Tuesday," Stefano pleaded. "We'll talk."

"No, non e' possibile." Eugenio marched down the street.

Stefano cursed loudly. He shook his head slowly from side to side. "Third one this month."

I turned to him. "Why don't you just close the store for the weekend and give yourself and your parents a rest?"

He touched Mary's shoulder and sighed. He looked at me as if I'd said something revolutionary. "That's the best idea I've heard all year." He cupped his mouth with his hands and shouted, "Mama, Papa', *subito."*

They joined us as quickly as their old bodies would allow, shuffling on their tired feet.

Stefano spoke rapidly in Italian, telling them about their forced vacation from the café. They listened carefully. Mama started to say something, then stopped, nodded, and turned back to the door.

Stefano looked at Mary and playfully ran his fingers through her hair. "Looks like you're stuck with me, kiddo."

Mary glowered at me.

ꕥ

Doing her hair flip thing, Liz pulled her compact from her purse and added some lipstick. "Bathing suit time. Come on."

I groaned at the thought of buying a swimsuit. "Fine, Liz. But I'm not buying one just because of this weekend. If I'm not sufficiently covered up, I'll go without."

Liz's eyes widened. "You'll swim naked?"

"I meant I just won't buy one. I'll wear a sundress and be done with it."

Mary nudged Stefano. "They forgot to throw in a swimsuit." Her smile was smug. "I always take a suit when I travel." She winked. "Just in case."

"Okay," I retorted. "You're smart, we're not. Enjoy the rest of the day. No plans for tonight? Tomorrow?"

"No plans." Mary nodded. "Everyone is on their own until Friday morning."

"Oh, wait," I slapped my head. "I forgot. Gabby said something about drinks on the patio tonight. Said there would be fireworks for some kind of festival...like harvest?"

"Fine," said Liz. "We'll all meet on the roof patio tonight." She stood up and grabbed my arm. "Let's go! You need a bathing suit, I'm going to find you one, you're going shopping, and you're going to like it."

Chapter Twenty-One

Shopping with Liz could be maddening. She dawdled over every decision. Fortunately, we were focused on swimsuits, which eliminated shoe stores and most boutiques.

"I need to stop for a cold drink." My feet hurt, and I was overheated.

"We've only been shopping for two hours."

"Look, Liz." I stopped and looked her square in the eyes. "Your narrow butt can wear anything. I've had kids, I have hips. I need to sit, think, and strategize."

We'd scoured the shops in the area of the Piazza Popolo. By September, the swimsuit collection was slim picking. Nothing like trying on these elastic nightmares to plummet one's self-esteem. I scanned the street corner and spotted a bar. It was filled with people, laughing, drinking and savoring gelatos.

"There. We'll go there." I grabbed her hand.

We inched our way through the tables scattered on the outside patio and found one sheltered by a dark green awning. I settled ungracefully on the chair, retrieved a loose tissue from my purse, and blotted my glistening face. No. I had to be honest. I was dripping.

"What's your problem?" Liz hadn't broken a sweat. She'd twisted her hair in a knot and pinned it to the top of her head. Her all-beige linen ensemble was richly wrinkled, her makeup still intact. I wanted to hate her.

"Look at me. I'm sweating, Liz. My eyeliner is probably a puddle somewhere between here and the D'Angelo's café. My white linen looks like I've slept in it. I need a cold drink. We need to ask someone where to buy normal bathing suits."

"What? You looked adorable in that two-piece suit...the red one."

"I need a bit more covering than you." My eyes darted about for a waiter. I spotted one and did what one never does in Italy. I waved him over to our table.

"Signora," he said, annoyed.

I swiped my face again with a tissue, cocked my head in his direction and smiled coyly. *"Mama Mia, fa caldo. Ho bisogno di...*uh, flat water, *freddo*, and a gelato limone." I smiled again and added, *"Per favore?"*

"Ah, certo." He smiled. *"Troppo caldo."* He fanned himself with the menu, indicating he understood.

He nodded at Liz.

"Ice tea, extra ice, *per favore?"*

"Si." With a cursory glance at Liz and a grin for me, he went to fetch our drinks.

Liz glared at me. "What is it with you and waiters? They always engage with you and ignore everyone else."

"I don't know, Red. But I'm starting to cool down. Don't ruin the moment."

The drinks arrived, and I held the cold bottle against my neck. "Cheers, Red. To finding a bathing suit that covers the body."

"Excuse me." A matronly looking lady at the next table sporting bright blue eye shadow and over-ratted hair leaned toward me.

"Yes?"

"If you want normal clothes, for a normal body, go to the department store."

Liz looked at her, astonished. "A department store? Here? In Rome?"

The lady nodded, her sunhat bobbing up and down. "Everything here is for the boutique body. But in this travel guide, it says that Americans might want to try *La Rinascente,* a department store on the *Via del Corso.* It's not far from here."

"May I see that?" I asked, taking another long drink of water.

She handed the travel guide to me and continued chatting with her friends. It was obvious none of them had boutique shopped. Their clothes screamed comfortable tourist, inclusive of muddy neutral tones, lots of pockets, and elastic waistbands, not to mention sensible shoes.

I located the store on the map. "We'll go there next." Liz rolled her eyes and took a sip of tea.

We finished our drinks. My gelato had melted. I returned the book to the lady.

"Good luck," she yelled after us.

"Thanks." I was on a mission.

An hour later, I settled on a one-piece black suit that offered a peek of white at the top and anchored my behind below.

"Liz, not to hurt your feelings, but I need some time to myself. Are you okay with my going back to the penthouse now?"

"You know I hate being alone." Liz pursed her lips. "Go ahead. I want to browse. And your impatience and rushing the shopping bothers me." She waved me off.

It was the first time Liz had ever shown annoyance with me. I felt bad. I turned to apologize, but she'd already disappeared in a store.

The coolness of my bedroom relaxed me. I snuggled into the soft blue wing-backed chair and stared at the bag holding my swimsuit. After several deep breaths, I came to the conclusion that the suit wasn't the issue. No. Everything was rooted in the fact that Ted knew me. Dante didn't. What would he think of my bulges, sags, and scars?

I'd felt like a giant eraser rubbed off all the hair from my body when I started chemo. No eyelashes, eyebrows, not a speck of hair anywhere. It rendered me invisible to myself and threw a curve to those who looked at me...giving me attention I didn't want. Erased and invisible? Weird and unattractive? Either way it caused devastation to my psyche.

Before I dissolved into self-pity, the phone rang, its flat tone jarring me.

"*Pronto.*"

"Ciao, Julie. This is Gabriella. Dante left a message for you. Said to pack a light suitcase with casual clothes, a swimsuit, and one nice outfit for dinner."

"Define 'nice.'"

"Just something you would wear to dinner in Rome. Linen is popular in Capri. And dress comfortable for the trip. Dante decided to take the train to Napoli and catch a boat to Capri from there."

"Really? I expected a limo."

Gabby laughed. "It'll be another fun Italian experience. The train trip will be an adventure, and the ferry to Capri...something new. Besides, driving is a nightmare in Naples."

"By the way, there will be eight of us. A friend of Mary's is going, too."

"Really? Male or female?"

"Male. It seems the draw to the Vatican was a man."

Gabby chuckled. "Good for Mary."

"So what time on Friday?"

"I've reserved the ten o'clock train to Napoli." She paused. "Julie, Dante doesn't bother with women. I mean, he dates, but he avoids affairs of the heart."

"Gabby, how do you know Dante so well?"

"It's a long story. Dante prefers to tell you himself. Don't worry about it."

Hanging up the phone, I stood up, retrieved the bathing suit from its classy red bag, and trudged into the bathroom, ready for the full-length mirror.

After much slithering and tugging and pulling, I faced my image. "This is it, Jules. This is a fifty-year old body. And it's not going to get better."

I turned to get a back view. "Hmmmm. Skin still looks good, no cellulite, butt not sagging too badly." I examined the dreaded bust line. "It'll have to do."

I wandered back to the bedroom and plucked the cover-up for the suit out of the bag. Sliding the filmy white and black material over the suit, I faced the mirror again. "Now that looks sexy, Jules."

I shed the suit and threw on a shift for comfort. Strolling to the kitchen, I opened the fridge and gathered some fresh tomatoes, scooped up some salt and olive oil from the counter and sat at the table. I salted the tomato, drizzled it with olive oil and ate it like an apple. In the silence of the bright white kitchen, I thought about the coming weekend.

For me, it would be the ultimate temptation. What were the sleeping arrangements? Gabby and Antonio would sleep together. They were lovers, after all. Mary and Stefano? Mary was still married, and with all her ranting at me...no way would she sleep with him. Liz still distrusted men, although very attracted to Matteo. Would he make his move? That left Dante...and me. Alone with a man so sexy he made my teeth hurt. In the soft Italian darkness, would I be able to resist him?

"What's up?" Mary walked into the kitchen, eyes roaming the table, noticing every dribble of juice from my tomato.

"Just thinking and having a snack."

"Look at the tomato juice all over the table." She touched a spot on the floor. "Olive oil? And look at your shift."

"Leave me alone, Mary."

"Are you okay?" Her voice softened.

"Actually, no."

"Why? What happened?"

"A stupid bathing suit is what happened."

She settled herself in the chair facing me. "Why is a suit such a crisis for you?"

"Isn't it obvious?"

"No. You look fab for your age. You're a head-turner, and your self-image is so low, you're always looking at the ground instead of seeing the attention you get on a regular basis." She touched my arm. "Look, Jules. It is what it is. You've battled cancer and survived. You're still Jules."

I stood and turned to leave.

She faced me, pointing her finger. "You're not the only one with problems. My life has been a living hell. You've only heard the half of it since we've been in Rome."

Hands on hips, I glared at her. "Then, open up, Mare. Don't be so bloody closed all the time. Are you trying out for the Mother Teresa opening? Tell me why you're so obsessed with my marriage."

Mary sighed and rolled her eyes. "Look, Jules, Italy is a make-believe world for us, far from our reality."

"And your point is?"

She spoke quietly. "I want the second part of my life to be different. I want to change, to be happy."

"That's all I want, Mary"

"Look, Jules, when I'm ready, I'll tell you more about my life. In the meantime, you and Dante? That's your call. I don't think you should sleep with him until you figure out your marriage. In fact, I don't think you could live with yourself." She shrugged. "Whatever your decision, my lips are sealed." She paused. "We need each other, you, and me, Liz...."

"Okay, time for a truce." I walked to her and gave her a hug.

The front door slammed. We looked down the hall and saw Liz, laden with bags. She joined us in the kitchen, tugging the handles from her fingers, and let the packages drop.

Mary grinned. "I see you've been drowning your problems in shopping?"

"Needed some new stuff for Capri." She reached into the biggest bag and held up a soft yellow sundress.

Mary and I looked at each other and laughed. Liz's shopping skills and endurance were amazing.

"You go, Red." I sat down next to Mary and enjoyed the fashion show.

Chapter Twenty-Two

I watched Dante stack our luggage as the Euro Star slid smoothly from the station in Rome. There were no porters on Italian trains, and it was clear why he'd warned us to pack lightly.

Dante glanced at the tickets. "Follow me." He pointed to two groups of four seats. "Here. Because of language problems, Giulia and I will sit with Liz and Matteo. That leaves translators for everyone, *sì?*" He repeated it in Italian.

After much shuffling and sighing, we settled into our seats.

Dante engaged everyone. His every nuance, from voice to clothes to his glorious seductive accent, turned me on. Knowing it was wrong, I compared him to Ted. As usual, it was unfair. Because they were incomparable.

Ted, a good-looking man by anyone's standards, would have boarded the train in a Southern California outfit consisting of a flowered cotton shirt, comfortable jeans, white tennis shoes and white tube socks. Dante, impossibly good looking, sported impeccably fitted khaki-colored linen slacks topped with a silk short-sleeved shirt in buttery cream. I loved the shadow of his beard, wanting to feel it against my skin. His feet stretched in front of him, crossed at the ankles. For a few delicious moments, I studied him.

He must have sensed my stare. He turned to me, and our eyes met.

I leaned in to him and whispered, "Dante, can we go somewhere and just talk?"

He grinned. "*Certo.* The dining car."

He stood, offered his hand, and we made our way to what I hoped was a quiet place.

Since it was morning, the car was quiet except for the occasional clinking of silverware and soft Italian pop music playing in the background. A few people sat alone at beautifully appointed tables topped with sage-green linens adorned with fresh sunflowers. Businessmen sipped cappuccino while working on their laptops; others read the morning paper. Dante slipped the attendant some cash and he ushered us to a cozy corner booth, with a promise that no one would bother us.

He slid close to me. "Alone with you. *Finalmente.*" He held my hand to his lips.

"I'm nervous about this weekend. It's where the rubber meets the road."

His brows furrowed. "Rubber? Road? Who are we meeting?"

I laughed. "It's an expression, Dante."

"Explain." His piercing gaze gave me chills.

"Dante, your relationship with Gabby seems—umm--mysterious. Were you and Gabriella lovers?"

"*Mio madre di Dio, no.*" He leaned back.

"*Va bene. Calmo,* Dante. Just curious."

A lock of hair fell onto his forehead, and I resisted the urge to brush it from his face.

I waited for him to explain.

"Giulia, remember when we first met? That day at the Caffe' Farnese."

"Yes, I remember." I felt a chill just thinking about the first time I gazed into those eyes.

"I knew of you long before that."

"What?"

"The penthouse you're renting. It's mine."

"Huh?"

"I own the building. I own many buildings in Rome, in Sorrento, on Lago di Como."

"I had no idea. Why didn't you tell me?"

"I'm a private person."

"So, what is your connection to Gabby?"

His eyes clouded. "Gabby. She's my half-sister, someone I never knew existed until ten years ago when my father died, and his will was read."

Sister?!

"It's a long story, Giulia. Gabby and I have the same father. It's difficult to talk about. But Gabby and I are close, now."

I loved his Italian protectiveness. His vulnerability made him even more appealing.

"Gabby told us about her mother revealing her 'dad' was not her real dad. But she never mentioned the connection with you."

"It's been a difficult adjustment for us. Now, I want to protect my sister." He took my hand. "Let's talk about us, *cara.*"

"Not so quick, Dante. *How* did you know me before I came here?"

"Your emails. Gabby shared them with me. We always work together when renting any of our properties to foreigners. Gabby has this fantasy that the penthouse is magic and always rents it below market price to troubled people." He cupped my face in his hands. "We argued about it, but when I saw your photo, the smiles, what you'd been through with the cancer." He leaned in to kiss my lips. "You are so different from Italian women. When I met you in person, I had to know you better. I noticed," he touched my hand, "that sometimes your smile is shadowed."

He glanced away for a long moment. He looked back and said, "I didn't expect to have these feelings for you."

"And your wife and child?"

"It's in the past. My son and I are close. Maria got what she wanted. A lot of money and a child. Her beauty was, as you say, only on the skin."

"Skin deep, Dante."

Dante pulled me close to him. "I know you're married. But you leave me breathless. You're fun, you're normal." He trailed his fingers down my arm. "You're passionate. I don't know. I just know I want to be with you. It's a risk I'm willing to take."

He kissed me, softly, then with a deep hunger. My body and heart responded with an ache of wanting.

Breath ragged, Dante pulled away. "I just want you to be happy." He buried his face in my neck.

We snuggled in the booth, sharing dreams and hopes until the attendant approached us. "*Signore, Napoli.*

Dante took my hand. "Come. We join our friends and talk this weekend. Know each other better." His smile was almost shy. "Maybe we meet the road?"

"*Si,* Dante. Maybe."

We walked in silence to join our friends. So Dante, with all of his outward perfection, carried wounds, too. I felt myself deeply attracted to each new layer of this man.

Chapter Twenty-Three

The train slowed, pulling into the station. People gathered their belongings and crunched into a tight line in the aisle.

"Gabby, take the ladies and wait at the wall right off the steps. We'll get the suitcases." Dante gave my arm a squeeze and pushed his way forward with the other guys to gather the luggage.

While we huddled, Mary elbowed me. "Where the heck were you two all this time? Did he rent a compartment or something?" Her dark eyes peered into mine.

"Shush, Mare. We just went to the dining car to talk. That's all. Why don't you concentrate on enjoying this weekend instead of worrying about me. Stefano, with those big sad brown eyes, is crazy about you. Feed on that."

"He's so blasted young. And I am STILL married." She turned to talk with Liz.

Relieved, I moved toward Gabby and lowered my voice. "Dante told me you were his sister. Why didn't you let us know?"

"We'll talk later, Julie." She touched my hand. "I'm glad you know."

Antonio waited at the exit to help each of us from the train. *Chivalry wasn't dead.* I clunked down the narrow steps, holding his extended hand. He lifted Mary down. Liz stepped off as if she were a runway model, hair swinging, make up perfect, a wide smile on her face. Several men stared at her. Who could blame them?

When I reached Dante, I leaned against his arm, feeling safe. He grabbed my finger and pulled my hand behind his back. Such a small gesture, yet it said to me that he cared and would take care of me. A smile tugged at the corner of his mouth.

"Guarda, per favore," said Antonio. He laughed. "Danger here." He looked toward Gabby, begging for help with the language. They exchanged a few quick sentences and Gabby turned to us.

"Follow Antonio. He's taking us to the end of this bin and then to an escalator. We'll find a cab there to take us to the dock."

The eight of us huddled together, the men carrying the luggage, the women clutching our purses against us.

On the escalator, Liz and I were directly behind Antonio.

His tight designer jeans, sandals, and t-shirt accentuated every taut muscle. Following him was a sensual delight.

"Beautiful, isn't he?" Gabby saw us watching him. She winked. Liz blushed. I grinned and nodded, embarrassed to be caught.

Antonio held the door open, and we stepped from the station right into the heart of Naples.

The noise was deafening. Taxi drivers swarmed us. The smell assaulted me. Fish. I hate fish. My hand covered my nose. The sidewalk to cross the traffic-laden street was filled with a mass of happy deodorant-free humanity jostling their way quickly to their final destination.

Dante took my hand and pointed across the street. There I saw a huge market, fish, fresh fruit, people haggling for deals, voices loud. But there was an underlying scent that was heavenly: rich sauces, oregano, garlic. Freshly baked bread.

Dante yelled at a lanky man with long unkempt gray hair, cigarette hanging from his teeth, one hand clutching a piece of paper. His voice was argumentative. I made a wild guess he was head of the taxi drivers.

"No, non capisce? Non e' possible." He pointed to his paper.

Dante gestured angrily at him. Finally the man stood mute, arms folded and shook his head, his expression stubborn, immovable.

"Imbecile." Dante snapped. "He refuses to let us move on to the taxis that hold eight people. Now we go with two taxis. Come."

He put Liz and Matteo, Mary and Stefano in one and gave the driver directions. The rest of us piled into the next taxi. Dante sat behind the driver, holding me tightly.

The Port of Napoli was a mass of gigantic cruise and cargo ships. Smaller boats bobbled and peeked at us in the distance. Antonio and Dante haggled a price with the cabbies, and then went to purchase boat tickets. We stood in a circle guarding our luggage. Dante's frustration was apparent. *Hmmm. He didn't like not getting his way.*

The hydrofoil taking us to Capri appeared as a speck on the horizon. But the swell of people lining up—not exactly lining, but shoving—clued us that it was nearer than it looked. Ten minutes later, the boat docked.

"Just stay with Gabby, Jules." Dante touched my nose and winked. "We'll take care of the luggage and save your seats. Go up at the stairs." He, along with Antonio, Matteo, and Stefano, were swallowed into the crowd.

"Hook arms, ladies," said Gabby. "Elbows out." We shoved our way in.

"Don't they believe in lines in Italy?" Mary said, annoyed.

"Deal with it, Mare." I tugged her arm and ran interference as best as I could.

"Stairs ahead," yelled Gabby.

I thought it was a double-decked boat. But no. There, behind the captain, was a small private lounge, just large enough to accommodate the eight of us. Antonio perched on the windowsill behind the couch and Gabby snuggled on the seat in front of him. The rest of us sat comfortably around the teak table in the center. Cold water bottles sweated invitingly on a bright yellow tray.

"Hey, where's our luggage?" Mary looked nervously through the cabin.

"Relax." Dante pointed to the bottom of the stairs. "They hold for us. Not to worry."

Always in charge.

"You like?" His dazzling smile, not to mention the body heat from sitting so close to him, calmed me and inflamed me. I felt cared for, cherished, fearful. And I needed to know more about him. I'd learned so much on the train ride; yearned to know him better. I closed my eyes, inhaling the salty air.

"Look, look!" Mary almost shoved Liz out of her seat to kneel and look out the window. "It's beautiful."

And indeed it was. The Isle of Capri.

Dante took my hand and led me through the door to the captain's station and up another narrow stairway to an open deck. I could feel the movement of the boat meeting the waves, the salt air smelled fresh, and the occasional mist of the sea dampened my body. And there ahead, Capri rose majestically from the aqua and purple of the waters. White villas hung on cliffs; flowers shown brightly in nooks scattered in the rocks.

"Dante, this...." He silenced me with a finger on my lips.

"Don't speak. Look. Feel the island." He stood behind me then gathered me against him, hands locked at my waist.

"We will know each other this weekend, Giulia. *Si?"*

He turned me to him, his gaze meeting mine. I almost lost the ability to breathe.

"*Si*, Dante." I touched his cheek. "We'll talk a lot, have some fun." I wondered what he meant by "know" me. Now, a raw fear surfaced. I felt foolish.

He pulled my arms to my side and stood there, looking at me, eyes reflecting the color of the water. He sighed.

"Dante," Antonio yelled from the bottom of the ladder. *"Paolo e' qui."*

"Va bene." Dante explained that Paolo was from the hotel to gather our luggage.

As we rejoined the others, Gabby said, "Let's wait until everyone's off the boat, then we go." She ducked her head down at the deck below. "Lots of tourists today."

"Gabby, you're talking to the stairwell. What'd you say?" asked Liz.

"Stay with me, Liz." Matteo smiled shyly and took her hand. "Stay with me."

Liz sat back and crossed her long legs. "Okay, I mean, *va bene,* Matteo."

The captain walked back into the private room. *"Signore, Signori, prego,"* waving his hands.

Climbing down the stairs was difficult since we had to descend feet first holding the ladder. I didn't want anyone grabbing my backside. But, when

I reached the last rung, I felt hands encircle my hips. I smiled and turned to the deeply tanned young man who'd helped me. *"Grazie."*

"Don't touch me," growled Mary. "I can do this." Obviously not understanding English, the young man who helped me grabbed her hips and pulled her petite body past the last three rungs and set her gently on the floor, his hands lingering a bit too long.

"Honestly," said Mary. "There's too much touching here." She smoothed her Capris and raked her fingers through her hair, miffed.

"Ciao, Paolo!" Dante yelled and waved to a distant man. He wore a navy uniform, hat covering his unruly salt and pepper curly hair, smiling with joy at seeing Dante.

"Ciao," Paolo said, hugging Dante, embracing him again.

I watched them, one man wealthy, the other serving him. The respect between the two startled me.

Dante waved us over to join them.

We disembarked. Mary, Liz and I stood back along with Stefano and watched this reunion. Had they forgotten we were there? The affection of Gabby, Dante, Antonio, and Matteo for Paolo was evident from their embrace.

"Ah, *Americani?"* Paolo walked toward us, arms open.

Mary stepped back. "Good grief, not another kiss and hug session with a total stranger.

"Mi chiama, Paolo! Piacere," he said, extending his hand. "I speak English good too. Welcome to Cesare Hotel."

"Piacere, Paolo." I shook his hand. Mary and Liz greeted him.

"I think we're hungry, Dante," Gabby said. There was a new easiness for me with Gabby. Knowing her connection to Dante made a huge difference.

He agreed. "Okay, we eat just a snack at the end of the dock. The Grotto's open. We need to take advantage of low tide."

Paolo finished placing our luggage on the resort's tiny toy-like truck and honked the horn, driving like a mad man on the narrow sidewalk flowing with pedestrians. *"Ciao,"* he yelled back, careening inches from the edge of the concrete pier. Dante motioned for us to start walking.

Before my eyes, Dante changed from take-charge to playful. "I love this island," he said. "While we're here, only happy thoughts, fun. Today the famous Blue Grotto, then a swim at the pool."

He continued to talk, but all I thought about was being seen in a bathing suit in public for the first time since surgery. My stomach felt like a fist had punched it from the inside.

It is what it is, Jules. Just deal with it.

Dante charged ahead, weaving in and out of the other people toward the end of the pier. He stopped, turned, and held up his hand. He looked like a Roman God. And when I reached him, I stood as close as possible. He hugged my shoulders while we waited for the others.

"Over there to the blue umbrellas." We followed him, relieved to escape the chattering tourists.

A waiter approached us. Dante ordered us drinks and salads.

He counted our group and arranged tables to accommodate us.

"I ordered light," said Dante, "because the Blue Grotto is best experienced on an empty stomach." His eyes twinkled. "You will see."

Gianni returned with the drinks and several bottles of water. The men had gallantly, by choice or accident, sat with their backs to the ocean with a view of the tourist rip-off shops. The women had a perfect view of the sea, and the bustle of the tour boats arriving for a day trip.

The tiny harbor held large boats to ferry people to the mainland as well as other islands dotted along the Amalfi Coast. Dozens of freshly painted wooden motorboats bobbled in the water, waiting to take tourists around the island or to the Grotto.

Mary didn't say much. But I noticed the excitement in her eyes. "Mary, what do you think?"

She poked her head forward to see around Liz and Gabby. "Jules, I'm happy." She glanced at Stefano, blushing. "I feel content and overwhelmed by the beauty of this place." Stefano reached across the table for her hand, but she shook her head.

Matteo spoke to Dante in Italian. Stefano and Antonio joined them. And we sat listening, straining to catch a phrase here and there.

Gabby took pity on us. "They're talking about plans for the weekend. Everyone has their favorite activity here, and they're planning a surprise for you. Be prepared for anything." She chuckled, looked at Antonio and blushed. Gabby blushing! Hmmmm.

Gianni arrived with the food, and the blue and white checkered table coverings were hidden by platters of fresh local food.

Something about sea air makes one hungry. And we devoured the eggplant, olives, bread, cheese and blood oranges. I tried not to watch while Dante forced tiny squid into his mouth. At that moment, my old life seemed distant, almost non-existent. I basked in this other new world. What could be better than this? Still, I felt a tug of something. Homesickness? I stared at the glittering sea.

"Earth to Jules. Earth to Jules. We're taking a trip to *il bagno.* No facilities on these little boats."

I gathered my purse and followed them into the main restaurant where a narrow staircase wound to the bathrooms.

"What the heck is wrong with you?" Mary asked. "You've been mute for twenty minutes, staring off into space. Shake it off."

"I'm fine."

Liz peered at me. "You sure?"

Gabby took my arm. "Julie's fine. We need to hurry. The guys went to buy the tickets."

Gabby almost had us at a run when we reached the pier again. Just a few meters from shore stood a shack with large black letters that said: BIGLIETTI. Tickets.

We followed Antonio to a boat that held about twenty people. No one else boarded. The teak on the outside gleamed, and the benches on the deck were clean with a scent of recent paint. The boat owner cracked a half-smile while helping us aboard. He was tall and tanned; a baseball cap covered his head. He readied the motor and backed out of a tight space, almost hitting the sand. The boat glided out of the harbor and gained speed once we passed the jetty.

I leaned my head back to enjoy the sea spray. I tasted salt stinging my lips. With the bright sun, the ocean's aqua, green, and purple intensified. I couldn't decide whether to enjoy the water or the sharp cliffs and villas balanced high above.

It was difficult to talk over the motor's noise. Gabby sat on Antonio's lap, staring into the water. Matteo held Liz's hand, watching the enjoyment on her face. And Mary, dear Mary, held Stefano's hand and was laughing with a joy I'd seldom seen.

Dante's body was warm against mine. "There, Giulia. Look. The boats for the Grotto. And there," he pointed up, "are the remains of the castle of Tiberius, Emperor of Rome."

Dozens of tiny white rowboats appeared and disappeared with the waves, tumbling up and down while the rower stood, balancing to avoid hitting the limestone cliffs. One large boat was anchored. An old man sitting behind a crudely made desk shouted to the rowers.

"Who's he?" I asked.

"The ticket taker," said Dante. "You pay him to go into the Grotto and the rower when you come out of the Grotto."

"What?"

"Americans call it...how you say...a rip-off." He chuckled. "But if you want to see the Grotto, it is the way for many years."

"Where's the Grotto, Dante?"

"Right there." He pointed to a small opening at the base of a white cliff. A rope looped away into the darkness.

"We can't go in there. The boat's too big."

"Ah, but we get in one of the rowers' boats. They take us in."

I heard Mary yell, "No friggin' way!" to Stefano. Liz just sat eyes wide. Suddenly, each man took off his shirt. Their bare chests were tanned and tight. We'd seen Antonio shirtless. But Dante?

I'd felt his muscles through his shirt when he held me. But to see the body.

Dante winked at me. "There's more." He removed his belt, unzipped his pants and folded them neatly on the bench. I didn't know where to look.

He was naked save for the Speedo and I averted my eyes, barely able to take a breath.

"Told you there was a surprise." Gabby chuckled as she wiggled out of her clothes, revealing a barely-there two-piece swimsuit. She giggled at our faces. "Haven't you ever seen bathing suits? Americans. So uptight."

"We're just not as comfortable in our skin as Europeans, I guess."

Gabby laughed, and so did I. But inside my discomfort grew like a lump of raw dough.

The quiet man guiding our boat cut the motor. A tiny rowboat sidled next to us. Dante helped me, Liz and Matteo into the rocking rowboat, and then hopped in next to me while the man rowing the boat screamed, "Lie down." With his oars pushing against the rocks, he guided the boat and held onto a thin rope that ran from a large hook on the outside of the Grotto to another hook inside. He leaned back, balancing the oar, and pulled us through a tunnel and into the Grotto.

At once, the boatmen started singing "O' Sole Mio." The melodies echoed in the cave. But the water...the sandy bottom reflecting sunlight from the sea. We were in a dark cave with water an unimaginable deep aqua.

I heard Antonio yell from another boat. "*Va bene?*"

"*Va bene*," Dante answered. The four guys jumped into the water, followed by Gabby. She held onto Antonio's feet, and they undulated in the water like dolphins, the color so clear, it was like watching them swim in a pool. Only it wasn't a pool. It was the most incredible ocean with four gorgeous almost-naked men, swimming, diving and playing in the water, their baritone voices bouncing off the stone.

Stefano swam to Mary's boat, a wicked smile on his face. Mary scooted away from him.

"No way. Don't even think about it."

I barely saw him in the dim cave, but Stefano was completely visible as he swam under the boat and pulled himself up behind Mary.

When the boat tipped, she screamed. Stefano caught her. But it was too late. In she went. She sputtered, flailing her arms. "*Mio Dio.* What were you thinking?"

Stefano laughed and dove to remove Mary's shoes. "Let's swim. You're wet anyway."

Mary's face and hair were still dry. She held onto him, hands digging into his shoulders. "I can't swim," she wailed.

"No problem." Stefano held her under his arm like a football, Mary screaming and kicking. He took her to the middle of the grotto and called to Dante. "Put her on my back." He swam, Mary clinging to his body, her voice pealing with laughter. Her black tank top and capris clung to her body like a gleaming wetsuit.

Liz and I enjoyed watching her loosen up and have fun. Which is why I didn't see Dante until his wet face and shoulders jumped up from the water in front of me.

"Come in, Giulia." I bent to speak to him, to say no, but he took my face in his hands and kissed me, slowly, deliberately. I tasted the salt on his lips. "You're going to get wet. You know that?" He reached into the boat.

"Watch out!" Liz yelled. "You're going to capsize us!"

His hand caressed my legs inching toward my feet. I held my breath while he removed my sandals.

"Come." I slid over the gunwale into the glowing sea. Dante held me tightly, keeping me afloat, kissing my neck.

"Hey, if I'm going to look like a wet rag, so are you." Mary splashed me, Gabby joined in, and I gave up. I dove under the water, the salt stinging my eyes, and explored the colors. My swimming was clumsy from the weight of my heavy linen clothes. But I didn't care.

The only dry person was Liz. We formed a circle around the rowboat, all of us smiling.

"Wait!" She held up her hand, fished in her pocket with the other hand and pulled out a hair band. Gathering her thick red hair into a knot, she closed her eyes, stood, and made a perfect dive into the water.

I floated on my back, watching my friends. Mary was childlike, clinging to Stefano, her hair in wet tendrils across her forehead. Gabby and Antonio swam vigorously in their skimpy bathing suits, their conversation loud within the rock walls. Liz and Matteo raced each other, splashing the water in their effort to win. Dante swam under water, his body moving with the grace of one born to swim.

"Time to go, Giulia." He pointed to his watch. We swam back to our boat, and the bored rower. Dante helped me into the boat, climbed in behind me and pulled me next to him, smoothing my hair away from my face. "Hmmmm. *"Ti voglio."* He sighed and pulled my head to his chest.

I shivered, and thought of the hotel, the sleeping arrangements, nighttime. My breath caught. In my heart, though, I knew I wasn't going to betray Ted any more than I had.

The rowers insisted we leave. Everyone piled onto their respective skiffs, settling on the planks.

We were lying flat on the floor of the rowboats watching the rower pull us through the narrow tunnel and back through the opening to the sea. The eight of us were back on the motor boat, wet, laughing like kids, like family, as if we'd known each other forever. The Blue Grotto had become the ice breaker for the weekend. Inhibitions melted, and we settled in for the ride back to the harbor. Gone were the attempts by Liz and me to always look perfect. We were at ease. What wasn't gone for me was sexual tension. I wanted to stare at the hard body of Dante, delight in it. He'd toweled off, but his naked chest rubbed against my arm as he held me.

Pulling my hairbrush from my purse, I attempted to untangle my dark curly hair. I toweled my face and hands dry and pulled out my lotion.

Dante took my hand. "Where's your ring, Giulia?"

My ring. My wedding ring was gone.

Chapter Twenty-Four

Trying not to panic, I rifled through my purse, searching each section carefully.

"Give it to me, Jules." Mary reached for the purse. "You never put anything in the right slot. I remember seeing you take off your earrings and watch before getting into the rowboat. Your ring is most likely there, too."

She rummaged, in an organized way, through each section. "For Pete's sake. Here." She looked at me; her short dark hair plastered to her head, eyes peering from pooled mascara, and slapped the jewelry, ring and all, into my hand. "You might want to look in a mirror."

"Thanks, Mare. And raccoon eyes become you, too, my dear." I didn't need a mirror to know what I looked like. I simply had to glance at the streaked faces of the other women, black circles around eyes, crusted salt on wild hair and on cheeks in place of makeup. And I didn't care. The trip from Rome, the boat ride to Capri and the Blue Grotto had done me in. All I wanted was a quiet room and a bed. I slipped the jewelry back into my purse, leaving my ring finger exposed.

When we disembarked, the port was crammed with tourists. Fortunately, two taxis were waiting for us and whisked our wet and tired bodies to our hotel. The taxis were open-air jeeps. The ride up the winding, narrow road was breathtaking and precarious, especially where the cliffs made a sheer drop from the no-guardrail road. Meeting another vehicle while coming around a hairpin curve had me holding my breath and clinging to Dante's arm. My salt-encrusted hair whipped in the wind.

The glass lobby doors of the Caesar Hotel were large and impressive. Paolo greeted us and handed room keys to Dante. Inside the lobby there was an atmosphere of understated elegance. Soft beige couches and chairs trimmed in burgundy cording huddled in small vignettes across stone floors. Palm trees loomed near the windows, fresh flowers adorned each table. Guests read books, some gathered to talk, and others sipped drinks and gazed at the Mediterranean. The staff stood silently by, waiting for Dante to acknowledge them.

"*Signore*, you luggage are in rooms." Paolo smiled at each of us. "You will much like rooms."

Dante went behind the front desk, and we lined up.

Gabby leaned in to Dante. "Please check Julie in. I want to have a word with her."

"Of course, *cara.* Please, go."

Gabby grabbed my hand and led me through the lobby to the pool area.

"I've got to show you something."

We took a lift down the side of a cliff to an infinity pool. It appeared as though the aqua water fell into space. Mt. Vesuvius welcomed us in the distance, and the harbor of Capri about one thousand feet below looked like a picture postcard, diminutive and peaceful, tucked away to the right of the hotel.

"Look." Gabby pointed to the hotel that rose up the cliff in sections, perched in white beauty. "It's my favorite place, coming here. Quiet and peaceful. We'd better join the others." She took my hand again and led me back to the lobby.

"Where'd you go?" demanded Mary.

"Gabby took me to the pool. Oh my gosh. We are so not in the real world."

"No kidding." But she had a smile that stretched across her face. "Or to quote you...I'll think about it tomorrow."

Dante beckoned us to follow him to our rooms.

Gabby patted my arm. "Dante always stays in the corner room, but I think he gave it to you. Enjoy this, Julie. Remove all from your mind and enjoy."

I caught her watching Matteo. But he was engaged in conversation with Liz.

Antonio opened the door into a room that took my breath away. The floor was natural stone. Two floor-to-ceiling windows looked onto the sea. Antonio smiled, but his dark eyes seemed to be clouded with anger. He glanced at Gabby and quickly shut the door.

Dante took my arm and told the others to follow Paolo. Liz and Mary were in a room together. Stefano and Matteo each had a single room. "We'll meet in the bar by the pool at seven." He propelled me away. "I can't wait for you to see your room, Giulia."

We turned right at the end of the hallway and stopped at the last room. The pure white door was emblazoned with polished brass letters: SUITE TIBERIO.

Dante opened the door. I stood there in wide-eyed wonder.

"You like?"

I walked to the window. "Dante, am I in heaven?"

Laughing, he came beside me, opened the window to the balcony. I couldn't speak. The corner terrace on the cliff edge provided exquisite views of the purple and aqua sea, the sharp rocks rising from the water, and the Bay of Naples with Mt. Vesuvius reaching into the surrounding clouds.

He touched my shoulder. "Let me show you the rest of the suite, and then I'll let you rest." He led me to a sparkling white bathroom with tiny splashes of aqua tiles. In the corner window stood a whirlpool bath allowing panoramic views of the sea. He pointed to the bed.

"Look, Giulia." He waved a hand toward the windows. "Without leaving the bed you can see Sorrento and the port of the Island."

He stood there, tenderly facing me, and then leaned to kiss my forehead. "I'll see you at seven." I started to get up. "I have the maid coming to draw a bath for you. Stay here until she comes."

"But I'm all salty and sticky from our"--I glanced up at him mischievously—"swim."

"Relax. She'll be here in a minute." He blew me a kiss and before he left the room said, "Oh, this suite has its own private entrance off the main terrace." And with a wink, he was gone.

Jules, you're in big trouble.

Really?

Yes. Big trouble.

Why didn't you put your wedding ring on again?

I just clumped everything together in my purse. It's safe.

The safe place is your finger.

I know. I know.

Do you think Dante has expectations for this weekend?

No. I trust him.

He's a man, Jules.

A knock on the door interrupted my internal conversation.

"Come in."

A petite woman in her fifties entered the suite. She smiled. "*Buona sera. Sono Angela.*"

"*Buona sera, Angela.*"

She curtsied and pointed. "*Bagno?*"

"*Si.*"

She turned, her black dress starched to a stiffness that made a sandpaper sound as she walked. The white lace apron and white hat were crisp. She carried a basket.

I tried to relax as she readied my bath. She returned to my bed and offered her hand. I stood. She placed a robe on the bed and started to undress me.

"No, no. *Non c'e problema.*" I gave her a cheerful smile, said, "*Grazie,*" took the robe and walked toward the bathroom. I looked back. She smiled, hands folded across her apron. I closed the door, began disrobing. The scent of roses filled the room. Pink and red rose petals floated on the water and lay across the floor. Opera music seemed to float around the room. I climbed into the tub, facing the window, and eased into the soft scented water. I heard a quiet knock on the door.

"*Si?*"

"*Per favore?*"

The maid. She was still here. What the heck?

She opened the door and came in. Humming to the music, she reached for some oils and a sponge and proceeded to wash my back. Modesty forgotten, I gave in to the pleasure of being cared for, pampered. She massaged my arms, flopped them in an effort to relax me, and sponged them clean.

I raised my hand in protest, starting to speak.

She shushed me and reached for my foot. She oiled and rubbed each toe and scrubbed the bottom of my feet, humming softly.

Reaching for the hand-held spray nozzle, she wet my hair and applied an olive oil scented shampoo. After the rinse, she applied conditioner, gently but firmly massaging my scalp.

Eyes closed, I heard more water. Back she came, holding a large white towel, and waved me out of the tub. She wrapped the towel around me and led me to the shower. I meekly went in and rinsed off, letting the large, powerful jets embrace me with water.

Angela appeared with another towel, handed me the softest robe I've ever felt, curtsied and left.

I was so relaxed I barely had the strength to dry my hair. Cuddled in my robe, I padded across the cool tiled floors to the bed. On the end table sat a plate of fresh fruit and a crystal glass filled with chilled water.

The bed had been turned down, revealing crisp linen sheets. I sank onto the bed, sighing, wanting to sleep. I took a long drink of water, ate one grape, and resisted the tiredness...unwilling to miss a moment of this luxury.

GABRIELLA

Chapter Twenty-Five

Gabby saw the anger on Antonio's face. "What is your problem?" Her stomach tightened.

"I not like the way you look at Matteo. He always stares at you."

"He's with Liz. I'm with you."

"Not enough." He pulled her to him possessively, thumbed her bathing suit top down and slid the bikini thong down her legs.

"Wait, Antonio. I want to take a shower." He kissed her hungrily, his hands touching her with soft sensual strokes.

"Now." His tone was demanding, not tender.

"Damn you, Antonio." She brushed away tears. "Is this all we have? Sex?"

He carried her to the bed, pulled the covers away, exposing white linens and laid her there.

She tightened her eyes and fists, sat up, grasped the linen around her and swung her legs off the bed. "No. No more solving everything in bed. I'm done with that. I feel used and cheap." She walked to the wardrobe and grabbed a robe.

Antonio reached for her, his face tight and flushed with anger *"Ti amo, Gabriella. Ti voglio."*

"I know you love me, but it's not enough." Tears spilled from her eyes. She whispered again, "It's not enough anymore."

"*Perche, mi amore?*" Why?

"Because I want all of you. To be together. I want to know your son. I need to be a part of you."

"It's the American women, *si?* You want to be independent like them?"

"No. I want us to be in the same world. You and me and your family. I want a child. I want you to stand up to your mama and let me do your laundry and cook for you. I want to travel with your son." Her voice rose. "I don't want to be your mistress anymore. I don't want to be like my mother."

"Matteo won't marry you, Gabriella."

"Matteo has nothing to do with this. I love you." She ran to the bathroom and locked the door.

Antonio heard the shower. He slumped naked, on the bed, his face in his hands until Gabby came back into the room, a too-large robe covering her tiny frame, hair damp against her oval face. Her eyes were puffy from crying, but there was a new resolve on her face, in her posture.

Antonio watched her for a moment then strode to the shower. He paused at the door and turned to Gabby. "*Ti amo.*"

"I know, Antonio." She stood with shoulders straight. "But I meant it. That's not enough. Choose me or your mama. Choose, Antonio. And Dante has arranged another room for you." She went to his suitcase and pulled out a pair of beige slacks and black polo shirt. "Here. The rest of your things will be transferred to your room."

He grabbed his clothes, dressed, and slammed the door.

Gabby took some fruit and a bottle of water to the patio, sat on the lounge chair and propped her feet on the balcony rail.

She closed her eyes, a satisfied smile on her face.

"The Americans learn from me, I learn from them."

An hour later, she wandered back into the room. The only thing left of Antonio was the scent of his cologne. Her heart quickened.

Chapter Twenty-Six

The mirror reflected a totally relaxed me! My skin felt like velvet, my eyes sparkled. *So this is how the other half lives?*

The flat drone of the phone pulled me from self-admiration. *A phone in the bathroom. Yes.*

"*Pronto.*"

"*Ciao*, Julie."

"Hi, Gabby. What's up?"

"I made him leave my bed, my room, Julie." Her voice choked. "I did it."

"*Brava*, Gabby. Are you okay? *Va bene?*"

"*Si*, Julie. I'm fine. Well maybe not fine. But I want to be number one with the man in my life. And I'm not. In fact, I'm really number four. Oh well, it doesn't matter. I did what I had to."

"Are you going to meet everyone as planned?"

"Oh yes. I'll be there. See you in twenty minutes."

Glancing at my watch. Seven. "Ah, you're coming on Italian time, making an entrance?"

"Exactly. *Ciao.*"

"*Ciao*, Gabby."

I patted the deep turquoise off-the-shoulder jersey blouse, hoping the color would enhance the kiss of sun on my face. Walking into the bedroom, I slipped into my high heels, tossed my head to loosen the curls and made my way to the pool bar.

The fire opal sun bounced off the darkening sea. Dante stood, one foot on a stool, elbow on the wooden bar, dressed in black linen pants and a soft aqua shirt. Delicious. He smiled. I walked across the patio to him, searching for air to breathe. His eyes were unreadable behind his sunglasses.

Fear, desire, and confusion fought in my stomach. But I kept walking and leaned in for a kiss.

"*MioDio, Giulia. Bellissima.*" He traced the outline of my jaw with his fingers. "The special bath was good, *si?*"

"Ah, Dante. More than good. *Grazie mille.*"

Mary scurried over to me. "What bath?"

"Good Lord, Mary. Dante arranged for the spa to do a body scrub for me." I lowered my voice. "We weren't in the tub together. Lighten up."

I glanced around the patio. "Where's Liz?"

Mary pointed to a far corner beyond the pool. Liz and Matteo were standing against the rail gazing at Mount Vesuvius visible in the twilight.

I heard a soft "*Ciao.*"

I turned and dropped my jaw. Antonio strolled to us, sporting that lazy-I-want-to-bed-you smile that reached beyond his lips. His designer jeans molded to him. His silk black long-sleeved shirt, open to the navel, billowed in the breeze. His black curls still wet from showering, he looked like a cover shot on GQ.

"*Ciao,* Julie. *Che bella,*" he murmured. His cologne moved in cadence with him. I felt a jolt of electricity and knew exactly why Gabby was addicted to him.

Dante raised an eyebrow, looking for Gabby, who usually came attached to Antonio. Then Dante's jaw dropped.

I turned just as Gabby entered the patio area, blonde hair spiked and straight. Dressed in white, cleavage prominently displayed, midriff exposed, legs erupting from spiked red heels, face framed with red chandelier earrings, she walked in slow deliberate moves toward us.

Antonio sucked in a breath, following her with his eyes. She ignored him and greeted everyone with a "*ciao*" and a blown kiss.

Dante was speechless, and cocked his head in surprise.

Liz and Matteo had quietly joined us. Matteo stood, heart in his eyes, looking pensive.

"So," I said. "Everyone's here. I'm starved." I walked to Dante's side. "What's the plan for food tonight, Dante." I nudged his arm.

"Ah, yes. First drinks. Let's sit." He waved his arm to an oblong table, the cover shimmering gold, the crystal sparkling in the soft lighting of the candles. Wild flowers were scattered artfully on the cloth.

The tense moment with Gabby and Antonio was broken. We strolled to the table.

Gabby grabbed Liz's arm. "So tell me, Liz, do you love it here? Isn't it beautiful? Mind if I sit next to you tonight?"

"Sure. I mean, no, of course I don't mind." Liz sputtered.

We gathered around the table, Antonio and Gabby at opposite ends.

Chapter Twenty-Seven

The lights of the hotel and the dinner candles on the patio table flickered in the darkness. The sea shimmered in moonlight.

Gabby kept avoiding any glances toward Antonio and chattered cheerfully with everyone else. Antonio ate, his eyes clouded with thunderstorm anger. Despite the tension between them, we enjoyed a delightful dinner conversation.

Dante clinked a glass with his spoon and stood. "I want to toast our American friends." The light from the patio caught the gray strands in his dark hair. "To a special three days in Capri. To fun, good food, and laughter. *Cin Cin.*"

We extended our arms to touch glasses. "C*in cin*." The limoncello warmed my throat, and Dante's face warmed my heart.

"*Salute*." A voice drifted from another table.

I turned to see an elderly couple sitting just outside the light by the pool. His face was lined, his eyes faded. He held a wine glass in one hand while the other caressed the hand of his wife. He wore an old cap; her hair, gray peppered with black strands, was softly pulled from her face into a bun.

"*Ciao. Grazie*," said Dante. He motioned for them to join us.

The old man stood, his body stooped, and pulled the chair back. We saw she walked with a cane. Dante rushed to pull a couple of chairs to our table.

"*Buona sera.* I am Marcello and this is my bride, Isabella."

"*Buona sera,*" we echoed back in unison.

"You speak English well," I said.

"That's because we're Americans." He smiled, his eyes watered with age. "We were born in Napoli but immigrated to the States when we were young."

Mary asked, "Where do you live?"

"We moved to Miami twenty years ago from New York City," said Isabella. "We wanted to come to Italy one last time." Her voice quivered, her eyes of faded brown, twinkled. "It's our anniversary. Sixty-five years." Her husband gave her a squeeze.

A flash of sadness hit me. I resisted the urge to run to the refuge of my room. But Dante called to the waiter and asked him to serve espresso to everyone. Then he said, "After coffee, let's swim."

"*Perfetto*," said Antonio. "A perfect night for swimming." He stood and walked to the hotel entry.

"What about your coffee?" asked Matteo.

"I'd rather swim." Antonio disappeared.

He returned to the pool just as our espresso was served. He stood, dropped his robe, and dove in a perfect arc into the water. I heard Gabby gasp.

"So is everyone swimming?" I looked at Mary and Liz.

"Of course we're swimming. That's why we brought suits with us." Mary sipped her coffee.

Matteo took Liz's hand and gave it a soft squeeze. He drank his coffee in one Italian gulp, and went to his room to change.

I sat, frozen.

"You young people go," said Marcello. "We'll stay here and watch for awhile. But we're tired." He smiled at Isabella.

Dante helped me from the chair. "Are you okay? *Va bene?*"

"*Si, Dante. Va bene.*" But I wasn't okay. Something about the old couple fussed at the back of my mind. And, of course, the dreaded first-time appearance in a bathing suit since breast cancer. I forced a smile. "I'll be back soon."

The walk to my room felt funereal.

ಌ

I stood naked in front of the full length mirror in the elegant bathroom. I studied my body. My fingers trailed across my right breast, fully plumped with an implant, cancer hopefully gone. The horizontal scar running across the skin had faded to a soft pink. The skillfully made nipple and tattoo looked real from a distance. I stood at attention, and squeezed my breasts, wondering how they felt to a man.

Everything is different after breast cancer...the way people look directly at your chest when you tell them you had a mastectomy, as if they could magically peer through my clothing. I touched my hair, now full, dark, and curly and remembered the sadness of being bald.

You're still the same on the inside, Jules.

No, I'm not. I'll never be the same.

What's changed?

I'm a fighter now. A survivor. Strong. Sometimes bitchy. I often question what I once used to tolerate, like rude behavior, stuffing down emotions and reactions.

Of course. This has built up some backbone in you.

I felt a slight shiver and hugged my body.

There you go, Jules. Hug yourself. You deserve it. And if Ted, or any man, doesn't appreciate you, then they don't deserve you. Put that suit on, girl. Stuff those breasts into the cups, stand proud, because your anatomy is NOT who you are.

You're right.

I stopped the mindless prattling in my head and slipped one leg, then the other into the black swimsuit and started to pull. I wiggled into the "we-promise-this-will-make-you-look-ten-pounds-thinner" bathing suit, pulled the shoulder straps into place, and tucked everything in. Turning from side to side, I admired the fit. No breast scars showed, just a nice taste of cleavage. The scars from the pic line used for chemo were only faintly visible inside of my left arm.

Okay, then. Here we go. I was thankful for a separate entrance from my room to the patio. I strolled into the pool area. Everyone was in the water, splashing, laughing. Matteo and Dante had draped themselves on the edge of the infinity pool facing the sea and looked as though they'd fall into an inky pit.

Marcello and Isabella had moved to lounge chairs next to the pool and had wrapped themselves in the thick gold towels available to the guests. She rested her head on his shoulder while he held her hand next to his lips. They sat, looking content, black shoes peeking from the towels.

I walked to a chair in the dimly lit far right corner. I jumped as a cool wet pair of hands circled my waist from behind. It was Matteo.

"You're going to get wet." He lifted me.

Dante walked in front and pulled at the bathing suit cover. Before I knew it, they'd thrown me into the pool.

I rose to the surface, hair plastered to my head, sputtering. Dante dove in and grabbed me, whispered in my ear, "*Facile, bella.* See how easy?" He pushed the hair from my face. "You're beautiful, *si?* Enjoy." And he swam away. Could a man this sensitive really exist? My head nodded side to side with a definite "no."

I heard Mary and Liz laughing. "Come on, Jules. Swim to the edge." Mary's voice was clear and happy. Her face shone. "Have you ever seen such beauty?"

We clung to the side of the pool, our chins resting on the flowing water, and gazed at the black sea edged with silver.

"Love your suit, Jules." Mary squeezed my shoulder and leaned in for a whisper. "You look great." She patted my hand and pushed away, swimming smoothly through the water with the help of her floaties.

Everyone was relaxing, enjoying the pool. All the other guests were gone except for our precious old couple. Antonio and Gabby were swimming instead of entwined. Dante left me alone. My body and mind eased with the enjoyment of the moment. I had no idea what time it was, nor did I care. The massage and nap of the afternoon had left me refreshed.

I turned to face the hotel, a white gleaming layered building, hanging on a cliff. Marcello and Isabella were standing now, talking to Stefano. I heard New York and Miami mentioned. They waved and said good night.

Dante had ordered a carafe of wine, and the eight of us stood in the shallow end of the pool sipping wine.

"I'm exhausted." Liz stretched her arms, yawning. "Between the Grotto and this swim, I'm more than ready for bed."

"Same here," said Mary, handing her wine glass to me. She walked out of the pool, shivering in the soft breeze of the night.

"I guess the party's over," I said. I moved to the steps.

"Wait, Giulia," Dante whispered.

My body tensed.

"*Buono notte,*" Gabby said, putting on her cover-up. She glanced at Antonio, his wet body glistening in the candlelight. She turned, waved and walked to her room alone.

After everyone left, Dante and I swam back to the edge of the pool.

He didn't touch me or try to kiss me. We talked quietly about Italy and the island, and his family.

"What's your son like, Dante?"

"Alessandro is good son. Handsome. Smart. He teaches at University of Bologna."

"Really? No interest in the family business?"

"No. He has much money now and when I die. But he wanted to teach. It's his passion. The money is not so good. But he doesn't need it. He's a good man." His tone turned serious. "For awhile, we all worried that Gabby would upset the flow of money. My son didn't like her at first."

"And his mother? What was she like?"

"She is good woman. She married again, an older man. They live a quiet life in Sicily. She was very young when we married. It was arranged, really. I didn't know how to love then." His voice softened. "I do now. I just can't find a woman to love...until now." He turned away.

I wanted this strong quiet man to hold me and assure me I was lovable and beautiful.

"Come, Giulia. It's late. We have big day tomorrow. Some surprises." We swam to the stairs. Dante held a towel for me and gathered me close. His body felt so good. I heard him sigh.

He picked up my suit cover and folded it across my arm. We walked to the end of the patio and down the narrow path that led to my room. My heart raced. I feared he would want to come in. And feared, even more, that I would let him.

Dante took the room key from my hand and opened the door. The bed was again freshly turned down, with chocolates on the pillow. The maid had dimmed the lights and soft music floated through the suite.

"Giulia, dormi bene," he whispered in my ear. He kissed me then, his lips tasting of coffee and pool water. The towels dropped to the floor, our bodies wet and chilled, at the same time feeling heat from within. "You have no idea of your beauty," he murmured. He pushed the wet hair from my forehead. *"Che picatta.* What a shame."

He wanted me. I threw caution away and, for the first time, I initiated a kiss, raking his hair with my hands, enjoying the scents of pool, coffee and the hint of cologne. My hands ran over his smooth back. I screamed inside… my body stiffened. And I pushed him away.

"Domani, Giulia." He pulled way and cupped my face in his hands. "Tonight, no. *Domani, Giulia.* " His fingers trailed from my neck to my breasts and across my stomach. And then he was gone.

I stood there for a long time, water pooling at my feet on the cool tiled floor, feeling foolish and lonely. I walked to the phone and dialed Liz and Mary's room.

"Ciao," answered Liz. I heard Mary laughing in the background.

"I need company. Are you ready for sleep yet?"

"Are you kidding? Mary and I have been howling ever since we got in the room." She giggled. "None of us are drinkers. So two glasses of wine has rendered us foolish. You could say we're drunk with happiness."

Their laughter was just what I needed. "Please, girls, come on down. I'm taking a quick shower. What time is it, anyway?"

Liz giggled some more. "I don't know. We'll be down in five. We're in our jammies." Another giggle followed by a bellow of laughter from Mary.

I ran to the shower, peeled off my bathing suit, and sponged the day away with the heavenly lemon-scented soap and shampoo.

Toweling off, I slicked my wet hair back; put on my soft lounging pj's and waited for my friends.

"We're here," said Mary, knocking loudly.

"Shush, you two." I opened the door. They stumbled, giggling, into my room. To my surprise, Gabby had tagged along, holding a bottle of Birra Moretti, a light Italian beer. She looked disconsolate.

"Hey." I waved them over to the chairs in the living area of the suite and scurried to gather a fourth one. "Make yourselves comfortable."

They passed across the stone floor and settled into the art deco chairs.

"How you doing, Gabby?" I rested my hand on her arm.

She patted my hand. "I'm fine. I should have done this a long time ago." She wiped her cheek with the corner of her fluffy robe.

"Done what?" asked Mary.

I looked at her, marveling at her insensitivity. "Broken her relationship with Antonio. Duh!"

Mary tipped her head to the side, face thoughtful, as if trying to focus. "Oh, right. Sorry."

"He filled my room with flowers." Gabby looked at us through puffy eyes. "Beautiful flowers. But it won't work this time. I've decided flowers are cheap apologies. And to Antonio, I say...nice try."

Mary swirled her wine glass. "I never get flowers. Mr. Beast says flowers die."

"That's what Ted says, too. But he sent me some, remember? And I think the effort was sincere."

A piece of foil winked at me from a half open Swiss chocolate bar lying on the table next to me. "Anyone want to share?" I waved the bar in the air.

They chorused, "Yes."

"So, again, I ask, what's wrong with flowers?" Mary broke off a piece of the candy bar.

"Flowers mean Antonio's sorry. And profound apologies always follow flowers." She paused, pulling on her fingers. "Then he wants to bed me." Her hands were clenched. "And I always gave in."

"Really? No, really? I'm sorry I asked." Mary glared at Gabby.

Gabby leaned forward in her chair, revealing a soft pink silk nightie under her robe. "So, Mary, does talking about sex make you uncomfortable? Have you ever had good sex?"

"Why the heck are we talking about this?" Mary frowned.

"You're so right, Mare." Liz gulped down some wine. "After my jerk of a husband did what he did to me, my body totally closed itself to sexual thoughts. I can still see him with my friend." Liz blinked tears.

Mary's brows furrowed. "Can we please not talk about this anymore?"

"Calm down, Mary." I reached over to touch her hand.

Her eyes closed. "Leave me alone."

"Get yourself something to drink, Jules." Mary pointed to the cabinet of treats in the corner. She leaned forward. "*Vai, Vai.*"

"I'm going, Mare." I walked to the cabinet and chose a chilled sparkling water. Pouring a glass, I sat down. "Let's talk."

"First, we toast." Liz held up her glass, we followed. "To learning about men, making right choices, and the next fifty great years of our lives."

"Cin cin," we chorused, clinking our glasses together.

"So, Mare," I said, grabbing a piece of her chocolate. "What do you think of Stefano? Is it going anywhere? Do you like him more or less since you've had this time alone with him?"

"Good grief, Jules. I've not had a moment alone. The eight of us have been together all day, pretty much."

"Well, do you like him?"

"Of course I do."

"I saw him kiss you goodnight, Mare." Liz smiled. "He's so cute. Those big brown eyes always look so sad, yet at the same time twinkle when he looks at you."

"Yeah, well, twinkle is as twinkle does." Mary bit off another chunk of chocolate.

"Mary," I said, stretching my feet from their tucked position. "He's cute, he's American. Stefano oozes charm despite being raised in New York City."

"Are you insinuating New Yorkers' are rude?"

"No. I grew up in New York. New Yorkers can be perceived as abrupt. Stefano is not." I rested a hand on her arm. She pulled it away. "He's kind and never been married. Think of the possibilities of molding him."

"I'd like to mold Matteo." Liz sighed.

Gabby laughed. "Remember the *mammoni* lecture? Trust me, Liz. Italian men over forty are not moldable." Gabby raised her hands, pretending to hold a fishing rod. "You have to reel them in, let go, reel them in again. Always keep them guessing. It's a lot of work."

"Who's reeling whom?" Mary rolled her eyes at Gabby. "You seem to be under a spell with Antonio. Seems to be a very volatile relationship."

"I've had enough of that." Gabby stretched. "I just want to be loved with no complications."

Mary cast a disparaging glance, then hiccoughed.

A knock on the door interrupted us. "Must be room service." I got up and opened the door. A young man stood there dressed in a delivery uniform, hat and all. "Flowers for Giulia Walden?"

"I'm Julie. Do I need to sign something?"

"No. From Signore Capoferi." He walked quickly to the coffee table in the center of the living room area, deposited the vase of flowers, turned and hustled out.

Gabby started to laugh. "Poor kid. I mean, think what this looks like. Four women, giggling, and, Julie, I'm sure Dante thought you'd be alone." She gave me a knowing look.

"Jules, these flowers. They're breathtaking." Liz touched one of the petals. Purple and yellow wild flowers draped gracefully in a brilliant gold-veined Murano glass vase.

"Remember what follows flowers?" Liz snorted. "Apologies, begging for forgiveness. What's he asking forgiveness for, huh, Jules?" She sat on the floor laughing. "I want some flowers, too."

Soon we were all laughing, unable to stop. "Door again," gasped Gabby.

I walked to open the door. A dignified older man in a starched white service uniform stood ready to roll a cart full of goodies and wine into the room. He gave us a disapproving stare.

The perturbed man set the chocolate desserts on the dining area table, along with everything else I'd ordered, opened the three wine bottles, bowed and waited.

I walked to my purse on the bed and grabbed ten euro.

He took the money, smiled slightly and left.

We dissolved into giggles again.

Gabby covered her mouth to stifle her laughter. "Italian men disapprove of drunken women, you know."

"Yeah. They can deal with it. What the heck did you order?" Mary stared at the goodies on the table.

"Well let's see now. There is chocolate gelato, chocolate mousse, chocolate chunks, cappuccino." I turned to her with a grin. "In case we over-indulge, there's some *limoncello* to help digest this stuff; and, oh yes, I was craving olives."

Gabby held up her glass for more wine. She turned to Liz and patted her arm. "And are you feeling any attraction when you're with Matteo?"

"Uh, well...yeah. I guess so." Her face turned the color of her hair. "He treats me like a lady and is a perfect gentleman. No seducing on his part."

The phone rang. "Who on earth? Shhhhh."

"*Pronto, chi e?*"

"*Ciao,* Giulia."

"Dante?" I shushed them again, but they were all giggling helplessly.

"Are you alone?"

"No, I'm not alone. We couldn't sleep, and everyone came to my room for a nightcap."

"Did the flowers arrive? You know, Giulia that it's tomorrow?"

"Oh yes, the flowers are beautiful. And, yes, it is tomorrow, Dante." My face flushed.

He laughed. "You're safe tonight, *caramia*. But we must meet at nine for breakfast. Try to get some sleep. Tomorrow is a long day."

"That shouldn't be a problem. I'll see you for breakfast at nine." I crossed my eyes. "What time is it now?"

"It's two a.m."

"Oh. Okay. Well, we should all get some sleep, then. Right away."

In his sexy, sleepy voice, he whispered, "*Ti voglio.*" Then he whispered more Italian. It sounded seductive, but I was too fatigued to understand him.

Heat rose in my body.

"*Si, Dante. Buono notte,*" I whispered. I sat on the edge of the bed, suddenly sober. "If you girls weren't here, I might have broken my marriage vows."

"Get a grip, Jules." Mary rolled her eyes. "We all could have been in trouble tonight. Now let's eat, forget about the real world, and enjoy some girl time." She scurried over to the table, gathered a demitasse of espresso, grabbed a cup of melting gelato, and plopped herself on the floor, humming the tune from West Side Story, "I Feel Pretty."

"Wait a minute, Mare. We're not done with you yet." I grabbed one of the desserts. "Do you think Stefano is too young for you? Because he's not, you know."

Mary scowled. "Have you forgotten I'm still married? Granted, the jerk is going to leave me. But I can't think of anything or anyone until I get home...to my reality."

Liz sipped some wine. "Mary, did you like Stefano's kiss?"

"Wipe the grin off your face, Liz. You're free. But you don't make good choices in men, either. Matteo is not your reality. He's a fantasy. And kissing isn't something I've experienced much in the last twenty years."

"Come on, Mary. We've all shared things. What's bugging you?" I tried once again to touch her arm.

She stood up, arms to her sides, hands clenched. "Sex for me has mostly been an endurance contest. A demand, a duty." She padded across the tile floor, leaned on the windowsill, looking out onto the now black sea, and sighed.

"We had to get married. Good Catholic kids didn't do it. We did. It was a shotgun wedding in the office of a dour priest with two sets of parents who were ashamed of us."

"Ah, Mare," I said. "I'm so..."

She held up her hand, still facing away from us. "Sex was what brought us together. It was wild and passionate. We were both needy young kids, and I fell for the line that 'If you love me, you'll not let me suffer like this.' So I let him have me in the front seat of his dad's red Chevy pickup truck. I was sixteen, he was twenty-one."

She studied the ceiling. "Today I could have put him in jail for statutory rape.

"For the first couple of months, we got along. Then I got heavy in my pregnancy. I could smell perfume when he came home late. I knew his affairs by the scents, knew when he changed women.

"After the baby, it was like he had a Madonna complex. He'd wake up in the morning, roll on top of me, take me, shower, and leave for work."

She started to pace, her shoulders rigid, hands still clenched.

I spoke softly. "Mary, what happened after you lost your son?"

"Ah yes, my son." Pain radiated from her face. "George never had much use for women. He was, as you can imagine, a demanding father also. My poor daughter still suffers because of him. To have his second child be male meant everything to him. But when his SON died, he poured his bitterness onto me." She turned to face us. "That's when I began sleeping with the enemy. Every night was like a rape." She leaned against the wall and slid to the floor. "He told me I was too stupid to earn a living, demanded perfection in the house, and became obsessed with neatness."

Mary covered her face with her hands. "The irony is, my son was not his. And the subject is closed."

"Mary, it's okay." I sat on the floor next to her and hugged her close. We both cried. "You're going to be okay. Because we're all going to stand by you."

Mary, lips quivering, looked at me. "I miss my little boy." Her cheeks were streaked with tears. "But what kind of man might he have been with George as his father?"

We looked at each other, speechless.

Chapter Twenty-Eight

In the history of mankind, or rather, womankind, I am certain four exhausted women had never showered, shampooed, and dressed as quickly as we did that morning.

Nevertheless, only an hour late, each of us entered the breakfast area by the pool at ten, looking refreshed, except for our puffy eyes, which we'd covered with glamorous sunglasses.

The sun was blinding. White villas sat like tiaras on the surrounding hilltops. And there sat four handsome men, obviously finished with their coffee and food, waiting patiently.

Okay. Not all of them looked pleased. Antonio and Matteo appeared relaxed. Stefano, whose mind ran on American time, sat drumming his fingers, eager to start the day.

And Dante...his eyebrows were raised. I smiled and croaked. "B*uon giorno.*"

"What time did you go to bed last night?" he asked.

"Late. And I'm sorry we're late for breakfast. I hope we didn't mess up your day."

He stood and held out a chair for me. "No, it's fine. Coffee?"

"*Si*, lots of coffee."

Mary sagged into a seat next to Stefano. "Do they have pills in Italy?"

Stefano rolled his eyes and shook his head. Antonio and Matteo leaned back in their seats, arms folded, smiling.

"What?" asked Gabby. "We had some quality girl time and forgot to look at the clock. Stayed up late."

Dante ordered coffee for everyone and a Bloody Mary for Mary. "We have to hurry. A car is picking us up in about thirty minutes. Don't worry, ladies. I said nine but knew it would be ten before everyone was up and about."

The charming older couple we'd met last night, Marcello and Isabella, strolled to a table nearby, holding hands. Isabella carried a small bundle of flowers. He seated her, and then leaned down to kiss her neck. She giggled.

"Drat," murmured Mary. "Look at them. She gets flowers and giggles after all these years. Flowers have many meanings I guess." She moaned while letting out a heavy sigh. "That sweet couple. They're living my dream.

"Shush, Mare." I glanced at Liz, who was blushing. Gabby looked down to avoid eye contact with me. But it was useless. We dissolved into laughter, remembering Antonio always brought flowers to Gabby to "make up."

"Flowers? They won't work for me anymore." said Gabby.

"I'm sorry, Dante." I looked at him, his face so serious, trying to understand this woman-speak. "Please, tell us what we need for the day. We'll eat fast and be ready soon."

"There are two things I've arranged for today. One is a surprise, but you need your walking shoes. The other will be dinner tonight at Quisiana." He stroked my chin. "You'll all have plenty of time for a nap, a swim, whatever you want before dinner." He leaned down and kissed my cheek. "See you in the front lobby in about thirty minutes." He waved and walked away. His cell phone rang, and he turned into a serious businessman as he strolled through the door.

ꕥ

By eleven thirty, the eight of us were piled into a six- person convertible Jeep. Dante and I were squeezed next to the driver, Mary sat on Gabby's lap, Antonio in the middle, and Liz perched precariously on Matteo's knees. Stefano crouched on the floor between Mary and Antonio's feet.

We squealed around the treacherous 'guard-rail-less' roads and screeched to a halt next to twenty tour buses.

"Where are we?" My nose was buried in Dante's shoulder.

"Ana Capri. We stop here for a treat."

A *carabiniere* strode rapidly to our taxi. *"Signore Capoferi."*

Dante opened the car door and hugged the young man, Uzi and all.

"Tutti va bene, Signore. All is ready." He bowed his head in my direction, face solemn. Then looked at Dante and winked.

Hmmm. What was that all about? Must be a fab surprise. Alone time for Dante and me?

"Grazie." Dante offered me his hand. Our companions piled out of the back seat, exhaling, shaking themselves loose.

"Follow me."

We pushed our way through the groups of sweaty tourists. Dante led us through a gate to a ticket booth. He gave his name to the young woman. "Capoferi."

She handed him an envelope. *"Buon giornata, Signore."* And with a bow, she came from the booth and led us ahead of the others waiting in line.

"Che cosa, Dante?" What?

"What are we doing?" Mary stood on her tiptoes, trying to see around the rest of us.

"We go to the top of Capri. Is beautiful sight. Have cameras ready. Matteo, you first. I go last." He reached for my hand.

We walked up a narrow stairway, and I heard Mary yell, "No friggin' way." I smiled. Mary was back. Then I saw what she saw.

It was like a ski lift. Only these chairs were single riders, seats enclosed with a single bar. I watched Matteo back into the seat. Stefano gave Mary a gentle shove as the lift operators propelled her into a seat.

Stefano made clucking sounds of assurance. She held on, white knuckled.

Gabby, Antonio, and Matteo had been on this lift before. Gabby yelled back at me, "It'll be worth it, Jules."

Liz gracefully settled on to the chair, and with the first movement of wind in her hair, she pulled a rubber band from her purse and swept her red locks into a pony tail.

Liz, Liz...this is your opportunity for a wild look. What are you doing?

I backed into my seat and Dante followed me in the next chair.

I was terrified.

"Just look around at the beauty, Giulia. It's quiet and breathtaking."

And that it was. I held on to the rope, thinking that OSHA would never approve this chair. But as the ascent to the top began, I could only hold my breath in wonder. The sea vistas of blue and green were incredible. White villas clung to hillsides in the distance. Lemon trees and gardens swept under my feet. The warm grass, lavender, and lemon blossom scents of Capri rose to greet me. And I reveled in the twenty minute silent ride to the top of the island.

Getting off the lift proved just as difficult as getting on. With an awkward, "Oomph," my feet hit the ground and I walked to the side of the chairs to join the others. We waited for Dante and walked up a flight of worn rocks. When we reached the summit, I gasped.

I saw the whole of the Island, the deep aqua of the sea, dotted with purple hues. Seagulls, bright white in the sun, flew below us like white angels. Vesuvius stood proudly in the distance and the port below looked like a toy village.

We hiked further, rounded a corner and came to a delightful coffee bar. Green canvas lounge chairs were scattered under the covered patio. Tables and chairs nestled into corners with astonishing views of the sea.

"You're on your own now," said Dante. He pointed to different hiking trails. "The *cappuccini* and *panini* at this little bar are wonderful. They also serve cold water."

He took my hand. "Come, Giulia. I want to show you my surprise."

He led me past the bar and down a narrow path, around a large rock. "Hold onto the rope, *cara.*" I looked down the sheer cliff, clinging to the rope for dear life. It led to a bed of violet flowers tucked into the side of the rock, making a tiny cave-like room with nothing but the sea and pounding surf below us. Waiting for us was a white blanket, a basket, and a brass container filled with a bottle of water nestled in ice.

My heart stopped. This was his surprise. This intimate hideaway.

"Sit here with me." He pulled me down onto the blanket, cradled my head in the crook of his arm, where I could smell the sweet scent of his cologne. The sun brightened the intense blue of his eyes.

I held my breath.

"This is my special hideout on the island. It's for everyone, but I wanted you to see this first.

He rolled my body flat and kissed me, slowly, agonizingly sweetly, then deeper. I struggled for a breath, opened my eyes and saw the raw hunger. With a moan, I pushed him away, fighting between desire and intense fear. I yearned to give in, but felt my entire body tense.

He buried his face in my neck, his breathing ragged, and whispered, "I'm sorry."

He kissed me again. And for the first time, Teddy's face filled my mind. I erased the present with my mind and cleaned it as though dusting chalk off a blackboard.

"Dante," I gasped. "Stop, please. I'm sorry. This is wrong." I began to tell him about my husband.

He listened, his face fixed and grave. He looked down and took my hand and held it gently for a time. He lifted my chin and looked deeply into my eyes.

"It's okay, Giulia. I understand...and yet, I don't."

Mary's voice grated loudly from the distance.

For once, thank you, Mary. Wonderful, obnoxious Mary.!

"Come on, guys. I think I see Julie's shoes."

"Ma dai!" My shoes lay a few feet away, close to the entrance of our hideaway.

"Sempre!" Dante scrambled to a sitting position, hitting his head on the rock. *"Madre di Dio."* Rubbing the back of his head, he peeked out and yelled, *"Un momento."*

The voices of our friends drifted into the cave.

"Accidenti." I struggled to sit up.

Dante sat Indian style, put his face in his hands, and heaved a sigh. "Mary! She seems to always know...to deliberately try to separate us." He looked at me, frustration evident. "I think God is trying to tell me something." He took my hand, kissed it, and turned his attention to pouring some cold sparkling water.

"To Giulia, my gift."

I took a sip of the crisp, bubbly water, touched his cheek and said, "I'm sorry, Dante."

He winced, then gently combed my hair with his fingers, thumbed away streaked makeup, and fixed my clothing back into place.

I reached for his hair, loving the feel of the curls, the thick texture, my hands trembling...guilt filling every inch of my body.

"Tonight, Giulia? I make sure no one disturbs us tonight." He kissed me.

Tonight? No. There will be no "tonight."

He helped me to my feet. We tucked in our shirts and smoothed our hair. Dante gathered the glasses, putting everything back in place.

"*Cara.*" He held my face in his hands. "You look like a woman who's been loved. " He kissed my forehead. He broke into a smile. "No one will believe we had a picnic."

He took my hand. "Be careful, *cara.* Hold onto the rope."

We carefully edged ourselves along the narrow path and stepped back onto the main trail. Our six friends sat on large boulders, laughing, licking their quickly melting gelato cones.

"There's still food left. And biscotti." Dante waved his hand.

"Come on, girls." Gabby tugged at Liz, and Mary followed.

Gabby paused for a moment, looked back at Dante, and mouthed, "I'm sorry."

Dante shrugged.

She turned away, the three of them giggling their way into the cave. Their laughter was raucous.

I glanced at Dante, wondering if our voices of passion had carried for others to hear.

Antonio shrugged. "Women. No understand."

Stefano chuckled. "Antonio, women are to be enjoyed, not understood." He patted him on the shoulder. "Come on, let's hike."

Dante glanced my way, eyes begging me. He leaned in and whispered, "Let's go back to the hotel. Now."

I couldn't breathe. My head turned back and forth into a solid NO.

"Hey, you two gonna hike with us?" Stefano stood waiting, obviously clueless.

"Go ahead, Dante," I said, pushing away the hunger for him. "I'm going to wait for the gals on the patio and cool down." I smiled as he touched my chin.

"A presto, cara."

"See you soon, Dante."

With the men enjoying the climb and my friends howling laughter in the cave, I walked up the rough stone path leading back to the café. The number of people had tripled since I'd been to the hide-away with Dante.

I sought a cool, secluded corner away from people. I lost myself in the seascape and startling white ocean birds. But my mind had only one view... Dante. I closed my eyes, reliving the short moments alone with him; struggling between sensibility and fantasy. I watched the tourists. Homesickness tightened around me like a closed coffin.

Soon I heard my friends, sounding like they'd reverted to childhood. Their laughter was refreshing.

"There she is," yelled Mary, pointing to me, waving to the others.

They reached me and immediately scanned the patio for a larger space. We settled at a table with another glorious panorama of the sea below. A waiter brought us a large bottle of water, glasses, and our hot drinks.

"Well, Jules, never thought I'd say this." Mary leaned her elbows on the table. "But you sure picked the right landlady for this trip, who had the perfect half-brother, both of whom have given us the gift of the real Italy."

"We've been lucky." Liz kept poking her cheek with her finger, indicating she'd consumed too much wine or too much laughter. She wound the string around her teabag. "I love Italy. And the shopping...well, needless to say, it's been the best. And I love how the shops are so small and intimate. It's a beautiful place."

I nodded my head in agreement. "Italy must be savored." And I knew the part of Italy I longed to savor. I turned to Mary, shaking off a chill. "So, have you thought about going home?"

"Heck, no." She held the cold water bottle against her neck. "I'm in the moment. Don't ruin it. I'm taking a page from dear Scarlett. I'll think about it tomorrow."

Mary sat in quiet contemplation for a few moments, an unusual feat for her. "I've been smart enough to hide money. I did it in fear, but I did it. I'm not stupid." She tapped her spoon.

"Yeah, Mare." Liz smiled. "And guess what? Matteo told me he's always wanted to visit the States." She blushed. "I don't think he wants to marry again. But I'm hoping he'll visit California." She took a long sip of her tea, and then grinned wickedly. "However, if he sends me flowers before I leave..."

"Hmmmm, ah yes, flowers." Dante's cave kiss still had my stomach in knots.

"And, you, Jules?" Mary waited for an answer.

"I know one thing. Rome and its people have changed me. I feel...more confident."

Mary looked at me, lips drawn in a tight line. "You ARE going to give your husband another chance, right?"

"Probably." I grinned. "But I DID receive flowers last night. And you know what that means."

We laughed so loud people turned to watch us.

I tried to put tonight out of my mind. I wanted to be with Dante. I enjoyed his company. I could think of nothing else. His phone rang constantly while waiting to take the lift back to town. By the time we made the trip down and walked to the Jeep, he'd said goodbye and taken off in a taxi. Antonio went with him.

"Look at him." Gabby pointed to Antonio. "He makes pouting an art form."

The ride to the hotel felt long. The Jeep now held six of us. We agreed to meet by the pool and wait for Dante to give us our dinner plans.

Paolo greeted us at the front door of our hotel, helping us from the Jeep.

"I'll see you at the pool in a few," Mary said as she and Liz walked to their room to change.

"See ya." I wandered through the pool area to my private patio, and noticed Isabella sitting at a shaded table by herself.

"Ciao, Isabella. Where's Marcello?"

She shaded her face with her hand. "He's sick. Feeling very nauseous. The hotel desk has called for a doctor."

I sat next to her and held her weathered hand in mine. "I'm so sorry. Is there anything I can do for you?"

"You can keep me company."

"Shouldn't you be with him?"

"I came out here for a break, to cry where he couldn't see me. He gets upset when I show sadness about his health."

"I understand that."

"It's over, you know." She gazed into the distance, voice resigned. "He's had congestive heart failure for years. Doc said he shouldn't make the trip. He insisted. And when he makes up his mind, he's a stubborn fool." She blinked back tears.

I didn't know what to say. We sat for a few moments. I sensed she wanted to gather her emotions and waited for her to speak.

"Honey," she said, still looking straight ahead, "life is short. Fix things with your husband if you can and then make a decision."

"How..."

She turned to me, her eyes faded with age. "This handsome man is not your husband. He's like a new love. Something you must need for some reason. But don't give in. Love the husband of your youth always. I overheard parts of your dinner conversation last night."

I glanced away.

"You might not think so to look at me now, but I was a beauty in my day."

"I believe you. You're lovely now."

Isabella's lips curved into a subtle smile, remembering. "My husband, for many years, had a terrible temper. He's always been stubborn."

"You seem so in love. Sixty-five years is a long time. He looks at you adoringly, holds your hand. And I noticed you're always pulling his ear. Very cute affection between you."

She chuckled. "The ear pulling is my signal for him to shut up."

I laughed. "A silent signal. I love it."

The hotel clerk approached us. "Signora, the doctor is here now."

I saw her stiffen.

"I'll come with you." I squeezed her hand.

When we entered the room, the doctor was standing by the bed. He looked up. *"Mi dispiace.* I'm sorry. His heart was too weak."

She sat on the bed and stroked her husband's face. "It's been a good life."

"I've arranged for an ambulance to come." The doctor bowed to her. "The staff has contacted your family."

"Would you like me to stay with you?"

"No, dear." She stiffened, her fists clenched, her face shriveling in depair.

"I'll leave my address and phone number at the front desk. You'll call me?"

"I promise. I need to say goodbye. I should have stayed with him."

I sat beside her and held her close. "He didn't want you to see him take his last breath."

I hugged her, slipped quietly from the room, and joined the others at the pool.

Gabby sat on the edge of the pool, splashing her feet. "What's wrong, Julie?"

"The old couple...Marcello died."

"Oh, no. Has everything been handled for them? I can call the front desk and help them with arrangements."

"It's already handled, Gabby. This hotel has really come through for them."

I watched Liz and Matteo swim; Mary and Stefano were sipping iced tea at a shaded table. "I think I'll go inside where it's cool and read for awhile."

"Something is still bothering you, Julie. What?"

"I'm sad. They had what I've always wanted, a long marriage, and growing old together, total contentment with each other. I need some time alone."

I started for my room, turned back to Gabby. "Is Dante coming back?"

"I'm not sure. I think he left a note for you in your room." She frowned. "You'll see him tomorrow when we get back to Rome. He left on business. In Italy, when a decision is made regarding the sale of a property, you act on it." She shrugged. "One never knows when the buyer's mood will change. It's the Italian way. Dante's a good businessman because he understands."

"See you at seven," I said, waving to her.

Gabby followed me. "Dante's infatuated with you. I think the same for you. He's a hopeless romantic and will never commit." She took my hand. "You've had your romance. Go home to your husband."

We stared at each other, silent.

She was right. I turned and walked to my room, opened the door,and was amazed. No sign of the girls' party the night before existed. The place was pristine. On my bed lay a single white rose and a card. I sat on the edge of the bed and pulled the note from the envelope.

Cara Giulia,

Business has taken me away. The staff informed me about Marcello. I hope they've taken care of everything as I instructed. I know you will feel sad and wish I could be there with you. I hope you will think of me. Ci vediamo a presto, Dante

P.S. I cannot forget today. Tu hai mio cuore.

"You have a part of my heart, too, Dante." I held the smooth paper next to my face. Dante's scent lingered. I knew tonight would not be filled with temptation. Once again, I was spared from making a huge mistake. God must surely be protecting me from myself. I turned my thoughts to the sad and lonely face of Isabella. She had committed herself to sixty-five years, the ups and downs, solidified by their determination. I walked to the phone and called Teddy.

"Walden's. Leave a message."

"I miss you, Teddy." I placed the receiver back on its black stand.

My body felt stiff, and, for a moment, I didn't know where I was. I'd fallen asleep. Rubbing my eyes, I caught a glimpse of the flowers on the coffee table, but they had no effect on me now.

I stretched and stared at the ceiling. I thought about my time in Rome, the people, my friends, the heartbeat of the city. I thought of Isabella, now alone. With fingers pressed against my forehead, I remembered Ted and our life together. We'd had passion once. But today...I thought, too, of Dante. Even this caused me grievous sadness.

There was a soft knock on the door. I rose to answer it. Gabby.

"*Ciao*, Julie." She walked past me to the cabinet that held the wine. "Do you have a minute to talk?" Without waiting for an answer, she poured herself a glass, set it on the coffee table, and curled into a chair. I sat across from her.

She looked into my eyes. "I know this is none of my business. But I have to say it. I truly believe there is one soul mate for each of us. My mum had that with my real father, Dante's father." She sipped her wine. "I think, for you, Dante is that person."

My heart did a little leap.

"Antonio is my soul mate." She heaved a sigh. "It doesn't matter that he's married, or if he'll ever divorce his wife. He's the air I breathe. I am committed to staying away until he can be mine completely. I pray for strength not to give in."

She reached for my hand. "But, you're different. You've had a life with a man for twenty-five years. You have children."

"Gabby, I haven't slept with Dante."

"In your mind, you have. And you want to. But, if you do, Dante will always be in bed with you and your husband."

She gulped her wine. "My mum stayed in her marriage because she thought she had no choice. But it ruined her. Her heart always belonged to someone else. She told me it felt empty."

"I understand." My voice was a whisper.

"I know you do. But I don't think you can leave your husband and family, take a lover, move to another country...you're too established in your life, your traditions, your faith, your true moral compass."

"I have no intention of leaving my husband." I gripped the stem of the glass and stared at the flowers. "Gabby, have you ever wanted it all?"

"Yes. But, for me, unless a miracle happens or Antonio's mama is killed by a lunatic Vespa driver...whichever comes first...it's not going to happen."

Smiling wryly, she leaned toward me. "I have to decide. Do I want Antonio, or do I want to be alone. Because he's ruined me for another man."

"And, if I sleep with Dante, I'll be eaten by guilt.

I thought of Ted, then. Fondly. He was faithful and steady.

"No one would ever have to know." I set the glass on the table and turned to face her. "No one would know."

"Here's the truth. When you and Dante came out of your little nest today, you had the look of a woman satisfied with the love of a man. Do you honestly think you can hide that if you actually experienced it fully?"

"I know tons of women who've kept affairs a secret."

She stood. "Dante has passion in everything he does. If he makes love to you, it will drive him insane to think of another man touching you."

I sucked in a breath.

"When he can have all of you, Julie, give yourself to him. But not until then. For both your sakes." She got up from her chair, walked to me and hugged me. "I have to go, Julie. Just think. That's all I ask. Think. Besides, you're too American. It would never work."

I moved leadenly from my chair and walked her to the door.

"Thanks, Gabby."

She kissed me on the cheek and left.

I held the white rose petals next to my cheek. "No one will have to know." I kissed the petals, then walked to the closet to choose an outfit for dinner tonight.

"I'll know what to do when the time comes."

The phone rang.

"Pronto."

"Ciao, Giulia."

I breathed deeply. "Dante."

"Tomorrow, *cara.* Tomorrow I prepare dinner," he paused, "in my apartment. *Penso di me."*

He hung up the phone before I could respond. My desire for him would never be fulfilled. Tomorrow loomed before me like dreaded test. And whether I failed or passed this test…it could determine my future. I buried my face in my hands, knowing what I had to do.

Chapter Twenty-Nine

The minute I stepped off the train and walked out of the terminal, the familiar rhythm of Rome and its chaos comforted me. After three days on the Isle of Capri, relaxed by the sun and sea, the contrast was startling as we waited for a taxi.

Matteo had his arm around Liz's waist, squeezing her intimately and possessively to him. His silver, curly hair framed a face bronzed by the weekend sun. The muscles in his arms were taut as he held Liz. He brushed some hair from her face, his hands strong and masculine, sensually appealing despite the specks of imbedded stains on his nails. He pressed his lips to her ear and whispered something. She blushed. Turning her enticing eyes to meet his, she nodded, then walked over to me.

"Jules, Matteo and I are going to his shop to pick up his motorcycles. We're taking a ride in the country."

"We'll be late," said Matteo. While they waited for a cab, Matteo stroked her hair, his artist hands strong, yet gentle.

"Then the four of us will share a cab," said Gabby.

"Uh, not really." Stefano threw an arm around my shoulder. "I promised mama and papa' that we'd have dinner with them tonight. Mama is excited to have a guest for dinner." He rolled his eyes. "I just hope she hasn't nagged my dad to death while I've been gone."

He grabbed Mary's hand, but she let go and waved for a cab.

I tugged at her arm. "Mary, have you learned nothing? No snapping of fingers and waving of hands to get what you want...it gets you nowhere."

Mary pursed her lips. "I'm trying. I'm getting better."

"Yes, you are, sweetie." I patted her hand. "Now let Stefano get the cab."

Stefano laughed and tousled Mary's hair. "See you later tonight, Jules."

Mary grinned. I noticed a glow of contentment I'd seldom seen.

"Just you and me, Gabby. Let's get that cab."

On the way back to our penthouse, I watched Vespas whiz by, and noted the mass of parked cars carefully crammed into impossibly small places. Roman workers, in their designer suits, walked rapidly, waving their hand, holding a cell phone to their ear. The exciting pace of Rome had drawn me in. I knew in time the lifestyle would drive me insane, but the tradeoff....

The driver sped through the streets and narrow alleys. Pedestrians flattened themselves against buildings to avoid being run down.

While careening down the alley leading into the Piazza Farnese, a gaggle of tourists walked single file toward our penthouse. I wanted to shout to them that it would be better to sit and sip a cappuccino while gazing at the Fountains of Caligula that graced the Piazza Farnese. But I remained silent.

The taxi stopped a few feet from the red door, the political graffiti still cluttering the side of the building. I remembered that first day in Rome. Everything seemed overwhelming and new. Mary and I were bickering, all of us felt rushed and tense. But today, Rome wrapped its arms around me. September's end would be here all too soon.

I paid the cabbie while Gabby unlocked the door. We walked up the many stairs to the penthouse. When we reached the door, I realized I wasn't huffing and puffing.

"Gabby, I climbed all sixty-four stairs, and I'm not gasping for air."

"Told you. Italy is so full of stairs and inclines, anyone will get in shape living here for a few weeks." She smiled wanly.

"You're thinking about Antonio, aren't you?"

"Yes. I don't want to be alone. Can we have a snack and just talk?"

"Sure. Let me change my clothes. I'll be right back."

When I returned to the kitchen, Gabby had prepared some fruit and cheese for us.

"When I'm depressed, I eat. Let's take this to the rooftop."

"Okay." I grabbed the carton of ricotta cheese and a pitcher of chilled water from the refrigerator. She followed with some bread and olive oil. I loved Italian comfort food...simple, earthy, bursting with flavor.

We set the food on a small round table between two lounge chairs. Gabby went to the small cupboard next to the trellis to gather some glasses.

The autumn sun spread its warmth over the patio. But the breeze carried a crispness of the October to come. We moved the ample green umbrellas next to our lounge chairs for shade.

I dipped some bread in olive oil and thirstily drank the cool water. Gabby savored the ricotta and started to speak, when her cell phone rang. *"Ciao, Dante. Ti dov'e?"*

She listened for a long time, and then gave the phone to me.

"Ciao, bella."

"Ciao, Dante."

"Mi dispiace, but the contracts on the sale have not been finalized. I wait now for the lawyer's signature. *Mi sento frustrato*."

"*Anchio,* Dante. Me, too." My body tensed, thinking of all the barriers stacked to keep me and Dante apart.

"*Domani.* I'll arrive tomorrow. Dinner at my apartment." His low masculine voice oozed sensuality.

I caught my breath. "*Domani*, Dante. See you tomorrow." I whispered the words, filled with disappointment. At the same time, a sense of relief swept over me. I had one more day to think, to ponder the relationship with my husband back home. I flipped the phone shut and gave it to Gabby. She looked at me.

"Business isn't done. He'll be back tomorrow." I paused. "By the way, where's Antonio? Have you heard from him?"

Her eyes were downcast. "I'm sure he's with his Mama, or at his studio." She pressed at her temples. "No, wait. His studio is closed until tomorrow." She scooped out a spoonful of ricotta. "I still don't understand why Dante took Antonio with him. It seemed disloyal to me. Maybe Antonio is still with Dante."

"I'm sure Dante had a reason. He adores you, Gabby. He'd never do anything to hurt you."

"We'll see. By the way, the hotel called. Isabella is on her way home and Dante instructed them to ship the body to the funeral home in Florida."

Gabby ate a few more spoonfuls of ricotta.

I observed her for a moment, knowing she didn't want to be alone. I felt an emotional pull discussing the old couple. After watching my parents grow old together, I wanted that for me. My determination grew to make that happen.

"You know, I hate to leave you like this, but, Gabby, I am desperate to be alone and think. And, for me, it's best done by walking."

Gabby patted my arm. "I understand, Julie. I really do."

"*Ciao*." I went to my room, put on some sturdy but fashionable walking shoes.

It was five o'clock and the streets bustled. Stores and banks opened at one o'clock on Monday afternoons. Restaurants that remained dark on Sundays now hurried to prepare for hungry diners. Aromas from simmering sauces and fresh herbs floated into the streets.

I wound my way through the Piazza Navona, past the Pantheon toward the Spanish Steps. It jolted me, how much I loved this city. The sidewalks of the Via Condotti were crowded with shoppers laden with bags. To be in the center of ancient Rome became an overwhelming experience for me. I felt a vibration of days gone by, walking on streets that echoed with ghosts from the past, yet I could see it today...the scents and power and people of present day Rome. The Roman rhythm had become a part of me.

I walked up the Steps to the first level, and settled in for some people watching. Sitting on the Spanish Steps was better than front row center seats at a Broadway Theater. This show was live and unrehearsed. I sorted through the tourists and gazed at the Romans standing near the steps cutting a *belli figuri*, people simply enjoying the art of looking elegant in public.

An elderly couple walked by, he in a worn suit, wisps of thick silver hair escaping his brown cap. His wife held onto his arm, her other hand on a cane. Her brown tweed suit was elegant, emblazoned with a silk scarf of orange and umber flowers. Her hair, dyed red, was thinning. They shuffled and talked. He patted her arm often.

A young couple approached the step in front of me and sat down. Within seconds their bodies were tangled in a kiss. He took a breath, holding her face between his hands, and kissed her again.

A flurry of *buon gioro's* and *ciao's* floated as their young friends joined them. The kissing of cheeks took forever. Watching Italians had become addictive.

I glanced at my wrist. Seven. I'd barely noticed the dusk settling over the Piazza. I walked toward our apartment, taking small alleys, and came to a beautiful cafe nestled on a corner with a view of the *Santa Maria della Pace* monument. The café, a meeting place for local intelligenzia, was spotlighted, showing balconies of wrought iron dripping with flowering vines. The tables were red and gray, interrupted by thick green plants. Tiny cars and Vespas lined the alley toward the church.

I sat down, waiting to order. A young, tall waiter with enormous brown eyes, long dark hair pulled back into a pony tail, took my drink request. I sipped the macchiato slowly, and thought about home. And Ted. I remembered the sweet companionship of my parents, of the old couple...the feeling of security early in my relationship with my husband.

More and more, I realized I was the only one changing. The brush with breast cancer had frightened me. Not knowing how to deal with my emotions had pulled me away and I had abandoned Ted. Ted coped by withdrawing and ignoring both my fears and his. We lost our easy connection, our humor and bantering. And the frustration buried us in silence.

Running away had also changed me. To be attracted so intensely to Dante had shaken me. Our connection was more than a simple physical attraction. We were drawn to each other as though magnetized. Yet, the relationship could never be. And everyone involved was going to be hurt.

After paying the waiter for my drink, I meandered, stopping occasionally in small stores along the way. The intimacy of the little stores was so pleasing and tasteful, quite unlike the impersonal department store mentality I experienced at home. I stood in front of a shoe store and caught my reflection in the window. I liked what I saw. I felt pretty, sexy, confident.

I smiled and thought of Liz. No wonder she loved the shopping here. I wondered where Liz and Matteo were right now. Matteo's body language had screamed his attraction. But I hoped Liz would fight a night of pleasure and think of developing a friendship first. She still needed to forgive her ex-husband; to rid herself of the bitterness against men.

Mary, on the other hand, was probably enjoying Stefano's company and the sweet attention he gave her, no strings attached.

I turned the corner onto the next alley and found myself at the Piazza Minerva, directly adjacent to the Pantheon. The Egyptian obelisk standing in front of the church of Santa Maria above Minerva cast a shadow on a gaunt female beggar sitting on the steps. I tossed a coin into her cup and walked to the large brown doors.

The interior was hushed, and soft organ music played, while sinners knelt, seeking forgiveness. I found a chapel off to the side, put my coins into the receptacle to illuminate the area, sat and prayed. And cried. I wanted my life back, the life I'd had before everything fell apart. But there was no going back. Only forward. I didn't want to erase Dante. He had, after all, restored some self-confidence in me. I wanted my husband and my family. To see my sons marry and have children.

A hand touched my shoulder. I looked into the pale gray eyes of a nun. "*Te ne prego, signora,*" she whispered.

"*Grazie.*" I needed all the prayer I could get. I stood, smiled, bowed to her before walking out of the church. The dusky gray of twilight had faded to dark. I had to call Ted again before Dante returned.

GABRIELLA

Chapter Thirty

Gabby sat cross-legged in the living room chair, a dimly lit lamp casting shadows on the photo book lying open on her lap. She flipped through page after page of pictures showing Antonio and her, together, happy. Her cell phone rang.

"*Pronto.*"

"Gabriella, it's Dante."

"*Ciao.*" Where are you now?"

"Still in Genoa. *Mannaggia.* This is frustrating. We're still waiting for the lawyer to finish the land contract papers. How are you? Have you heard from Antonio?"

"No." She fought tears. "I miss him. Am I wrong to want him to myself?"

"No. It is the way it should be. Antonio knows what he must do." He paused. "And Giulia?"

"She's confused. Why, of all the women in the world, and you could have many, do you want her so badly?"

"*Non so, Gabby. Non so.*"

Gabby heard the sadness in his voice. "You don't know? Then don't give yourself to her. She's not free. And, in the long run, it will hurt you. And Jules."

"You think I don't know that? *Merda!* I know. But we want each other. *Merdosa. Tutti e merdosa.*"

"I'm sorry, Dante. I agree the situation is shitty. We're a pair, we are. Just like our father."

"Don't compare me with our father. You know how much I don't want to be like him." He paused, and sighed. "Do you have any idea how much he hurt my mama? Watching her suffer, cry when she thought I couldn't hear her? It made me afraid to be a man. To love. To trust that I wouldn't do the same thing. No. I will not be like our father."

"I'm sorry. I know our father hurt many people."

"Tomorrow. I'll be alone with Giulia. I want her alone."

"But she leaves soon. What are you going to do? Love her, let her go? Dante, be reasonable."

"Love is not reasonable, *cara.* Neither is it fair."

"Wait a minute, Dante. The doorbell just rang." She set the phone on the chair and opened the door.

Antonio stood there, his expression anxious. "I have gift for you. Please."

Gabby waved him in, and returned to the phone. "Dante, I have to go. I'll see you tomorrow. Think. Please."

"Ciao, ci vediamo domani."

Gabby hung up the phone and stared at Antonio.

Antonio stood next to her, a manila envelope in his hand. "Here." He handed it to her. "Please read."

Fingers trembling, she opened the envelope and pulled out the papers. It was a legal document. She saw *"DIVORZIO"* in bold print, followed by Antonio's name.

"It's why I left with Dante. He made appointment for me...at my request." He took the papers from her hand and crushed her to his chest, whispering *"Ti amo. Ti amo.* I can't live without you."

Gabby drew her head back and gazed into his deep chocolate eyes. She looked hungrily at his lips. She quivered with relief and happiness that he'd come back to her.

Antonio swept her into his arms. "Forgive me. *Sono stupido."* He held her against his chest. "Never make me go away again," he murmured. "Please, Gabby."

She clung to him, running her fingertips through his hair. "Forever, Antonio. Promise me we'll be together forever."

"*Promesso, cara. Promesso.*"

"I love you, Antonio. And this might end 'us.' But I will not ever sleep with you until we're married." Her breathing was uneven almost like panic. She took his hands in hers and gazed into his eyes.

His eyes widened in disbelief. "No, please, Gabby. I need you. Please."

"It's wrong, Antonio. We can't solve every problem in bed." Her vision blurred with tears. "I need to know who you are, and I yearn for you to see me as a person." She reached up to cradle his face in her hands. "You are my soul mate. We are one. But I cannot, will not, continue this relationship based on sex."

Antonio's fists tightened. He sat there, staring out the window by the bed. Heaving a sigh, his fists relaxed. He whispered her name.

"What, Antonio? What did you say?"

"You win, Gabby. You win." He held her tenderly, showing no passion, but caring.

"Thank you, *caromio.* I know now you love me."

He took her hand and led her to the door. "*Dormi bene.* Sleep well. I can't stay here with you."

He opened the apartment door, turned, and pleaded, "Promise me, a small, quick wedding."

"*Si, sono promesso,*" she answered, her face lit in happiness.

Gabriella closed the door, sat on the soft worn leather sofa, and hugged a pillow to her chest, feeling content.

Chapter Thirty-One

I stood in the living room awash with dim golden hues from the brightly lit piazza below and stared at the black phone on the table by the window.

"Make the call, Jules." I repeated the command over and over in my head. "Make the call." Leaning against the wall, I lifted the receiver and dialed. The familiar American telephone ring droned on six rings until the answering machine picked up.

"You've reached the Waldens. Please leave your name and number."

Damn machine. "Ted, you there? Pick up, Ted." I heard a click, then a fumble.

"Hello! Hello? Hi, Jules."

"Your voice sounds breathy, like you've just run a marathon. You okay? You sound winded."

"I'm fine. Just ran in the door. How ya doing? Still mad at me?"

"Mad—no, that wasn't it when I left L.A., Ted."

"Well, the problem with marrying a man eighteen years older than you...."

"Stop using your age as an excuse to not do things, okay? I thought you'd buried the 'I'm so much older than you thing' long ago."

"Let me finish. I just...." His pause was long. "I've discovered something since you've been gone. I hate my life without you."

An uncomfortable silence. I waited.

"You're so beautiful, Jules. I'm looking at those email photos you sent. You're more beautiful now than when we married."

"I'm glad you miss me." I wanted to crawl through the phone and be home.

"Jules, age, at this time of our life, makes a huge difference."

"Sweetheart! Good grief, you're only sixty-eight. You make it sound like you're eighty. I hate when you talk that way."

"Let's not argue, Jules." His tone was tired and resigned.

"Are you sure you're okay?"

"Everything's fine. Please don't worry."

"I'll be home soon. Seems like I've been gone for a year."

I paused again. "It's—it's magical here, Ted. Just Rome, the city and people. If a city can help me discover the magic of life, we can find it too."

"Jules, I'm glad you're coming home. I've missed you." His breathing again seemed labored. "I admire your courage to learn a new language, appreciate your adventurous spirit."

Silence.

"Ted, we need to work hard on our relationship. I mean...I hate feeling so distant."

"Jules, what do you want from me? We've had twenty-five years together. At my age, I want comfortable in my marriage, my life. I don't want to work so hard, the constant watching what I say or how I act, or arguing. Peacefulness, contentment. That's what I want."

"Want? I don't 'want' struggles either, now or before, or at all. But I NEED for us to find a way back."

"I hope it isn't too late, Julie." He sighed. "Jules, I've done nothing but think about us. I know I'm not perfect, but I was there for you. I held your hand, walked through chemo with you. I remember. You were the one who pulled away from me." There was bitterness in his voice, sounding like the words themselves were weeping.

I struggled to keep Dante from my thoughts, tried not to see those blue eyes, or to feel his touch.

"You pushed me, Ted."

"How?"

"By expecting me to be the same. I couldn't be the same. You do still love me?"

"Of course I do. I'll love you until the day I die. Flowers, Jules. I sent you flowers."

"I know. It's huge." I chuckled awkwardly. I'd begged for flowers all these years. And I get them from my husband while salivating over another man. Ted wanted points for flowers, while another man had romanced me.

"I do love you," I said. "I'll call from the Rome airport. By the way, how are the boys? I've only had two emails from them."

"Dreaming about a perfect world. Self-absorbed, like most college kids. Doing just enough to keep me from cutting off their money pump. Like we were, remember?

"Yeah. I remember. Love you."

"Love you, too."

"I can't wait to see you, Ted."

"I just want to hold you again. You make me feel like a better man. And I love you for that. And Julie, I'll change. I know we can't have what we had. But I'm willing to do anything. It won't be easy, but I'm willing." He sighed. "I simply love you," he said, and hung up.

I clung to the receiver, trying to hold on to his voice, his image. "Dear God!" I sank deep into the soft cushions of the golden sofa.

I stared at the wilting flowers. One huge bouquet from Dante, the blooms full, soft petals floating onto the table. Ted's roses had reached their peak, the petals blending with Dante's. Silver petals...colored petals. There was my life... a table of fallen petals mixed together. My fists were clenched, and I was so deep in thought, I didn't hear anyone come into the room.

A pair of shoes settled in front of me. I rubbed my eyes and peered into the always soulful eyes of Stefano. He was holding Mary's hand. For once, she was silent. I saw hesitancy in her smile.

"Can I tell her, Stefano? Please?" Her smile brightened.

"What's up, Mare?"

"This man is a genius. Pure heart. His Italian buddy in Los Angeles came through for me. No-fault divorce. No problem. And I get half of everything." She sat on the arm of the sofa and gave me a hug. "George had me so scared, I couldn't see beyond his bluff."

She jumped up and ran back to Stefano.

"And, guess what, Jules?" Her smile shone stronger.

"I give. What?"

"I'm staying in Rome and helping out in the coffee bar until Steve, here, gets his parents' affairs in order." She bounced over to me and hit me on the arm. "Can you believe it? I'm staying. In Rome."

Stefano settled an arm around Mary's shoulders. "My parents love Mary. And my mom appreciates her neatness. That's all she talks about...'Stefano, you've got a good woman here. Look how she cleans.'"

I laughed.

"And," said Mary, "she understands my Italian, sort of. I mean, we can communicate. I'll be living in the little apartment above the coffee shop."

Every inch of Mary seemed ready to burst with excitement. If she'd been a ball, she'd have bounced all over the apartment.

I stood, walked to Stefano and gave him a hug. "Thank you. Thank you for giving Mary back to herself. Thanks for helping her."

"Hey, she's helping me. Are you kidding? Mary has my folks obeying her every command." Stefano gazed sweetly at Mary.

"Yeah, well, that doesn't exactly surprise me." I laughed and hugged my friend. "I'm happy for you, Mare"

"Liz back yet?"

"No." I glanced at my watch. It was after midnight. "And I don't think she'll be back tonight."

"Well, good for her," said Stefano. "Matteo seems like a great guy."

Mary harrumphed and for a moment retreated back to her old way, her mouth crimping. "Too soon for them to, ya know, get together."

"Oh, for goodness sake, Mare. Liz is almost fifty-one. I'm sure she knows what she's doing."

"He'll never marry her. Antonio said that, remember?"

"I'm sure Liz is aware that one romantic night won't lead to marriage. She's not stupid nor rash in any decision. She's deliberate. And marriage is the only way for them to have a satisfying relationship. Let's not draw conclusions until we talk to her. Frankly, Liz is too sensible. I imagine all that happened last night was a lot of talking. I'm going to the kitchen to get some wine for a toast. See you on the rooftop."

Chapter Thirty-Two

The scraping and banging of cans and yelling from the drivers of the garbage trucks beneath the kitchen window were deafening. Garbage day, which started early and lasted late, was another rhythm of Rome I would miss.

Mary was plunging into plans to remain in Rome with Stefano's parents. And the lawyer from Los Angeles had filed the papers for Mary's divorce.

I stretched and strolled to the refrigerator for a bottle of water. "You going to join me at the café, Mare?"

"I can make time for that." She hummed her way to the cupboard for a glass. Still dressed in her mix-and-match black, Mary looked more petite than ever. She'd lost fifteen pounds from climbing and walking. Her shoulders were squared back, the pursed lips were relaxed, and her snarky attitude had melted somewhere between the Isle of Capri and Rome.

She slammed her glass on the counter and yelped.

"What's wrong?"

"Liz? Did Liz come home last night?"

"I don't know. Her door was shut. Let's check."

We scurried down the hall, tapped on the door, and pushed it open. Her room was the usual chaos, but the bed was empty.

"Aha." Mary raised an eyebrow. "She slept with him."

"You don't know that. And what difference does it make?"

"She hardly knows the man."

"Hmm. Let's see. You're moving in with two old people you've known for three weeks, you'll be working as a counter waitress to help out this younger Adonis, who, I might add, is helping you get a divorce...and you're concerned about Liz? Puleeeze!"

We padded back into the kitchen. I felt a tingle thinking of Liz and Matteo having a romantic night. I blushed when I thought of Gabby and Antonio. And my heart pounded at the thought of being with Dante tonight. "Being with." I struggled what that meant for me.

After our late breakfast, Mary hurried to join Stefano. Waiting for Dante to return to Rome today had stiffened every muscle in my body. Yesterday had brought nagging thoughts about giving up twenty-five years of marriage. Without Mary and Liz around, I was restless and decided to walk to Trastevere...the bohemian section of Rome, where real Italian life reportedly took place.

I scanned through the book Gabby had given us on our first day with recommendations for restaurants and "must- see" places. An entire page had been dedicated to Trastevere. I checked the map. A long walk. I changed my shoes, and began my journey.

The stroll along the Tiber relaxed me. The tree-lined street and stately villas offered shade and luscious vistas. I loved the fresh smell of a river. After crossing the bridge, I eventually found the Piazza Santa Maria. The alley leading into the piazza was a maze of narrow lanes. Garden terraces with geraniums and bougainvilleas scrambled down walls amid lines of clothes hung out to dry. And a multitude of nicked and peeling Virgin Mary's peered down on me from street corner shrines. Separated from central Rome by the river, this was a charming working-class neighborhood. I noted dingy-looking beggars, most likely here illegally from third world countries, and several drunks sleeping off the night-before binge. The church of Santa Maria brightened the beige square. A fountain graced the center of the piazza.

My cell phone rang. Dante's voice rumbled of Rome. *"Ciao, Giulia. Dov'e?"*

"I needed to walk, Dante." I looked around and described the piazza to him.

"Ah, you're in Trastevere. *Perfetto.* Meet me at the fountain at four."

I took a deep breath and managed to choke out, "*Va bene.*" I trembled with anticipation, and with dread at saying goodbye.

My ankles hurt from stumbling over gaps from missing cobblestones. I tried not to notice the holes stuffed with cigarette butts and goodness knows what else. Grass struggled valiantly to peep up between the missing stones.

With time to kill, I tried to concentrate on the unique neighborhood. The place veered from chic to boisterously vulgar. An old lady sat in front of one of the restaurants, shelling beans, her large brown eyes watchful, enjoying the sights as much as I knew I'd miss them. Saying goodbye to Rome was becoming painful. Saying goodbye to Dante...I couldn't think about it.

The aroma of coffee enticed me. I noted a crowd of tourists near the *Gelateria alla Scala*. I couldn't resist ordering a cinnamon-flavor gelato to go with my espresso. I sat down to enjoy my surroundings.

The view of the piazza and church was lovely. It was evident, however, that this area was much more casual and earthy than that around the Piazza Farnese. Young people were dressed in blue jeans, T-shirts without slogans, designer shoes and leather jackets.

Right at four o'clock, Dante strolled to the middle of the Piazza Santa Maria, his jeans and polo shirt fitting in with the nattily dressed locals.

His sheer maleness took my breath away.

"*Ciao, bella.*" His strong hands rested on my shoulders as he greeted me Italian style. "Have you been waiting long?" He brushed the hair from my face, his touch intimate.

"I've been enjoying my walk, Dante."

"There is perfect restaurant here with typical Roman food. I think you like." His smile lit the late afternoon. "But first, we visit church." He tucked my hand in his arm and led me to the ancient church.

He told me the history of the *chiesa Santa Maria,* speaking rapidly.

"This *chiesa* was built in 350 A.D. and was the first cathedral dedicated to the Virgin Mary." He pointed to the incredible mosaics, all picturing Mary, her life, her coronation, the Assumption of the Virgin. Romanesque in style, it felt peaceful. "This site is on several floors, two earlier foundations...." He stopped speaking; an expression of resignation shadowed his face. "Giulia, you've made a decision?"

"*Che cosa?*"

"A decision." He cradled my face in his hands and kissed me softly. "There's a difference," he said. He rested his chin on my head, breathed inward, then exhaled slowly. "There's a difference," he repeated softly.

He placed his arm around my shoulder and walked me to a restaurant. It felt secure, safe, yet burned my skin.

The jovial owner, Carlos, hugged Dante and shook my hand. He escorted us to a table alfresco, under canvas umbrellas, with a view of the neighborhood's nonstop comedy and art. He handed us the menu for *La Tana de Noantari,* Italian for den of thieves. Jugglers and singers had already begun setting up their props near the fountain as autumn dusk settled over the Piazza.

A soccer ball skidded under our table. Dante bent down, picked it up and threw it to the young boys playing in the alley. "Tonight, just pizza, some wine. We talk?"

"Si, Dante. We talk."

"Tell me--" he stopped, thought for a moment. "I want to know about your husband."

"Dante, this isn't fair."

"Tell me." He leaned in, his face inches from mine. "I need to know."

"He's a good man. Several years older. Fun. Has a great business which he plans to sell soon to our boys, when and if they ever finish college."

"Is he good to you?"

"He's good." I rested my hand on his arm. "We've been married a long time, twenty-five years. I pulled away from him, so many changes in my life. I have to try to fix it." I looked into his glacier blue eyes, and my heart ached.

"*Non capisco.* No understand. We belong together. And some day?" He kissed me softly, his eyes sad.

While munching on a pizza, we talked about family, his ex-wife and son, my parents, work. We laughed at the mime's, threw money into the hats of the strolling singers. It felt comfortable. Dante charmed me with his humor, stories of his childhood. I hadn't experienced this back-and-forth conversation with a man for a long time.

Then he stopped, his brows furrowed.

"Giulia, I'm leaving town tomorrow. I won't see you again. But tonight, tonight I want to be with you." His hand rested on my thigh, his gaze unwavering and his breathing shallow. "Come. It's our time together."

I stood and let him take my hand. We strolled down the now-dark alleys to the main street, where he hailed a taxi.

Neither of us spoke. I didn't know where we were going. I knew I wanted to be with him, one last time. The cab pulled up to the edge of the Piazza Navona.

His apartment. He's taking me to his apartment. My heart leaped, my thinking blurred, my body aching to be with him. My throat tightened.

He led me to the front door of an old building next to the church, and then to a small lift. When it stopped, he walked me to an over-sized door accented by polished brass handles and hinges, put the key in the lock and opened it. We went through a sleek minimalist living room of white and beige. With the flip of a switch, lights came on. He backed me against the wall and began to kiss me. I pushed him away, afraid of myself. The tug of guilt was too much to bear.

He led me to his garden patio. It was breathtaking, the view of the Navona at night. He encircled me from behind, and we stood, silent, our breathing in soft rhythm. Could I live without him? I fought the tears welling in my eyes. I wanted him to remember me smiling.

He slipped his arm around my waist and led me to the bedroom. "Tonight belongs to us." He quietly shut the door and took me in his arms, his kisses tender, yet underlined with passion.

I felt his muscles tense. Barely able to breathe, I pulled back to look at him. Raw desire filled his eyes, along with something else.

"*Non e' possible, cara.*" He walked toward the window, stopped, and pounded his fist against the wall.

Sono geloso." He hit the wall again.

"If I take you now, Giulia, I could not live with the thought of another man touching you." He stood beside me and led me back into his living room. We sat on the white leather couch.

JOURNAL - ROME

It's okay, Teddy. It's finally okay. I'm coming home where I belong. To you. We're going to work on our marriage, I'm going to get over this stupid mid-life crisis, and most of all, we're going to show our boys that a marriage can last, survive all the ups and downs.

I've loved you from the moment I first saw you. There are times when you frustrate me to a point of anger I never had before I met you. But in the end, it is all about the two of us and our boys.

I'm not going to write anything more. I almost did something that would have destroyed our marriage forever. But my fantasy is over. I'm still Julie, I'm willing to work. I want to grow old with you. Ah, Teddy, I hope this cancer doesn't get me in the end. I think my problem is that I've been thinking too much about the future and need to concentrate on each day I'm given. Can you help me do that?

I'm coming home. Stronger, happier, less selfish.

I love you, Ted.

Chapter Thirty-Three

The sun grinned through the windows. The comforting buzz of conversation echoed from the piazza below. The curtains fluttered and swayed.

I pulled the zipper shut on my last bulging suitcase stuffed with Italian memories.

Although Mary had annoyed me beyond belief for the first half of the trip, the apartment seemed empty without her. Our goodbye had been hugs and tears. The three of us had formed such a close bond.

Liz had squeezed in every moment possible with Matteo. I heard her humming as she stuffed each new clothing item into her cases, one of them new to hold her Italian purchases.

She glowed when we met in the living room with our now heavy bags. The car would be here soon to take us to the Hilton Airport Hotel. Our flight left at seven in the morning, and we'd decided to stay at the airport for the night.

I phoned Gabby. "We're ready."

"I'll send Antonio up for your bags." Her voice caught. "I'm going to miss you, Jules."

"I'll miss you, too. But I'm a faithful e-mailer. We'll keep in touch, I promise."

"And I promise the same."

A few minutes later, Antonio knocked on the door. He stood there, same outfit as the first time we'd seen him...loosely tied pajamas, a bare chest...still looking delicious.

Gabby had remained firm on not being together until marriage. In spite of this restriction, Antonio looked happy and in love.

My feet leaden, I descended the steps. For the first time, I wished there were more of them. I walked onto the Piazza Farnese and stood rooted to the ground, my gaze taking in every building. The driver of our van flicked his half-smoked cigarette onto the cobblestones and ground it with his heel. He opened the van door, and we waved goodbyes to Gabby and Antonio.

Rome faded as we approached the airport hotel, the red Hilton signage glowing brightly. Another sign of a finished vacation in Rome. The driver wrestled our luggage onto the sidewalk, I tipped him, and the hotel attendant put the bags on a cart and pushed them into the lobby. We followed and the doors to the hotel lobby shut behind us.

The next morning, the sun still hidden, Liz and I hefted our shoulder bags and walked through the long tunnel from the hotel to the check-in terminal. We'd checked our bags with the concierge at American Airlines before going to bed.

"See you in LA, Liz. Wish we were on the same flight."

"Me, too." Liz paused and took my hand. "I want you to know Matteo and I talked all night. You know I'm not a one night stand person."

"I know, Liz. And…?"

"We agreed to email. He might come to America to visit." She took my hand again. "I've grown up on this trip. Really. Thank you."

She flashed me a contented smile and entered the security line for coach passengers. Reaching across the ropes, I hugged her, and walked rapidly to the First Class check-in. The gentleman behind the counter smiled. "*Buon giorno*," he said, handed me my ticket and a sealed blue envelope.

"Er, what...?"

He turned it over and pointed to the writing on the front.

"Guilia, Put in safe place. If you are ever free, open it."

The scent of Dante's cologne was fresh, and I looked around. Was he here?

"*Signora?*" the ticket man said. "Something is wrong?"

"No. No. *Grazie,*" I said. "I am—I am fine." I held the envelope close to my heart, sighed and moved toward my gate.

The customs line at Los Angeles was annoyingly long. I peered around the line, trying to see my driver.

After gathering the last bag, I pushed the wobbling cart holding my luggage toward the exit, glanced to the right and saw the name "Walden" on a whiteboard. A man wearing a tuxedo, sporting a mustache, held the sign. Sunglasses covered his eyes, and a chauffeur's cap shadowed his face. He reminded me of someone.

I waved to him, and he pushed through the crowd. He walked with his arms behind him, the cap still hiding his features. There was something familiar in his walk. With a flourish, he handed me a bouquet of red roses and spoke softly. "From the man who loves you and will always give you flowers."

The driver took off his cap and glasses, ripped the mustache from his face and stood, grinning at me.

"Ted!" His sense of humor was back. It was what I'd always loved most about him. Good, kind, and very funny Ted. But a wave of worry swept over me. He'd lost so much weight while I'd been gone. Tears spilled at the sight of him, followed by a bubbling laughter.

"Jules." He drew me to him and kissed me, with hesitance and then urgency. "Welcome home. I bought you a cappuccino machine." He grinned, and brushed a finger across the tip of my nose. "I was hoping you'd make me lots of Italian coffee." Pausing, he glanced at me and said, shyly, "I'll take any 'Jules' that's here, the new, the old...I hated being without you. You're my light." He choked on the words and was dearer to me for his awkwardness.

Taking my hand, he pushed the wobbly cart toward the terminal exit. His hand felt oddly frail, and I felt the fragility of life. Like the awkward cart, fixing our marriage wasn't going to be easy. But I knew I'd made the right choice.

Epilogue

Three Years Later, Orange County, California

Alessandro watched the women from the bar behind the piano. Hiding probably wasn't necessary; none of them had met him. But he worried he might look too much like his father, Dante. He wasn't going to take a chance. So he sat like a half dozen other men, laptop perched in front of him. He observed.

The small party was taking place at a round table, topped with a centerpiece of autumn flowers in the opulent lounge at the Ritz-Carlton in Laguna Niguel.

How elegant they appeared. He studied the photo of the three women Dante had sent via email: Giulia, Mary and Liz, smiling and sipping a coffee at the Caffe Farnese.

Gabby kept in close touch with the three women who had rented the penthouse three years ago. When Dante discovered they were having their third Italy reunion, he'd arranged for his son to be there.

Giulia. That must be Giulia. She was seated with her back to the floor-to-ceiling window, giving Alessandro a perfect view of her face, now lit with a movie-star smile. She looked thinner now, the last few months taking its toll on her as she'd mourned the loss of her husband. Her black, tailored pantsuit, adorned with a cobalt blue scarf tied artfully around her neck, accented her gray eyes and dark hair.

He looked for signs of sadness but saw contentment marred by a hint of stress around the mouth when she smiled. He typed his observation - in detail and then turned his attention to Mary. Could this be the same woman his father had referred to as brash, feisty, and long on the bossy side? Her expression held a delicate softness. Tiny little thing, she was. Running a family restaurant in New York must agree with her.

Alessandro had no problem spotting Liz. She'd arrived late, arms laden with bags from the hotel's boutique. She was a looker. Her wild red hair glistened, her gold earrings fluttering in time to her movements, green eyes accentuated by her gold lame' top. She'd surrounded her feet with the bags after she sat at the table and handed Julie and Mary a small robin's egg blue box. He noted a flash of light and saw a large diamond on her left hand. She'd recently announced her engagement to a man she'd met at Ted's funeral…a widower with four grown kids, all of whom adored her. Guilia had sent photos to Gabby.

Alessandro continued the email, assuring Dante that Liz looked wonderful. Clearly her long-distance romance/ pen-pal relationship with Matteo had ended and she'd finally found happiness.

He laughed, watching Mary point her finger at Giulia. Mary's hair had grown from the cropped gamin cut in the photo to an elegant bob. Her dark eyes and pitch black hair commanded attention. And her bright red suit hugged her tiny frame. What had Dante said...she always wears black? Not tonight.

Alessandro dreaded relaying how radiant and content Giulia seemed. Giulia had worked hard on her marriage after Rome. According to Gabby, for two years they had managed to live in total happiness and love.

He typed the details of their faces, the way they were dressed, and their expression, and confirmed what Gabby had revealed. That Julie was a lovely widow, full of confidence, more beautiful than ever, but with an edge of regret in her eyes when she smiled.

Finishing the email, he hit send, pulled out a cell phone, and hit speed dial.

"Pronto."

Ciao, sono Alessandro." He described the scene to his father, told him a detailed email had been sent, and snapped a photo with his cell phone.

༺༻

Julie saw the flash and glanced over in time to see the phone snap another photo. She frowned, leaning forward to listen, faintly hearing Italian.

"Jules, what's up?" Mary drummed her fingers on the table. "Why the sudden smile?"

"Nothing. I'm just happy." She turned to face Alessandro. When he closed his phone, she winked at him. He quickly looked away.

"I'm thinking of taking a trip to Rome. I hear it's lovely in October. Anyone want to join me?"

She missed Teddy so much. Her boys were now her focus. Her future was here and she felt a strange contentment. Yet, she reached into her purse and felt the blue envelope, giving it a squeeze. She'd opened it, as promised, a year after Ted died. She knew the simple words by memory.

Cara Giulia, I will always love you. If you are free, and if you want me, I will be waiting for you...in Rome.

THE END

Acknowledgements

As a freelance author, I thought writing a novel would be a piece of cake. Was I ever wrong. It's daunting and lonely. It's hours of re-writing and being critiqued. It means using a lot of paper. And, finally, I can answer the question my friends have been asking for years. "When will your book be published?"

At last I can say, "Now."

For my wonderful mentor and tireless critique group leader, Louella Nelson…this couldn't have been done without you, my fellow authors, and the time spent at UCI Extension courses.

Particular thanks go to Dennis Phinney, Laura Taylor, Judy Whitmore, Kim Rapier, Brenda Barrie, David Spiselman, Scott Allen, Mary Gulesarian, and so many more over the years who gave wonderful input. And to a consulting agent, Bob Tabian, who encouraged me to set the novel in Rome. And to my dear friend, Dr. Jim Hills, who edited my first and second drafts.

About the Author:

Writing has always been an interrupted passion of Janet's…interrupted by life. After free lancing in magazines and appearing in The Baptist Bulletin, Travel and Leisure, and The Travel Section of The Orange County Register, she reversed course to write this novel. It is the first of three novels set in Italy.

Her non-fiction book, "An American Chick's Guide to Italy," will be coming out in the winter of 2012.

Her life interruptions have included teaching gifted high school teens… hopefully inspiring them to write, read, and think in order to release their inner muse.

For many years, she also ran a secretarial service which included serving as secretaries to corporate executives, editing theses for graduate students, and composing letters for busy small business owners who could not afford a "gal Friday."

While working in the marketing industry, she began to observe people and took notes on how people communicated in real conversations. She thanks all the customers who breezed in and out of her life while purchasing products, sharing freely their heartaches and joys.

Visit her website http://www.janetsimcic.com to find out more about her writing and to read her blog on Italy.

Book Club Questions:

Have you ever felt like running away from home as an adult? Why?

Can a marriage survive an emotional affair? A full blown affair?

How would you describe the path of falling into an emotional affair?

Have you had peripheral friends who became best friends after sharing deep secrets?

Why do you think men have problems accepting a breast cancer diagnosis? Does it indicate an already troubled marriage? Or is it about the core character of the man?

How did the age difference play into the marriage of Julie and Ted? Why do you think Ted closed down while Julie went through treatment?

Do you think Dante intruded on Julie's marriage? Was Julie right to let him? Did he have an ulterior motive? Did he really fall in love?

What are the specific wounds of each woman…Julie, Liz, and Mary… and how did it cripple their life?

Do you have a secret you've withheld for years? Does it cloud your life? Do you believe the truth can set you free?

Why do women stay in abusive situations? Fear, helplessness, security?

What is your opinion of how each woman treated her husband? Were the women cruel? Not cruel enough.

Which of the women in the novel were you most sympathetic to and why?

Which of the women's boyfriends were you most attracted to and why?

How does the Italian setting affect the novel? How might the novel be different if it were set in another country?

What steps will you take to open communication between your spouse or a friend after seeing the changes in the women of the novel?

What do you think is the key ingredient to having a real friendship?

How do you heal a broken relationship?

What part does forgiveness play in all of us? If you refuse to forgive, who controls your life?

Do you have your own ending to the story of these three women and the fun-loving Gabby? What do you imagine they will do next?